Hope you
as much
writing it!

A KILLER

— AND —

A KING

A TALE OF REVENGE AND REGRET

BY TOM DUMBRELL

19.03.25

PRAISE FOR
A KILLER
— AND —
A KING

"*An exciting, page-turning, whodunit murder mystery set in a fantasy world . . . This book is snappy, fun and filled with plot twists that will keep you hooked until the end.*"

–LIBRARYOFAVIKING

"*Dumbrell offers up his best novel yet. . . a fantastic job of injecting Christie into a powerful twist with a very surprising turnaround. . . no one leaves the novel unscathed.*"

–FANFIADDICT

"*Agatha Christie meets grimdark fantasy in this compelling, fast-paced whodunit page-turner.*"

–DANIEL T. JACKSON AUTHOR OF ILLBORN

ROYAL FAMILY OF FERMANTIA
AND OF THE CADRAELIAN REALM

KING YORICK III

QUEEN LIESBETH

PRINCE LEANDER

PRINCE OSKAR

THE MINISTRY OF FERMANTIA
AND OF THE CADRAELIAN REALM

JORAN RENSEN

MINISTER FOR WEALTH

ROEL DUBECK

MINISTER FOR FAITH

BRUNO BEKAERT

MINISTER FOR THE ARTS

LENNART DE MEIREN

MINISTER FOR JUSTICE

BRAM HOSTE

MINISTER FOR LAND

EMILE ROOS

MINISTER FOR WAR

For my girls, Breana & Steele

CHAPTER I

The guillotine snapped down, slicing through the flesh and bone of the man's neck. Appalled, Leander resisted his first urge to empty the contents of his stomach. He'd seen men killed in battle, of course, but this, well…this was something very different.

The head rolled away almost playfully, leaving a trail of gore. As the separated body fell limp, the operator of the killing device began cleaning the blade immediately. Clinical, but admirably efficient.

It was, altogether, a solemn moment, which, for whatever reason caused the crowd to cheer uncontrollably. The fabled fighting pit of Cadrael, once home to warriors of great valour and bravery. *Where is the honour in this?* Leander wondered. Men, guilty or otherwise, slaughtered for the entertainment of a baying mob and their bloodthirsty king.

A bloodthirsty king who it was Leander's misfortune to call father.

A man stepped forward to drag the body away. Clouds darkened overhead as rain began to fall in heavy droplets, dispersing the blood-trail in vascular streams of red. The sky blackened as if in mourning, thunder rumbling ominously, perhaps with the discontent of a higher power. The crowd, to their credit, were unaffected, insatiable. Execution days only came around once a month, and though the thought offered little comfort to Leander, it seemed to encourage all others in attendance to form a feral mob.

Some laughed, others whooped in excitement. Celebratory songs sounded out, the verses pitted with obscenities toward both parts of the newly butchered victim. In pockets of the crowd enthusiasm had boiled over into aggression, sparking senseless brawls along the stonework terraces fringing the square-shaped arena. *An honest fight at least*, thought Leander. However intoxicated, mindless, and devoid of skill, these contests remained closer in spirit to the historic bouts of old. The constraints of foreign campaigning had forced King Yorick to stall the fighting pits in order to preserve and secure skilled fighting men. Illustrious warriors had become mercenary soldiers, while their king, an undeniably resourceful man, found a single solution to two troubling problems. War invites unrest, exacerbated by boredom. The answer: round up the rabble-rousers and entertain the masses, or at least divert their attention, with monthly executions. It was either callous or cogent, depending on your viewpoint, but to Leander's mind, unquestionably despicable.

He clenched his teeth as the next victim appeared, dragged to the centre of the arena and the promise of the guillotine's inescapable pillory. The man's arms were bound, his mouth was gagged, and he tumbled into the puddle of blood left by the previous victim. The spectacle was abhorrent, but Leander knew better than to let this show on his face. According to his father, this was a rare opportunity, a privilege. As a private viewing area high in the terraces, the Royal Gallery was the concession of just seven men—the king accompanied by the six members of his prestigious council, The Ministry. Together these six men represented the most powerful families of the Cadraelian Realm, lands bound to King Yorick of Fermantia, who held his seat of power in the capital city, Cadrael.

Leander gripped his knee and tapped his foot nervously. As the first prince of Fermantia to enjoy such an honour, he knew the king would expect gratitude, and he was certain that he would not tolerate weakness.

Below, the action continued. Under duress, spurred on by the crowd, the man fell to his knees for a final time. Leander twisted uneasily in his richly upholstered chair, turning his thoughts toward the distinguished company who sat in a row beside him. A parade of entitlement, ambition, and self-interest—the privilege, he concluded, was entirely theirs.

Nearest to Leander, at the end of the line, was their leader, the all-powerful, King Yorick III. Leander had been aware of his father's gaze all afternoon, like a vicious Fermantian Gorehawk eyeing up its rodent prey. Though presented as an honour, Leander was under no illusion that this was, in fact, a test. The king dedicated many an hour to the trials and tribulations of rule, a pastime second only to hints at Leander's deficiencies. For all his mother's efforts to beg patience, it seemed that the queen's words fell upon deaf ears against the noise of King Yorick's displeasure.

"Enjoying yourself, son?"

Leander forced a smile. Honestly, he couldn't think of a worse way to pass the afternoon. He was about to reply when the Master of Ceremonies clapped his hands together to silence the audience, from his position at the centre of the arena. The announcer had straw-coloured hair tied at the nape of his neck, a broad grin, and a disconcertingly cheerful demeanour. A fresh wave of nausea washed over Leander. To the left of him, all seven men rose to their feet, as was customary. He turned to face his father and regretted it immediately.

"Join us, Leander." King Yorick gestured an upward motion as he spoke.

Leander obliged, legs trembling. He couldn't help but feel that the whole crowd was watching his every move. The king nodded, and the Master of Ceremonies began his enthusiastic address.

"People of Cadrael," he grinned. "I now ask you to consider the fate of one, Ferran Veraza." He pointed an accusatory finger at the ill-fated man, whose name prompted unexpected recognition in Leander. "Charged with not one, but two counts of sedition, this wretch before you was apprehended when demonstrating against the righteous overseas campaigns of our beloved leader, King Yorick III."

Fresh noise, this time, a mixture of jeers or calls for the king's good health. Leander grimaced before the host eventually called for silence.

The Master of Ceremonies smiled again, working the crowd like a master puppeteer. The man's expression was one of utter amusement, and it was unsettling to Leander to find that same unbridled joy mirrored on his father's face.

"Wine!" called the Minister for Land, Bram Hoste, cutting through the quiet. "Forget beheadings, I'm dying of thirst over here. My mouth is dryer than the Sands of Sumeya."

He was a middle-aged man with thinning grey hair, large ears, sagging jowls and deep bags under his eyes, which gave the false impression of a kindly old fellow. Bram adjusted the rounded eyeglasses that perched on the tip of his rosy nose, leering at the young girl who rushed to refill his outstretched glass.

Next, Leander's gaze settled on the Minister for War, Emile Roos, who was currently nudging an older man who sat beside him. Emile was the youngest and latest addition to The Ministry. Little more than thirty years old with a tidy beard and dark, shoulder-length hair, he was a handsome addition to the crowd of otherwise grim-looking fellows. Even the scar across his eye had a certain allure—an exquisite wound which added a heroic quality to his already striking countenance. An alleged memento from his time at war, the scar conveniently avoided any damage to the eye itself, causing Leander to wonder if Emile himself was responsible.

War wound or victory for Emile's irrepressible vanity? The very question typified Leander's distrust for the minister. The man's father, Arjen Roos, had once driven the expansion of King Yorick's realm, establishing a legacy of blood and bravery which should have made him one of the most celebrated generals in Fermantia's illustrious history. However, no man is without weakness, and his end was one famously mired in treachery, a scandalous betrayal still casting shadow upon his successor, even to this day. Emile was perhaps the most handsome man in all Fermantia, but the Roos name brought with it an ugly reputation.

"Did he say Veraza?" Emile's piercing blue eyes narrowed questioningly. The pink skin of his infamous scar paled to white as the skin tightened. "I had two men by that name during the siege of Ardalan. Both worthless bastards, of course…" he added, waving a dismissive hand. "If that's their father, then let's get this over with."

His company—Lennart de Meiren, Minister for Justice—was middle-aged with a full head of thick dark curls, accented by streaks of grey about his ears. The man's bushy eyebrows lifted as he chuckled in response, causing Leander's fists to clench with anger.

The siege of Ardalan had been Emile's finest hour and King Yorick's most prestigious victory. The conquest had led to the seizure of the capital of Tenesca, securing a successful conclusion to the Fermantian invasion, while securing Emile's reputation for tactical genius. Yet Leander knew better than to believe the songs and Emile's own claims to triumphant strategy. Then a younger prince and fresh-faced general, Leander had led his company to cut supply lines to the besieged city. Their efforts soon choked the river, and they had repelled attacks from rebels seeking to salvage the capital. The assignment was simple: starve the people of Ardalan into peaceful submission. It was a patient, calculated technique quite uncharacteristic of his father, so it was perhaps no surprise when Emile's reinforcements were called in only days into the siege. King Yorick's patience was already exhausted. As always, brute force was to be the alternative—the man to deliver it, one desperately seeking to restore his family name.

Leander still remembered the order as though it was yesterday.

"Your men have been reassigned to me, Prince Leander. Our orders are to take the city, no matter the cost."

Emile's voice, but the words of the king. Reckless tactics employed to secure a quick victory; a legacy for King Yorick III, written in the red of Fermantian blood.

Rolan and Elias Veraza had been good men as far as Leander was concerned. The campaign had been his first command, and though he had feared resistance to his inexperience, the popular brothers had never challenged their unproven leader, instead choosing to sway the company in full support. War was so often a test of forbearance and attrition, but Rolan and Elias were seasoned campaigners, skilled with a blade, and never short of a joke or story about the campfire. They would have made great captains, but Emile made meat of them.

A futile charge at the heavily defended walls of the Tenescan capital led Leander's men like lambs to the slaughter, another worthless sacrifice in pursuit of a king's wild ambitions. To this day, he wondered if he could have done more to prevent it. Could he have refused Emile and defended his men, just as Rolan and Elias had done for him previously? Leander was a prince, after all. Surely that should have counted for something. He'd sworn an oath to protect the lives of his compatriots with his own; they all had.

Worthless was a fair word to describe Leander's part in that sorry saga, but Rolan and Elias had unquestionably been men of worth. If this soon-to-be-executed man was their father, likely he would be little different.

The Master of Ceremonies turned to gesture in the direction of the royal gallery. Leander felt a sheen of sweat form on his brow as thousands of eyes suddenly landed upon him.

"For judgement, we look to those responsible for guiding our great realm," the host continued. "When questioned, the accused made no attempt to deny the charges, accepting guilt and placing himself at your divine mercy. Thus, in time-honoured tradition, I ask whether any man will stand for this traitor. Will you choose clemency or sentence this, Ferran Veraza, to his final reckoning? In your judgement we trust, in your footsteps we follow…"

The man gave a timely bow, and the arena turned deathly silent. Leander peered down the line once more and winced as Bram returned to his seat without a second thought, already calling for someone to refill his wine.

Following him closely was Roel Dubeck, Minister for the Faith, whose assortment of gold chains and bangles clinked as he took his place. As always, the man's brow furrowed with deep lines, though Leander knew this unease to be less concerned with the fate of Ferran Veraza than the creases in his shimmering silk robes. Sighing with disinterest, Roel scratched at the thick beard that hugged his well-defined jawline. As he did so, a wayward raindrop bounced from the top of his liver-spotted pate. Leander had always found the man to be wily and unpredictable, but Roel's lack of compassion was no revelation. Roel's greatest devotion, after all, was the pursuit of his own best interests.

Ferran Veraza had everything to lose, and Roel Dubeck would gain nothing from saving him.

It came as no surprise when Emile dropped to his seat, laughing dismissively, and Lennart soon followed, his face expressionless. These barbaric spectacles only served to make Lennart's life easier in his role as Minister for Justice. There are, after all, few challengers to the laws of a dangerous and impulsive king. If the public needed reminding of the consequences of treason, Ferran Veraza's beheading offered a very useful example.

This left only two ministers who could intervene. Leander's hopes first turned to Bruno Bekaert. The Minister for the Arts was a diminutive man, but one with no lack of presence or personality. As always, the minister's skin shone, his features accented by the application of powders, while his well-groomed beard and moustache were characteristically pristine. To many, the minister would have appeared picture perfect, but the brushwork was no longer faultless up close. In truth, he was fighting a losing battle, with the undeniable presence of wrinkles as scars.

Cultured and gentle, Bruno claimed to counsel his king from a position of learning. However, much like the others, the Minister for Arts had grown wealthy in the tailwind of King Yorick's relentless campaigning. Predictably, the man lowered himself without hesitation, perfecting his white hair so that it parted neatly to one side, his attention soon lost to the glimmering gemstones adorning his bony fingers. The way he pawed at them had Leander in mind of a playful kitten with a ball of yarn, the minister a perfect picture of feline conceit.

Last but not least: Joran Rensen, Fermantia's infamous Minister for Wealth. *The Moneyman* was remarkably tall and thin, towering over the others when stood at full height, even more so when all around him were seated. Balding, sour-faced, with dark, deep-set eyes and a wide nose, Joran's unsmiling mouth was framed with gritty stubble that completed his list of rather shabby attributes. But he was, as always, smartly dressed and never anything less than serious, this particular occasion no exception. Joran considered Ferran Veraza's fate only briefly before seating himself with a typically stern expression.

The Minister for Wealth had spent many years helping King Yorick realise his ambitions, and Leander knew it had been foolish to expect any different. Perhaps carried by a wave of momentum, or simply unwilling to swim against the tide, all six ministers were now in their seats. This left the decision in the hands of one man, much to Leander's considerable dread.

Plainly unbothered by proceedings, it took a brief but unexpected coughing fit to delay the king's inevitable conclusion. The hacking noise sounded painful, but was not unusual, and a servant soon arrived to deliver the king's prescribed tincture, which Yorick swigged deeply before clearing his throat. He straightened himself, a vision of good health, then turned to his son, nodded, and sat immediately.

Leander was now the only man standing.

"This is your moment, boy," the king said, grinning widely. "You've heard the charges. The decision is yours."

Leander froze, his body turning cold. His eyes widened, but the king offered no reprieve, no empathy, and no opportunity to change his mind. *This* was the test as always intended: a simple choice, with grave consequences. Of the thousands in attendance, Leander alone would decide the accused's fate. Leander who, through his own inaction, had sent Ferran Veraza's sons to an early death.

He let his head drop as he sat to confirm the man's fate. Was it disappointment at himself, or perhaps at his father? *No*, he thought, steeling himself to arrest his nerves. Good, bad or indifferent, Ferran Veraza was a man who had challenged the king's authority. The man was a traitor, while his sons had been warriors. Rolan and Elias had known the risks of service. The brothers had willingly offered their lives for glorious victory. Certainly, none of this was Leander's doing…

But if this was true, then why did he feel so sick?

The crowd erupted with a new chorus of bloodlust. Leander's despairing gaze turned upon his father, and he wondered, briefly, if they were really so different after all.

Physically, the comparisons were widely acknowledged. Although the king bore a grizzled complexion and a little extra around the waist, Leander shared his father's fair, sweeping hair, grey, deep-set eyes, and square jawline. On close inspection, Leander was a little taller than his father, but the king's confident gait and stately presence worked to nullify the marginal difference. This left the two men remarkably similar, a thought which failed to bring a smile to

Leander's face. The king was stubborn, hot-headed and insatiably ambitious. He was a warmonger, a neglectful father, and Leander hated him, though he couldn't fail to acknowledge the man as one of Fermantia's most illustrious rulers. He only wished that his brother Oskar had been born first, heir to the throne. Sadly, this was not the case, and the consequences were increasingly evident, perhaps never more so than in that moment.

A temporary hush fell on the arena.

The guillotine blade plummeted, and Ferran Veraza was gone.

"Drink!" called Bram, startling Leander, who jumped in his seat. The man smiled as the young maidservant returned to fill his glass with wine appropriately blood-red in colour. He then winked across at Lennart and laughed as he slapped the poor girl's rear unexpectedly, sending her stumbling forward.

Leander winced but couldn't bring himself to turn away and face the carnage. Carnage for which he was ultimately responsible.

Noise in the arena had returned to full volume. Roel mouthed incantations to The Goddess, while Yorick barked words at Joran, who strained to listen. Bruno held a small mirror aloft to review his appearance, and the only outlier was Emile, who had turned from the bloodbath below, face pale and eyes wide with revulsion. It seemed the Minister for War had seen enough blood for one day, though Leander suspected there was more behind it than sudden, uncharacteristic compassion.

Sickness bubbled in the pit of Leander's stomach as help arrived to reclaim Ferran's head and remove his severed body from the centre of the arena. Rolan, Elias, and now Ferran Veraza. Blood on Leander's hands. Death on his conscience.

The Master of Ceremonies stepped forward once more, his voice again bright with unaffected cheeriness. It was all Leander could do to prevent himself from rushing to throttle the man for his insolence. The speaker was just about to draw a close to the ceremony when a lithe girl with dark hair emerged from the audience. Her shrill cries cut through the feral din, and everyone watched as she ran in pursuit of Ferran's trailing body, at length falling to her knees and weeping inconsolably in the wet mulch of newly crimson sand. Her small frame shook as she draped herself over the headless body, a bloody image of harrowing despair.

A wife, or perhaps daughter? Leander couldn't be sure at this distance. His regret deepened, but some strange sense of responsibility compelled him to keep watching. He had done this, and he had to face the consequences, the human cost. His knuckles whitened as he gripped the arm of his chair, lost in his self-imposed penance. Only when the meaty hand of his father suddenly grasped his shoulder did his mind return to the present.

Cheers turned to boos, and the atmosphere soon soured. Either frustration that the spectacle was over, or belated anger at the injustice of proceedings. Perhaps the girl's appearance had served to hammer home the grim reality of death. For many in attendance, Ferran Veraza was just like them.

Or at least, he had been anyway.

Leander was sure he had heard a relevant quote from Bruno. *Bodies are empty; love makes us full.* The words of one celebrated scribe or another. In that moment he finally saw the sense in it.

His father's concerns, unsurprisingly, were much closer to home. "Come, son," said the king. "Time to leave, lest your head be next."

Crowds lined the wide streets of Cadrael as King Yorick III made a swift departure from the arena. His gold carriage glistened despite the inclement weather, and heavy raindrops bounced from steel-plated armour as guards fought to contain the revelry. In their wake, a young stable hand brought Leander his horse, a powerful chestnut gelding named Remi. The prince mounted without hesitation and Emile followed suit, ascending his own shadow-black steed. The remaining members of The Ministry had already ridden ahead.

"Animals, aren't they?" Emile made no effort to hide his revulsion, nose wrinkling as he spoke.

Leander forced a smile, lifting Remi's reins to pursue the king. He had no desire to argue with Emile and preferred to avoid conversation with the minister altogether.

It seemed as if the whole city was present: a colourful palette of age, race and religion, all demonstrating the breadth of responsibility bestowed upon a king. A weight that would, one day, fall upon Leander's shoulders. He shuddered at the thought, pushing the fear away. He reminded himself that he would be different. Assured himself that he would be better.

They passed through the thoroughfare at a canter, Leander paying little heed to the attending city folk and the tall, wood-beamed buildings that cast shadows upon them. That was until Remi reared and stopped, and a guard stumbled backwards, falling clumsily into their path. A small figure then broke free from the crowd and began to rush in Leander's direction before he had chance to reach for his sword.

"Prince Leander!" The girl's desperate voice carried a thick accent. The Veraza girl, Leander realised and gasped, concluding, on closer inspection, that she was the daughter of the recently deceased. He remembered her brother Rolan speaking of their family origins in Irazar, a nation formerly independent but since consumed by the jaws of the Cadraelian Realm. Conscription was typical for able-bodied Irazari men, and many, like Rolan and Elias, found themselves consigned to the front. Like her brothers, the girl had olive skin and raven hair that stuck to her face, wet from the rain. She certainly bore some likeness, though remnants of her father's blood obscured her appearance, large red stains discolouring her simple dress. She reached for Leander's leg and grasped him by the ankle. Shock crashed through his body like a wave, yet he steadied himself and prepared for the worst. For all his uncertainty, he knew one thing to be true: this girl was a very real threat.

Grudgingly, he paused in his failed attempt to release his sword. He heard Emile calling to him, but the words drowned in the renewed fervour of the crowds. The fallen guard stumbled on the wet flagstones as he tried to return to his feet, and Leander had no choice but to turn and face the girl.

For better or worse, he owed her his attention.

"He took them all," she cried, tone so desperate that it carried Leander back into the arena and the moment of Ferran's passing. Anguish that sent him crashing back even further, to the siege of Ardalan and news of his fallen companions, the girl's brothers among them. Her eyes were wide, wild, and unpredictable, but there was no sign of a weapon. Leander allowed himself a breath of relief. He was safe, or at least felt so in that moment. She was just a girl, inconsolable and all alone. She wasn't dangerous, surely. To his surprise, her next words said otherwise.

"The king must die!" she yelled, falling backward and wriggling like an eel as the guard, recently returned to his feet, fought to restrain her. Her arms and legs flailed as she released her grip on Leander, and though her cheeks glistened with tears of sadness, her eyes were angry. Feral.

A reactionary elbow slipped inside the guard's helmet to crush the man's nose, sending him reeling once more. Emile's horse reared nervously, but the Minister for War steadied himself to hold safe distance as the watching crowd laughed and cheered, surging against those sent to contain them. The whole world shrank to Leander, the girl, and the small space between them. For whatever reason, Leander did not attempt to escape.

"He has to die," she repeated, solemnly but with no lack of conviction. "It's the only way that things will change—"

Her last word trailed off as two further guards appeared for reinforcement.

Though Leander called for pause, his words fell on deaf ears. It seemed the girl's fight was gone, and she was soon overwhelmed, arms constricted and mouth silenced. The third guard returned with his bloodied nose. He cursed as he returned to full height then stepped forward to punch the girl in the gut, causing her legs to give way from under her.

"Don't worry, my prince, you're safe now. This treasonous wretch will hang for her impudence."

Bruised, bloodied and breathing heavily, the man probably deserved more of Leander's gratitude than he received, but in that moment, it was hard to take him seriously. Was Leander ever really in danger from the poor girl, and could anyone blame her for her actions, in light of all she had lost? The past was unchangeable, but the future was in Leander's hands, and while there was nothing he could say to make things better, he certainly wasn't about to make them worse.

"Release her." His words came as a surprise to the guards. Their eyes tightened with doubt, but found certainty in Leander's steely countenance, his best impression of authority. To his credit, the guard with the bloody nose remained silent despite his obvious outrage. Emile's horse manoeuvred to halt at Remi's side, and the Minister for War gave voice to his displeasure as the guards relaxed their grip and the girl wriggled free.

"You can't be serious," he said, somewhere between shock and disgust, as though he himself had fallen victim to the girl's elbow. "She's a traitor, a malcontent," he continued, pleadingly. "A troublemaker, just like Veraza and the others..."

That Emile had failed to make the link was no surprise to Leander. The girl never reacted, but Emile's passionate plea had left the guards hesitant. The man with the bloody nose displayed a newly hopeful sneer, while the girl remained expressionless, awaiting Leander's judgement.

He wasted no time to repeat, "Release her!" with a determined glare.

Respectfully, the girl nodded, turned and disappeared into the bedlam. Her departure shared the same abruptness with which she had appeared.

In her absence, Emile tutted. "Big mistake. Wait until the king hears of this."

Leander gave an audible gulp. The *right* choice, it seemed, was rarely the easiest.

CHAPTER 2

"**Y**ou insolent little shit!"

An open-handed slap sent Leander reeling. Emile had been right—it would have been an understatement to call King Yorick displeased.

The king paced around the royal bedchamber like a caged animal. His voice boomed from the wood-panelled walls and tall ceilings, echoing around the palace. Leander was used to frustrating his father, but this was something altogether very different. This was rage.

"Treason!" The king threw fists into the air. "Public treason, from the daughter of a convicted dissident. Is it any wonder these fools continue to challenge my authority, with the threat of mercy for consequence? I should have known you would disappoint me, Leander, that it was too soon to start grooming you for kingship. Your brother is as slow as a snail on an incline, but even he understands the rules of the game. At the very least, he demonstrates some respect for me and our family. Your mother has turned you soft," he said, directing a glare at his wife, Queen Liesbeth, who stood watching in the doorway. "No doubt she has filled your head with her romantic ideas. Her notions of peace, and love…" The king elongated these final words to ensure they sounded every bit as ridiculous as he considered them. He paused to look Leander from head to toe, tutted, and then walked to the window, where he peered out in silence, a brief respite for Leander who took the opportunity to massage his newly swollen cheek. Eventually, however, the king turned back and fixed his son with a familiar frown. "When a dog bites its owner, what do we do?" he asked. His eyebrows rose, but Leander saw straight through the question.

He sighed, and then answered, "We put them down."

A savage smile returned to the king's face instantly, making him look like a cat who had cornered a mouse. "Exactly. Perhaps I was wrong. Maybe you are not a total lost cause after all. We kill the mutt lest it develops a taste for blood. Our blood. We make examples of these creatures, Leander. A king is far more than a silk chair and a golden crown. Leadership is about strength, control, trust. The people of the realm trust me to keep them safe, and that task becomes a lot more difficult when miscreants run amok, spreading their bile. I know what you think of me…" The king glared in Leander's direction. "You think me cruel, ham-fisted; in all truth you probably hate me. But you know what, boy? I am your king. I am king of Fermantia, sovereign of the Cadraelian Realm. I am the final word around here, and you will learn to respect that, or I will ensure that you never live to enjoy the same standing. I'm sure it all seems so easy to you," he continued, pausing to straighten a framed picture on the wall. A portrait of himself no less. Leander remained silent. "Do the right thing. Treat people with kindness, blah, blah, fucking blah. Well, I'll tell you one thing, boy. Realms are not built on nice ideas. Ambition and drive are what led me to conquer half the known world and establish the greatest dominion in all history. Belief in the righteousness of my actions and the single-mindedness to lay all who would oppose me to waste. This, Leander, this is what truly makes a king. These are the lessons I had hoped for you to learn, the very reason I invited you to the arena. Success is sacrifice. Is that so difficult to understand?"

"No, Father."

"Finally, we agree on something." The king shook his head dismissively. "So, tell me, boy, why is it that you continue to undermine me?" Another trap. This time, the king raised his shoulders in question. "You call for peaceful resolutions yet you're only too happy to shirk your responsibilities and surrender your values when called upon. You well know the importance of our alliance with Eluria, and the part you might play in preserving our western borders. King Jannick is a patient man, but not without his limits. Jannick fears the increasing size of our humble realm and seeks some assurance of our...support for Elurian sovereignty. His request that you marry his daughter, Princess Sanne, is, I believe, very reasonable; I would not have agreed otherwise. Do you deny knowledge of these plans?"

Guiltily, Leander let his head lower. The king made to speak, then halted as a hacking cough escaped him, that same rasping sound like something stuck painfully in his throat. His face turned bright red, angry veins protruding from his temple. He covered his mouth with a silk handkerchief and then reached for the small glass phial in his surcoat pocket. A long swig seemed to end his temporary suffering. Eventually, he wiped his brow, cleared his throat, and then turned his attention back to Leander. With his father's gaze upon him, the prince gave an uncomfortable gulp of his own.

"Then tell me," the king said, voice still dripping with spite. "Why do you continue to defy me, and persist with the servant girl?" He stomped forward to close the distance between them, and a gasp escaped Leander as his father grabbed a fistful of shirt. "It is beneath you, Leander, and no good can come of it. You knew about this, I presume?" He released his grip and turned his glare upon the queen, an accusation that provoked little from Leander's mother.

She moved a long strand of red hair from her eyes before stepping out of the doorway, moving toward the centre of the room. "Come now, Yorick, were you never young and foolish? Perhaps memory fails me, but I seem to recall a few *reservations* of your own when our courtship was first agreed." Though subtle, the inference was not lost on Leander.

Surprisingly, the king's skin reddened, while Leander shared his mother's smile. He had always known the queen to be eloquent and glamorous, but his father's temper was volatile, and Leander had rarely seen his mother use her wiles to challenge her husband so openly. The sight was inspiring, and best of all, she was not yet done.

"Look at us now," she said, resting her hand upon the king's shoulder affectionately. The colour in Yorick's face softened, and his body wilted as his temper calmed. "Thirty years later, and we've never been better. These things require time, drive, *sacrifice*. Relationships can no more be built overnight than realms, and every great king was a fanciful prince once. Surely you of all people can understand this, my king." She let the compliment hang between them. It was masterful, and Leander could scarcely contain his relief.

Meanwhile, the king's expression shifted to one of puzzlement. In lieu of rage, he appeared frustrated, outmanoeuvred. Yorick's brow furrowed in deep thought. Clearly, he was not naïve to his wife's strategies; the bigger question, was how to act in response.

He forced a smile and said, "You're right of course," through gritted teeth. "Think on what I've said," he added, eyes flickering to Leander menacingly. The king's face fell into that familiar scowl. "I do what I must, and I won't be taken for a fool."

He turned and stormed from the room to leave them in silence.

Leander felt like he was walking on air. The horrendous ordeal with his father was over, and his mother, the queen, had proven kindness to be a most potent form of attack.

Above all else, Leander felt liberated. Though the circumstances of Ferran Veraza's execution were unquestionably regrettable, he was at least able to comfort himself in the knowledge he had saved the man's daughter. It occurred to him that if he had once known her name, he couldn't remember it, and the thought gave him momentary pause in the long, marble-floored corridor. Likely, it didn't matter, he reasoned, pushing the slight sense of unease away to keep moving. To Leander's thinking, she could keep her name, and with it, the small mercy of anonymity. She had her life, her freedom, and a chance to avoid the notoriety that had caused her father's downfall.

I did that, he thought to himself, smile appearing on his face for the first time that day. *I saved her…*

Onward, he drifted through the seemingly never-ending walkways of Cadrael's majestic palace. In his wake, a medley of extravagant gilded doors, stained-glass windows, decorative suits of armour, and assorted palace staff bowing reverently in passing. With each step, Leander's thoughts turned further from the Veraza girl, shifting to more present interests and the other subject of his argument with the king: "the servant girl," better known to Leander as Perrine Delport.

It had been two years since Perrine had joined the palace staff, but Leander remembered it as though it was yesterday. With shimmering copper-brown hair, ivory skin and soft pink lips, Perrine had captivated Leander from the moment they were introduced. She wasn't the first girl he had noticed about palace, but Perrine was different somehow, capturing Leander's attention with her enchanting brown eyes, light dusting of freckles and slim silhouette, which drew his eyes to her like a moth to flame. He wanted her from first sight.

To begin with, his father had put it down to foolish infatuation. Reluctantly, Leander even conceded that he was possibly right, and the vast difference in their respective upbringings would soon unravel the illusion. However, Perrine was a woman of many surprises. Beautiful? Undoubtedly, but smart too, and funnier than Leander had ever known in a woman. He soon found himself addicted to Perrine's company and was greatly relieved to find the sentiment shared.

Leander paused and gazed through a nearby window, where the heavy sun was disappearing beyond the horizon, leaving a sky that was pink and purple like Cadraelian passionflowers—nature's masterpiece, too beautiful for the hand of man.

Early evening already.

It was time.

His private chambers now loomed before him, and he opened the doors to find his hopes realised. Perrine, alone, intricately plaiting her hair in front of a tall mirror. She didn't notice him at first, or at least she chose to give this impression. Indifference was one of her most striking qualities. She never ventured to flatter Leander, irrespective of the societal distance between them. Perrine was genuine and often brutally honest. Perhaps best of all, she was a realist. In a world of princely excess and sycophancy, here was a woman that Leander could really trust. In this sense, their relationship was perhaps the most real thing he had ever experienced. Outside of war, anyway.

In a rush of excitement, he crossed the room and wrapped his arms around her. She gasped, and then laughed as he squeezed tight, lifting her from her feet and spinning the two of them around with reckless abandon. He loved these moments, and his cheeks ached with a smile as he eventually slowed to return her to her feet, her eyes sparkling like precious stones, her lips inviting.

Every urge drew him toward her, and his fingers brushed her cheek delicately but deliberately as he reached in to kiss her. In that instant of perfection, his eyes closed, and his mind wandered. He never wanted it to end, and his heart sank a little as Perrine pulled away, her hand pressed to his chest with the same tender purpose he had demonstrated only moments before.

She looked at him, eyes narrowed, and nose scrunched in an expression that stoked the fire within him. "I see someone has put a smile on your face. Should I be concerned?"

He startled then spluttered, "Yes, well…no. It's my mother—"

"Your mother?" said Perrine. Her eyebrows quirked with the same incredulity found in her voice. "You really are a master of bedroom discourse, aren't you, Prince Leander? Don't let me stop you. Do tell me more…"

Leander blushed then gave an exaggerated grin. Perrine had a real penchant for verbal sparring, and though she stuck out her tongue to goad him, he conceded defeat and chose to change tack. He knew better than to fool himself; he wasn't going to win.

"You should have been there," he said excitedly, keen to relay the story. "The king was up to his old tricks, lecturing me about the Elurian girl. The same old story, *duty and sacrifice*," he mimicked his father's booming voice. Perrine giggled, but the moment was short-lived. "You know what he's like. Too absorbed in his campaigns, too wrapped up in his damned legacy to notice what's happening in his own palace. He knows how I feel about you." Leander paused and reached to take Perrine's hand in his. "He knows that I want this. Us. He says he cares about me but treats me with the same disdain he extends to everyone else around him. In his eyes, I'm nothing more than property, an object to be bought or sold for his ambitions. He would have me marry that princess," he scoffed. "A woman I've not even met. A woman who could never be you—"

"But a princess nonetheless…" Perrine interjected. She blew out her cheeks, and let her hands fall from Leander's grip. "You don't know a thing about the girl. Maybe she is as awful as you imagine, or maybe she's perfect. Perhaps she isn't as smart or sharp as yours truly—" she flashed a playful smile, "but there's every chance that she's beautiful, educated and rich to boot. At the root of it, she's something that I will never be: royalty. You know I share your frustrations at your father, but Yorick is the king and this fantasy is putting both of us in danger, of that we can be sure."

"I can handle my father."

"Is that so?" Perrine's tone suggested she wasn't as confident. "How do you explain this then?" Leander recoiled as she reached to touch his cheek with tenderness not afforded by his father. His reaction drew a sad, knowing smile. Leander wondered how things had fallen from his control so unexpectedly. He'd arrived full of hope and energy, but as always his father had left an indelible mark. A cloud to rain on Leander's happiest moments. For all his early optimism, it felt as though he was about to lose the one person he truly cared for. He had to find the right words. He wouldn't let his father win.

"That?" he asked, gesturing to his swollen cheek. "That's nothing—a misunderstanding nothing more, I can assure you. Look, I don't deny that father has grand plans for my future. I know he wants this treaty with King Jannick, but I've spoken with him now and he knows my position."

"You spoke to him about us?"

"Well, loosely yes…"

"So, no." Perrine shook her head, but she didn't seem at all surprised.

"My mother—"

"Ah, your mother. We're back to this again…" This time she rolled her eyes. "Do you always bring mother into conversation when you're under pressure? Does she need to be here, or can you handle the rest of this conversation alone?"

A question in jest, but one worryingly close to the truth. While Perrine smiled, Leander blushed. She was right, and he started to wonder if he truly deserved her affection after all. Maybe his father was right, and no good could come of this. The thought sent a sickening feeling through his body. Nevertheless, he pressed on undeterred.

"The point is, that mother spoke to the king and he just, well…he walked away."

"Walked away?"

"Yes. No argument. No reprisal, he listened to her thoughts and let the matter go. I would be lying if I said we had his blessing, but it's a start, isn't it?' He reached a hand to Perrine's lower back to draw her close. They were almost nose-to-nose, and he fought the urge to close the remaining distance and kiss her. "Maybe we've been doing this all wrong, sneaking around, meeting in private the same time each week, kissing in the shadows." His cheek tugged with a smile. "The king is not without his flaws, but perhaps he can be reasoned with. If he can just get to know you, spend some time with us, see us together." He felt the momentum building, and the sparkle of hope in Perrine's eyes encouraged him. "King Jannick may want his wedding, but I'm not the only prince of Fermantia. Oskar is young and hot-headed, but he is his father's son after all. Likely, marriage will be good for him."

"More so than for the princess anyway!" They both laughed, Perrine's a quiet snort that Leander never ceased to enjoy.

"I'm just asking you to trust me," said Leander, drawing a loose strand of hair from her eyes. "I'll try to speak with Father, and yes, if needs be I'll ask Mother to entreat on our behalf. Whatever it takes."

Perrine sighed. "I trust you, of course I do. I just…"

"What?"

"I just know how things work around here. It's not just the king either; you know how influential The Ministry can be. Do you really think they'd allow a prince to fraternise with a lowborn girl like me?"

"Perrine—"

"No, Leander. I may have been foolish enough to fall for a prince, but I'm not stupid. You of all people should know that. Your father is a powerful king with a frightful temper. Even if he is as suggestable as you think and able to coerce those bastards from The Ministry into sanctioning our relationship, what then? Will you receive the same support, ascending to the throne with a low-class queen, or will our union create rifts even deeper than those known by your father? You are to be king, Leander. You know I think the world of you, but this alone is the reason for King Jannick's petition. You are the most wonderful man and you will make a fantastic ruler, but you belong to your country. This is about more than just you and me, you know that."

The words stung, but Leander sensed some truth in them. "I can change things," he said, hopefully, but with all the conviction of a small child. "I don't care what anyone else thinks. We can be together; I can look after us, after you…"

"Really?" Perrine frowned to reinforce her doubt, "Because, I may love you Prince Leander, but you know I'm not alone in this. There will be no shortage of glamorous princesses and other noble suitors for the future king of Fermantia, but I will be risking everything. I'm not just talking about my heart either, that can mend. My job here in the castle, though? My father is an old man, and his condition worsens with every day. He needs me, and I need this job so that he can focus on getting well again. You understand that, don't you?"

Leander nodded.

"I'm not saying this isn't what I want," Perrine added flatly. "Goddess knows, I'd look good sat beside you in that fancy golden chair." She laughed, then seemed to shake the last of her angst away. When she spoke again, her voice was soft and seductive. "I'm just asking you to think about it and remember how many people are affected by your decisions. Do the right thing, but do it for the right reasons. Most importantly though…" she added taking him by the hand. Her eyes flickered toward the bed, and she began to lead

Leander in the same direction. "Save all that deep thinking for tomorrow. There's no harm living in the here and now."

A golden sun blazed overhead. Leander sheltered his eyes to peer at the cloudless blue sky, warm breeze ruffling his hair as he went. About him, that same familiar sound of crowd noise, punctuated only by Remi's snorts as he rode along. The moment brought a smile to Leander's face. The road ahead was one of Cadrael's famously wide flagstone boulevards. Adoring citizens lined the thoroughfare, casting flowers before him, carpeting the path with a sea of wildflowers from the lanes and pastures that surrounded the city. Most notable was the infamous Blue Meadow Lily, whose azure petals emitted a sugar-sweet scent, belying their notorious and effective application in poison. To his left, Perrine Delport smiled from the mount of her own shimmering white mare and waved at Leander, her delicate hand dressed with precious stones.

A lustrous diamond wrapped in white gold. A wedding ring, he realised, squinting from the dizzying rainbow of colour. He glimpsed down and found a thick golden band of his own upon the same finger. Of course, she was his princess now, he remembered, feeling more than a little foolish.

Loved, and in love, this was a perfect moment.

"Keep up, son!" King Yorick turned in his saddle and called for Leander to close their distance. The king grinned and his face seemed softer than Leander could remember, younger somehow. His boyish smile seemed to have eased the deep lines that once stood testament to many years of kingship, and the queen, majestic as ever, regarded her husband with a look of young love.

A perfect moment, which would stretch out forever. The watching crowd cheered and whistled, summoning good health for the king and his family.

A young woman broke from the crowd to pay her respects. Barefooted, she moved at great speed, her shabby dress becoming a pinkish blur as her unruly hair waved in the breeze like wild grass. She made for the king, who reached to greet her. There was something in her hand, most likely a gift. Was she familiar? Leander's smile twitched as recognition passed through him. He made to call for the guards, but found none present. Where did they go? The crowds had already started to close in on them, smiles turned to malevolent grins that sent Leander cold. A new chant was rising through the ranks, and Leander strained in attempt to hear the words. When he discerned them, they sounded with murderous clarity.

"The king must die! The king must die!"

The king! He turned from the encroaching madness to search for his father. The royal horse ran loose and unsaddled, and King Yorick lay sprawled on the ground, arms twitching with the last semblance of life. At the tip of his fingers, another body, Leander's mother, with cold, dead eyes. Her silk bodice was blood red, and a pool of gore and entrails connected her lifeless form to that of her husband. The perfect moment had become a nightmare. The girl hacked and slashed, showing no signs of tiring. She snarled and wailed, cutting through flesh. Leander froze on the spot, terrified.

Suddenly, she stopped. She turned her face to consider him, her expression indistinguishable behind a mask of violence. Blood matted her hair, stained her growling teeth. She looked like a wolf driven mad with the uncontrollable hunger of a wild beast. Savage.

The Veraza girl—the one that he himself had set free. *I did that*, he thought, surveying the butchery and trembling at the terrifying injustice of it all. *I let this happen.* He wanted to cry, to scream, to take vengeance. Instinct led him to reach for his sword, but his hand closed around nothing more than a wilted tulip. Hopeless and lifeless. Leander knew he was not long for the same fate.

He righted himself in the saddle as the girl rose and began sprinting toward him. Her knife gleamed red, sharp edge aimed in his direction. The promise of pain and death. "Run!" he yelled to Perrine, turning to find the same horror reflected on his new wife's face. "Get the fuck out of here!" He left no room for negotiation.

Words too coarse for someone so beautiful. The fear on Perrine's face turned to shock, and she quickly obliged, spinning her horse to set off in the opposite direction. The crowd around her surged forward mindlessly like an army of the dead. Hands reached out and grabbed at her in an effort to haul her back, and Leander said a silent prayer, his last hope: her survival.

But what of his own? And where was the girl? He twisted to find his worst fear upon him.

Teeth bared, the girl cut fierce shapes in the air. "The prince must die!" she shrieked and lunged at Remi's throat. The horse backed up, whinnying and rearing in retreat.

Unbalanced, Leander reached for the reins, but it was too late. He fell away.

Falling…

Flailing…

He gasped, and sat up with a jolt.

Perrine's tired voice asked, "Leander, are you okay?"

A dark room lit by the glow of the moon. His room. A dream then, or more accurately, a chilling nightmare. He turned and found Perrine beside him. She was concerned but safe. Tired but alive.

"Bad dream?" she asked softly, reaching out to caress his arm.

Leander nodded, but words escaped him. A sheen of cold sweat lined his brow, and his heart pounded at double speed. The sense of relief was palpable, and he relaxed his head into the welcome embrace of the silken pillow. Little by little his breathing calmed.

Perrine leant across to kiss his cheek tenderly. "Sleep now," she whispered, and Leander obliged.

A crashing noise startled Leander awake. Bleary-eyed, he squinted in the bright orange light that filled the room. Morning and the familiar surroundings of his own chambers. He felt Perrine shuffling beside him, and his initial concerns drifted like a breeze. It wasn't a dream, however much it felt like one. He sat up to stretch and a yawn escaped him, his face relaxing into a contented smile that suddenly soured as soon as it had appeared. Panic descended, and Perrine pulled frantically at the bedsheets in an attempt to cover herself. At the end of the bed stood six palace guards, all armed. More concerning was the sight of Lennart de Meiren. He had an excited look, which was rarely a good sign.

The Minister for Justice cleared his throat before speaking. He paused to remove a piece of parchment from his pocket, unravelled it, and then began to recite his instructions.

"Perrine Delport, you are charged with unauthorised trespass upon on royal property beyond assigned working obligations and acts of subversion intended to undermine the wishes of his majesty, the king. By the order of King Yorick III, you are hereby arrested and shall be detained under Fermantian law."

Perrine's gasp filled the air, but Lennart stood expressionless, unaffected. A subtle nod sent two armed guards marching to the bedside, where they stamped their boots in unnerving unison. Their halberds cast menacing shadows across the silk bedcovers, and though Leander's head was awash with fear and anger, in that moment he could not put this into words. Had he really hoped to influence his father? He cursed himself for his naivety. A mistake, for which Perrine would face the consequences.

"A full and thorough investigation will follow, with your trial date to be determined in the coming days." Lennart folded the scroll to return it to his pocket. "It is, of course, in your best interest to acquiesce peacefully. Guards, please detain and remove our prisoner."

To Leander's surprise, Perrine surrendered in stoic silence. She gathered her nightdress and stepped from the bed, where the guards apprehended her, securing both hands with heavy, clattering chains. Overwhelmed, he scrambled to try and stop the unfolding madness. "Stop!" he yelled, like a young boy demanding attention, angry, frustrated and outmanoeuvred by his father. Was Perrine really going to leave without saying a word? Without any sign of affection? The most she managed was a fleeting "I told you so" smile.

His face knotted with confusion. Did she blame him, and if so, what could he do to change things? This was not the whim of a father, but of a king. "I'm going to sort this," he called to Perrine pleadingly. "I'll speak to the king, or Mother…Mother will know what to do." As he uttered these final words, he was hit with a fresh wave of helpless embarrassment. He remembered the series of events that had led to this moment, and watched as Perrine's head dropped, shaking slowly. Long gone were the playful jibes she had levelled at him the previous evening. The king was going to get exactly what he had wanted, and Leander wondered if things had ever been in any doubt.

"There is one more thing," said Lennart, causing the guards to pause in their path toward the doorway, snapping to attention with Perrine between them. Leander winced, considering how things could possibly worsen. "His Majesty has concerns over the threat posed by you and your family. Your father has been informed of these very serious allegations, and has since been taken into custody by my men—"

Perrine's cries brought Lennart to an abrupt halt. "You fucking shits!" she screamed, thrashing her arms in violent protest. Rarely did Leander see behind Perrine's veil of composure. This was raw and uninhibited, an instinct for survival. An instinct to fight and protect a father she loved above all others.

Sensing danger, Lennart tentatively backed away. Tears streamed down Perrine's face, and her cries echoed about the room. "Not my father..." she sobbed, but the guards were under clear order not to give an inch. On Lennart's instruction, they dragged her toward the door.

Leander jumped from the bed, "Just hold on, I'm going to fix this, I promise."

The best of intentions. As always, too little, too late.

"Mother!" Leander's protests began in the corridor. His voice reverberated among a series of ornamental marble columns bound by verdant climbers, his boots thudding to an eventual halt in front of the queen's door. Recognising his urgency, the guard soon stepped aside. The thick slabs of mahogany crashed open as Leander rushed into the queen's bedchambers. She was standing at the window with her back to him, refusing to turn despite the noise. Her hair rippled gently in a warm summer breeze. Beside her, Leander clocked a wine bottle. Empty.

"You'll never believe what he's done this time! It's Perrine," he said, pausing to maintain his distance. His back was sticky with sweat from storming through the castle, and the uncomfortable dampness of the cloth only served to irritate him further. "He's had her arrested, something about trespassing and subversion. Lennart came to my room to take her. Can you believe that? Mother…?" The deafening silence caused his eyes to narrow. "Is everything okay?" he asked, edging the final few strides that stood between them.

Finally, she turned, and Leander's jaw dropped. Her eyes were black with bruising, her lips swollen and split.

"What the fuck happened?" he asked, cursing himself at the naivety of his question. He rushed to take his mother's hand and asked, "He did this, didn't he?"

Tears formed in the corner of his mother's painfully discoloured eyes. "It's nothing," she said, turning away, before Leander pulled her back, to summon that pool of courage reserved for times when a loved one is suffering. Like Perrine, his mother was another victim of the king's spiteful obstinacy. A matter, which, when added to the indignity of Lennart's earlier, unwelcome appearance, caused Leander's anger to finally boil over. He swiped the empty wine bottle from the table, and it smashed into tiny pieces on the floor, the shattered glass feeling like an accurate portrayal of his life in that moment. He determined to make good on his promise, to stand up to his father and make things right.

"I'll sort this," he said, standing a little taller and adding a confident resolve to his voice that couldn't have been further from his own feeling. "I won't let him get away with it. I won't let him do this to you."

He made to leave, but it was the queen's turn to take his arm.

"Don't," she said, before her head lowered and her shoulders sagged. She was the strongest woman Leander had ever known, but a shadow of herself in that moment, bruised and defeated. The very sight tied his stomach in a painful knot. Only hours earlier she had left him awestruck, but for all her efforts, he now saw the futility of their circumstances. Beholden to a stubborn father and husband. Victims of a vengeful king.

"I know you mean well," she continued, barely holding herself together. "But you know what he's like. It will only make things worse."

Leander shook his head. "I can't let him do this to you, to Perrine. They have her father!"

The queen pulled away to bury her head in her hands. "*Single-mindedness*," she murmured, quoting the king and their exchange from the previous evening. She turned her attention upon Leander once more and said, "I know it's hard to hear, but perhaps it's time to…remove yourself from the situation. I thought I could get through to him, but look where that got us. Your father has made no pretence about his ambitions for you and King Jannick's daughter. If you really care for the Delport girl, perhaps it's time to step away."

"But I want to be with her," he pleaded, despite his mother's careful logic. For the first time, he wondered if she had ever experienced love quite like this. Hers had been a political marriage, akin to his own engagement with Princess Sanne. Had his parents ever loved each other at all? Were he and his brother Oskar the product of duty? Leander had never felt so worthless.

Observing his spiral, the queen took Leander's hand and led him to the edge of the bed where they perched side-by-side. "It's not easy, you know," she said, steadying a tremble in her lower lip. "Being king, that is. It puts a lot of pressure on your father. I was just eighteen when we met, and they told me he was rash." She smiled, but only briefly, split skin causing her to wince. "The Precipitous Prince is what they called him in those days. My father was desperate for the alliance with Yorick's father. He told me I would be queen someday, but warned me against your father's…impetuous nature. There was no shortage of rumours about Prince Yorick and his headstrong temperament, but you know what? I was not so different myself. With each new account I grew more convinced that I would be the woman to change him. I steeled myself for the challenge, and dreamt of the king that he would become and the Fermantia that we would create together. It wasn't easy, but I endured, and I persisted with the same stubbornness that has since passed to you and your brother."

They shared a smile, and his mother dealt him a playful slap on the leg.

"It may not have been perfect, but it was certainly love." The queen fussed with her wedding ring, and her cheeks pinched with a knowing grin that accentuated her dimples. "Your father was challenging but he was good. He was kind and generous, and we shared some special memories, I want you to know that."

Leander nodded. How was she always able to read his thoughts?

"Of course, it was no time before you arrived and then your brother," she continued. "He loved you boys in his own way. He still does. Your grandfather was a tough man, and Yorick was a mirror for his own father's failings. The two had a withdrawn relationship, which only added to the grief and regret when King Audrick passed. Kingship is no easy burden, a truth that you'll come to know before long. Though your father did his best, sorrow and stress will do mad things to a man."

"I can't imagine." Leander murmured. In spite of everything, he couldn't help feeling some sympathy for his father.

The queen nodded. "It was subtle at first, but he was soon enveloped by the responsibility of rule. He became distant, so much so that he could scarcely hear my voice anymore. The pressure seemed to give him strength and eat away at him at the same time, taking a fresh piece of him each day. More than anything, I know he wanted to surpass his own father. Audrick made no secret of his disappointment in Yorick. His son was never ambitious enough or as decisive as Audrick would have liked." She paused to laugh. "What am I saying? You know this of course. The sad reality is that in spite of my efforts, you are living it. You and your brother. I'm sorry I couldn't have done more."

"Mother…"

"The point is," said the queen, squeezing his hand. "When I first met your father, he surprised me. He was caring and considerate, some distance from the man described to me back home. He was every bit the gallant prince I had hoped for, and people always used to tell me how different he was when we were together. *Different…*" She sighed and let the word hang between them. "Therein is the issue, Leander. There is a proverb in the Tenescan language which when translated reads: *Different is unexpected and temporary. Change is permanent.* Your father will never change. He is a man of moods and fancies. I'm not saying that you should let him run over you, or that you have to give up your dreams. I would just caution patience; use some of those smarts I've given you," she said with a wink. "Pick your battles, bide your time. Don't let your emotions get the better of you, like I did the last time we were together." She sighed. "I'm just a foolish mother who cares too much for her children, but you, well, you will be king one day, Leander, and when that day comes, I know you will bring true change. I, for one, will do anything to support you." Here she lowered her voice to a conspiratorial level. "In some ways, I think that's what keeps me going. The thought you will someday eclipse your father. That for all his efforts, yours is the legacy that will endure. Call it mother's intuition." She smiled, then winced.

"I just hope I don't let you down," said Leander. "But the same goes for Perrine. I can't just abandon her. I have to do something."

His mother's eyes lowered in thought, then eventually, she answered.

"Leave it with me. I'll think of something, I promise. Older? Yes. Wiser? Maybe. One thing is for sure, I'm no less stubborn than the woman your father married, and I still love a challenge. Plenty happens in this palace without him knowing. For now, keep your head down and try not to upset him."

At that moment, a new presence appeared in the doorway. Oskar's long, golden hair made him difficult to miss.

"There you are," Oskar said breathlessly. "I've been searching everywhere for you, Leander. It's Father. He's called a meeting of The Ministry, and he expects you in attendance. You're already late."

CHAPTER 3

ᕫᕤᕫ

Pick your battles, bide your time.

Leander resolved to follow his mother's advice, but suspected it would be far easier said than done. Bemused, he made for the Great Hall of the palace, arriving to join the full complement of The Ministry. Six similarly disconcerted expressions, and at the top of the gilded banquet table, a provoking smile from his father, the king.

"Ah, Prince Leander, so nice of you to join us." Yorick inclined his head to the opposite end of the long rectangular table. A chair sat empty, awaiting Leander's arrival. It was a simple piece of furniture that shared none of the ornate woodwork or added comfort enjoyed by the other attendees. Perhaps worst of all, it was extremely low to the polished marble flooring. The ministers snickered as Leander straightened in effort to meet them at eye level. The king didn't try to hide his amusement. A chance to observe and learn or simple humiliation? This was Leander's first meeting of The Ministry, and with a father like King Yorick, he saw no reason why it couldn't be both.

Right on cue, the king stood to speak. He introduced the meeting and the ministers all silenced in unison. Distracted by concerns for Perrine's wellbeing, Leander fought to contain the angry scowl that tugged at his jaw. His mother was a victim to the king's vindictiveness, but she was strong and she held position, vigilant to her husband's schemes. Perrine, on the other hand, had trusted Leander and was merely an innocent caught in his struggle with his father. He'd promised to keep her safe and not only failed her, but her father too. He wanted to storm out and do something, but his contributions were at least partly responsible for the current problem. He had to trust his mother in the same way he had asked of Perrine. For now, his role was that of dutiful, attentive son. He sat forward in his chair and listened on intently.

"To business then," his father barked. Though deeply flawed, the king certainly knew how to control a room. "Emile, what of our conquests in The Clanlands? I'm in a good mood, so I encourage you to avoid disappointing me."

Obligingly, Emile stood, sweeping long, dark strands of hair away from his eyes. His features creased with the typical, self-satisfied smile that Leander found irksome. Memories of the incident with the Veraza girl only added to his feelings of resentment. To Leander's dismay, the smile widened as Emile announced, "Good news," to which the king sat back and steepled his fingers contentedly.

"As always, your timing is faultless, Your Majesty. Only this morning I received a pertinent update from Commander Lars Cornelis, stationed far to the south in the desert city of Udresh. You're a busy man, so I'll cut to the heart of his report. Our offensive action has proven successful as expected. King Soliman is dead, surrendered by discontented locals, and with him Udresh has ceded to Cadraelian rule. Commander Cornelis writes to apologise for his somewhat hasty decision to terminate your rival, claiming the action to have been prudent in attempts to stifle any insurgence. The Commander has remained in the city to maintain your presence, but the message is clear. It's over, Your Majesty. The last pretender has fallen and the Clanlands are yours."

A round of enthusiastic applause rippled around the table. Another king dead and a way of life soon to follow. Leander clapped along, but his overwhelming feeling was one of sadness. From what little he knew, Soliman had been an honourable man. Was this really cause for celebration?

For whatever reason, the king appeared to agree with him. Yorick sat back in his chair, but his face remained expressionless. His bloodlust, it seemed, was far from sated.

Finally, he reacted, "You mention insurgents…"

"Yes, Your Majesty." Emile gulped before answering, appearing more than a little off balance. Presumably, he had expected the news of victory to garner greater praise. His next words were hurried, and Leander took some pleasure from the Minister for War's discomfort. "There were but a small number," Emile added. "Identified quickly and dealt with effectively."

This time the king smiled. "Very good. Gibbets?"

"Yes, Your Majesty, all as instructed. Their bodies line the Road of Dust between Udresh and Dalarr. A message to those who would deign to challenge you."

The rest of The Ministry jostled in their seats, letting this information wash over them before joining the discussion. Bram's jowls shuddered when he cleared his throat to speak. "A fine victory indeed, my king. We now have a realm like no other, one which spans forests, mountains, deserts and open plains. A single people, united from Fermantia to the tip of Salmanus on the shore of the Southern Seas."

"An expensive venture, but one of great opportunity." Joran added, pausing from scribbling notes to share his considered thoughts. "Udreshi silk, as we know, is of the finest quality, while the city itself will provide a welcome staging post for caravans and traders. This hard-fought development will enable quick, safe passage across the Sands of Sumeya, effectively opening your realm from north to south."

Bruno shuffled in his seat to draw attention. "*A realm under one rule means peace for us all. United we stand, divided we fall.*"

"But not one faith," said Roel bitterly, and with none of Bruno's poetic flair. "We speak of a single people, yet these southerners live in heretical enclaves with scant emphasis on piety and virtue. More must be done to share the word of our creator."

Lennart raised a cautionary palm. "Patience, Roel, you must give things time. Did your Goddess complete the measure of her work in a single day? As Bruno will tell you, 'Peace is Progress.'"

Bruno gave a respectful nod at this reference to one of the esteemed Elurian philosophers, whose name, in that moment, Leander could not recall. The king, meanwhile, seemed less impressed. He shook his head, and then stood to speak.

"Peace?" The legs of his chair scrapped against the flagstones. "Peace is a project, a work in progress. I fear we are too quick to congratulate ourselves, too eager to declare victory. I had hoped to find Fermantia's greatest minds above hubris, invulnerable to complacency. No…" he added, turning to pace dismissively. "Welcome news though this is, we are merely another step on the road to immortality. I don't doubt that Queen Orsolina has been watching our progress from the Vicentian capital with a keen eye. Our gains are likely to render others…*uncomfortable*."

"Queen Orsolina is no fool," said Emile. "You can't imagine she'd be tempted to test us."

The king shrugged his shoulders. "I have an imagination for many things. To defeat an enemy one most ultimately learn to think as they do. Put yourself in Orsolina's throne for a moment. Does the expansion of Fermantia suggest peace and progress as you have suggested?"

"I'm sorry, Your Majesty, but what are you proposing?" Joran gave voice to a question that Leander himself was keen to ask. It seemed that, irrespective of status, the king alone was privy to the sum of his thoughts. The glint in his father's eyes caused Leander to shift awkwardly in his seat.

Somehow, the king's next words were even worse than expected.

"Tenevarre," he announced, returning to slam his hands against the polished wooden surface of the table, the noise serving to mask the collective gasp that greeted his proclamation.

Bram Hoste was first to react, scratching at the scalp of his diminishing hair. "Forgive me, Your Majesty, but are you proposing a fresh campaign in the north?"

A small state separating Fermantia from Vicentia and Queen Orsolina, Tenevarre was a neutral, if contested, frontier. Although not officially recognised as a nation in its own right, Yorick's father, King Audrick, had signed a peace treaty with the Vicentians decades previously. Tenevarre was to represent a harmonious front for the cultivation of relations, and while wealth and trade had grown exponentially during peace times, strategic positioning remained Tenevarre's most desirable trait. Forbidden from forming central governance, Tenevarre was a collection of disparate provinces, where power belonged to those with the deepest pockets or, indeed, those with the heaviest hands.

"The time has come to pursue our northern interests," said the king. "Progress is persistence and initiative is key. I understand my late father's preference toward peaceful solutions, but we have strong historical claims to the land that I have every intention of seeing fulfilled."

Bram's jaw fell a little. "But Your Majesty, this action is tantamount to all-out war."

"He's right," said Lennart. "There's no way that Queen Orsolina will accept this."

To Leander's dismay, the king seemed entirely unmoved. "I don't doubt she'll dislike the news, but those concerns are for the minds of your Vicentian counterparts. My considerations start and end with Fermantian interests. What our flourishing realm needs now is safety and stability."

"And to this you propose war?" Roel gave voice to a room of concern.

"That decision rests with Queen Orsolina." The king raised a single eyebrow. "You speak of faith; well, I have every belief in our divine claim to the state of Tenevarre. In fact, I have every confidence that the people will welcome our realm and its many benefits with open arms. Better that, than fall prey to the talons of Vicentia. Our arrival will bring new wealth and opportunities to Tenevarre, and in doing so, secure the northern frontier against those who might seek to challenge us."

Joran's eyes narrowed. Clearly, he had his doubts. "It's an audacious idea, my king, and one for which I'm sure you have conceived suitable plans. I must say, though, that it will not be easy, and while the Cadraelian Realm has many benefits to infer, we are not without our financial challenges. You need look no further than the slums of Lower Cadrael, where discontent appears to be growing by the day. There's a feeling that wealth is…unfairly distributed, shall we say."

"Come now, Joran, always the naysayer," said the king. "I'm an ambitious man, but not entirely without subtlety. I understand that this complicated situation requires a certain amount of tact and that is why I intend to bring you all along for the negotiations."

The room sat silent, inviting King Yorick to elaborate, though evidently not upon the hardship facing Lower Cadrael. Leander chewed at his fingernails with a mixture of uncertainty and trepidation. If not before, he now realised that he had vastly misjudged his father's desires and the lengths the man would go to see them achieved. In the power struggle for Tenevarre, it appeared his father might be the most heavy-handed of all.

"I've spoken with King Jannick, and while he appreciates my objectives, neither he nor his allies will support a declaration of war against Vicentia without diplomatic efforts. He has suggested that we negotiate fresh assurances of peace in Tenevarre or renegotiate more agreeable borders," the king added.

"I must say that's some relief." Bram blew out his cheeks, before straightening the rounded eyeglasses that threatened to slip from his nose. Momentary respite settled upon the room. Joran, however, was characteristically sceptical.

"I'm sorry, Your Majesty, but I can't say that I share Bram's optimism. Queen Orsolina is a difficult woman at the best of times. I don't imagine she will stand by and surrender Tenevarre to the realm. It's the equivalent of inviting us to the gates of her own queendom. From what I can see, there are only two outcomes: either Orsolina submits to your requests, losing face and weakening her own position, or—"

"War," said Emile.

The room fell silent.

An unsettling smile emerged on the king's face. "As I said, that decision rests with dear Orsolina."

The implications finally dawned on all of them. Six of the most powerful men in all of Fermantia, quietened, powerless. Puzzled expressions gave voice to a world of concern—not only for the fate of Tenevarre, but also what this path of action would mean to each of them.

"Are you sure this is a good idea?" asked Lennart, drawing his thick eyebrows together in question. "Your southern campaigns have not been without opposition. I live to serve and enforce your peace, my king, but fresh conflict is likely to be met with staunch disapproval."

"And significant cost," said Joran, firmly. "Lennart's right to highlight your recent forays, which, as we know, have been enormously expensive. As your forces grow, so do costs for food, armour, weaponry and other provisions. We previously discussed plans to invest in infrastructures—roads for trade and taxation that will, in time, help to replenish our reserves. In your footsteps we follow, Your Majesty, but perhaps it would be prudent to…delay this course and pursue a different path?"

The king slumped into his seat. "Stagnate, you mean? Bruno, tell me all you know of my great grandfather, King Corentin."

Bruno's open-mouthed hesitancy said more than enough.

"Exactly," continued the king. "The man was quiet, considered, risk-averse and historically irrelevant. To stand still is to fall behind. I will see our realm flourish, and with it, my legacy."

There it was. The crux of King Yorick's desires. No doubt each member of The Ministry had cause to challenge their king's plans, but who would have the nerve to contest him, and what good could come of it anyway?

Surprisingly, it was Emile who found the courage to speak out, though his voice was lower and more nervous than usual. His finger tapped on the table, betraying his unease, and in a strange twist of events, Leander realised that he shared the man's apprehension. "Your Majesty, you know that I live to serve you. It is an honour to lead your armies, and a privilege to share your victories. The rightful expansion of the Cadraelian Realm is something I support with every ounce of my being, yet…" Here he paused, and a grimace of discomfort crossed his face. "The men are tired, my king. They are tired, hungry and missing their families. Your southern campaign has been hugely successful but not without loss and suffering. Of course, I would march these men to face Vicentia in a heartbeat, but it is only prudent to paint a full picture of your position. Your battles in the Clanlands were hard-fought, but these were, for the most part waged against ill-educated tribespeople, archaic settlers and nomadic hoards. Vicentia, well Vicentia is a very different situation altogether…"

"So, you don't think you can win?" The king hoisted his eyebrows. He sat back in his chair and crossed his arms expectantly.

"Well, no…" he stuttered, before Bruno came to his rescue.

"My king," he began, speaking with a gentle, obsequious tone clearly intended to calm the situation. "It is true that many great legacies are written in blood. Of course, the great poet, Manousos himself wrote '*Land with swords, leave with songs.*' He gave a self-satisfied chuckle at the allusion, but his recital harvested little reaction. Discomfited, he straightened his velvet surcoat and cleared his throat before continuing, "I wonder if your narrative might be different. You've made great strides in the south already; perhaps there is time for pause, time to cultivate and develop relations with these nomads and tribespeople?"

Evidently, Joran shared this sentiment. "Build roads to your cities and bridges to the people, my king. Reap the rewards of your labours, fill your vaults with gold and make plans for Tenevarre. Time is on your side."

"He's right," interjected Emile, his blue eyes widening with hope. "All we need is a little time. Let the men rest and return to their families. Sharpen blades, strengthen shields, and I have no doubt that we will be ready to regroup by winter."

Of all the contributions, this hit Leander hardest. If Emile of all people was reluctant to spill blood, he had to know something the king didn't. He had to know that they could not win.

"Enough."

A violent coughing fit briefly curtailed the king's sentiment. He raised his handkerchief to cover his mouth, and by the time he removed it the white silk was speckled red. Concerned expressions passed among the ministers until a servant girl furnished the king with his tincture. He hawked up any residual mucus with characteristic gusto, slammed his fist on the table and then proceeded as if nothing had happened. As he spoke, Leander couldn't help but notice the red hue of his father's skin and the thick sweat that lined the older man's brow. For all his bluster, the king looked frail.

"What surprise to hear this talk of *plans* and *rest*. I don't doubt that you'd all be happy to remain in your estates, fucking your wives and eating fine food. Perhaps Bram will do us all a favour and drink himself to an early grave." The Minister for Land choked on a mouthful of red wine under the king's glare. The others chuckled in an attempt to curry favour, but the mood was undeniably sombre.

"Son," said the king, shifting his attention. "Today's challenges are yours for tomorrow. What do you make of this complex situation, and what course of action would a prince of Fermantia recommend?"

The king reclined and picked at his nails. Once more the moth being drawn to a flame, Leander felt a quickening in his chest. He swallowed deeply, considering the options at his disposal. Was it wise to challenge the king, and was he any more likely to make a difference? Solidarity with his father would possibly improve relations between them, perhaps to the extent of a pardon for Perrine. Yet war with Vicentia would be ruinous and nonsensical. Moreover, his father would need support from King Jannick, and Leander knew his part in that bargain only too well. He swallowed again, his pride this time. For better or worse, he had to make the king see sense.

"You are a great king, Father. One that history will remember fondly. Your ambitions far exceed our expectations, and it is your vision for the realm that drives us forward." He paused, and his father inclined his head appreciatively. Even now, the reaction gave Leander a swell of pride. He only wished that he could continue the same tack, but the eyes of the ministers narrowed in expectation. He had to do the right thing, and he had to believe his father could change. If nothing else, he now had the man's full attention. "While I have every confidence in our claim to Tenevarre and your prowess on the battlefield, I feel that there is some truth in the words of our esteemed company.

Thus far, your legacy is scarcely beyond the preamble. You have already achieved so much, and there isn't a single man who would fault you for resting to enjoy the laurels. Take pause…" he said, in his most pleading tone. "Meet your people and show them the realm that you envisaged. Standardised coinage carrying your likeness, trade, education, and religion," His gesture toward Roel met with a smile. "Queen Orsolina is not so foolish as to challenge you. But, when the time comes, let her face an army most dangerous. One that does not just serve but *loves* their king."

He finished and let out a sigh of relief. Regrettably, the king did not seem convinced.

"Very good." The king clapped loudly, causing the others to wince. "A respectable monologue, which I would have expected from The Ministry. Sadly, my son, you were born above that. It is our duty as royals to be decisive. To receive advice and to make decisions. History will remember me because I am remarkable, a man who stands above all others, rewriting the past and shaping our future. I brought you here in the hope of uncovering those same qualities, but it seems I may have been overly optimistic. You are my blood, and when the time comes, I need to know you will not disappoint me nor sully our family name. For now, you will remain at my side and watch closely. You will join us when we travel to discuss the fate of Tenevarre. As for all of you…" he scoured the great hall to scowl at the ministers. "Make your plans but make them quick. And remember, I have the power to see you all removed with a single clap of my hands. In future, it would be wise to avoid disappointing me. Oh, and Emile, send a message to Orsolina requesting parley. The rest of you be ready to depart two days hence."

A wave of nods and murmurs of consent passed around the table before the hall began to empty. Though the king remained seated, Leander made for the exit, pausing when only he and his father remained. *A man who stands above all others* was how the king had described himself, but at what cost? The rigours of kingship were clear on his face. Bluster and self-assurance were no mask for a man that now seemed tired and surprisingly frail. Would Leander, in time, prove to be any different, and was he truly strong enough to bring about change?

His first Meeting of The Ministry left Leander with no desire to return.

Back in his own chambers, Leander experienced a deep sense of bewilderment. He felt like a puppet with his father pulling the strings—a player in a story set upon on the broad stage of the Cadraelian Realm, the plotlines already in ink.

He slumped onto his bed, troubled by his mother's words, continuing to wonder if his life was just another inevitable instance of history repeating itself. He was, after all, King Yorick's flesh and blood. Even if the king had supposedly once been caring and considerate, little evidence of that man remained. Any kindness had been eroded by many years of responsibility, veiled by the smoke and fire of war.

A knock at the door shook him out of his reverie. To Leander's dismay, Oskar walked in before he could say a word, his face beaming.

"I heard the news!" The prince's voice boomed with excitement. He strode to the centre of the room uninvited, halting suddenly to fuss with the long strands of his golden hair that had fallen to cover his eyes. Despite their visible similarities, Leander was the older by eight years, a gap which had become increasingly difficult to bridge. Immature and impetuous, Oskar was the archetypal younger sibling, and though Leander had hoped to recover the affection they had shared in childhood, this particular ambition was currently some way off.

Echoing their father, Oskar continued, "Tenevarre! About time I say, take back what's rightfully ours. I knew Father would tire of those petty scuffles for southern dirt and dust. Tenevarre, that's the future—and with any luck, Vicentia too."

Leander fought to swallow his frustration. "Vicentia?" he asked. "You're hoping for war?"

"Are you not?" said Oskar, scratching his head with disbelief. "The Cadraelian Realm would be the greatest the world has ever known. That's our realm one day, Leander. Why, you'd be the king of half the known world."

"Assuming father wins. What of the lives lost?"

"If Orsolina has any sense, she'll surrender Tenevarre and cede to the realm. She's lucky that father has given her the chance of peace. What is it with you, Leander, why must you challenge father? A place in the Royal Gallery and attendance at the meeting of The Ministry. Father honours you, and you do nothing but undermine him."

Leander rolled his eyes. "It's not that simple."

"Oh, I think it is." Oskar snapped. "You know your problem? You think too much. You're a prince, Leander. Firstborn and heir to Father's throne. I would kill to trade places and learn from the king. Remember, while you're travelling to meet Orsolina, I'll be stuck here with mother doting on me like a babe." A sudden thought appeared in the glint of his eye, followed by a smile. "You're just like her, you know. Slave to your own emotions, high-handed morals and Goddess knows what else."

This was enough to exhaust Leander's patience. He rose from the bed and moved to stand toe-to-toe with his brother. "Enough!" he said, caustically, clenching his fists. "You don't know how dangerous this is, and I pray you never have to learn the hard way. You talk about trading places; well, I'd take that deal in a heartbeat. While you were here with mother caring for you, I was sending men to their death at the siege of Ardalan. It's not a game, Oskar. Even The Ministry disagrees with him."

Oskar scoffed. "The Ministry? Who cares what those old fucks have to say? If I were king, I'd have them all thrown in the dungeon and kept in chains. A king's word is final, Leander. The sooner you learn this, the better for all of us."

At this a brief peace descended between them, the only sound coming from Leander's heavy breath. Oskar really was a frightening reflection of their father, but maybe there was some truth in his callous words. Perhaps Leander was the very image of their mother, and to Leander's mind, this was no bad thing. He would travel with his father and contain his emotions. Bide his time and pick his battles.

"You're absolutely right," he answered eventually. "I'm sorry, I'm just tired."

Oskar nodded. "Of course. I should leave you." He departed, closing the door behind him, leaving Leander's chambers silent.

Someday, I'll bring true change, thought Leander. *But first, I must see Perrine to safety.*

CHAPTER 4

For the second time in as many days, Leander woke with a start. A soft hand was clasped over his mouth, causing him to gasp as the blurry image of his mother standing over him came into focus.

"Shh," she urged, silhouetted by moonlight. "Come with me, but be quick and quiet about it."

She turned and moved for the exit, leaving Leander to leap from his bed and change into day clothes: a silk shirt, cotton trousers and black, highly polished boots. He yawned deeply and rubbed the tiredness from his eyes.

"Ready?" the queen asked without turning to face him. He could tell she was nervous, shuffling with an obvious air of impatience and watchfulness.

"Ready," Leander answered, prompting the queen to set off through the palace, Leander trailing in tow. The queen was remarkably fleet-footed, moving through the marble columns and polished floors with only the sound of her dress echoing that of a gentle breeze, soft and light. Leander refrained from asking questions, not wanting to break the silence that was only interrupted as they passed the royal chambers. If nothing else, the booming noise left no doubt that the king was sleeping.

"Red wine," whispered the queen, turning to flash a playful smile in Leander's direction. "To most, your father must seem wholly unpredictable. *A great man, above all others,* as he loves to tell us, but not above the effects of a good wine."

Leander grinned and continued to follow. They passed through the palace unencumbered by run-ins with guards or other distractions, arriving at the grand staircase moments later.

Here his mother halted, her calm, composed countenance beginning to return. "I'm sorry for all the cloak and daggers, Leander. I had to do something, I'm sure you understand. Do you remember when we used to play hide-and-seek when you were younger?"

"Of course," he said, recalling the memories with unbridled fondness. Happier times he would never forget.

The queen took his hand and pulled him toward a heavy wooden door to the side of the staircase. The path to the royal prison in the bowels of the palace, likely the place where Perrine was captive. Leander's heart beat a little faster as his mother's plan finally fell into place. "Come," she said, as the armed guard at the door stepped aside obligingly. "Thank you, Arnaud. Nearly there now, Leander."

The guard smiled reverently as he opened the door to reveal a stonework spiral staircase. Flickering torches aided their descent, but the space below was silent and foreboding. "I'm sorry, my dear, but it's the best I can do for now. Let's hope your father doesn't find out about this."

"She's okay then?" Leander's voiced echoed about them with a tone of desperation.

At the foot of the stairs, his mother finally came to a halt. "She's fine," she said softly. "But wouldn't you rather ask her that question yourself?"

Before Leander had chance to answer, another guard appeared to address them. "Your Majesties," he said, with an exaggerated if courteous bow. "The girl's up ahead. You'll face no complications, but be swift about it. We don't have long."

The queen thanked the man with appropriate haste. "Go," she said, urging Leander. "Now's your chance before I change my mind."

Torchlight danced on the ground to light the way ahead. The single pathway was cold and dark, but Leander felt his mood brightening with every step. That was, at least, until he finally saw her.

"Perrine," he exclaimed. "What the fuck did they do to you?"

The hazy half-light did little to obscure her suffering. She barely looked like the same person, her beautiful features obscured by black bruises that bloomed beneath her eyes. Dank, oily hair framed her face, and whatever rags they'd put her in were crusted with grime. The smell of human waste caused Leander to cover his nose reflexively, as murmurs of suffering echoed out from the surrounding cells. This place was no prison. It was hell on earth. He crouched and wrapped a hand about the cool metal of the heavy iron bars. "Perrine, are you okay?"

She didn't answer but pulled herself up from the filth of the floor, propping her back against the dank wall of the cell.

"Where is my father?" she eventually asked, the words barely audible. Then launching herself at the bars, gnashing her teeth like a caged animal, "Where's my father? You promised me you'd keep us safe!" She was scarcely recognisable, desperate and pushed almost to the point of madness.

"I'm sorry, I—I don't know," he said, stammering to find an answer. "Mother says she's going to get you out of here, but the king is threatening all-out war. He's demanded I travel with him to meet Queen Orsolina and—"

"Fuck Orsolina!" Perrine stopped him cold, gripping his hand until the knuckles were white. "This may surprise you, but the entire world doesn't revolve around you and your family. Where's my father? He's innocent in all of this."

Shocked and unsettled, Leander began to question his true intentions for coming down here. For his own benefit perhaps, an easing of his conscience? Perrine was right—what use were empty platitudes? Good intentions, hollow promises. He dropped his head, hating himself more than ever before.

"I'm sorry," he said. "I don't know where your father is, but I'll do everything in my power to see him released. Mother has connections with officials at gaols all over the city."

"Good. Perhaps she can be relied upon to do something useful. Leave mother to clean up the mess while you're away playing soldiers."

"Perrine, please, at least my father will be away from the city. I know you're worried, but with Mother's intervention, I'm sure this will pass."

Perrine scoffed. "Pass?" Leander's cheeks reddened as she shook her head. "Simple as that, is it, Prince Leander? Everything back to normal, all forgotten. You believe you'll just ride back into the capital and we'll just continue to see each other, playing out your sordid little fantasy. What is this to you, some kind of power trip? Do you enjoy having control over my entire life?"

"Perrine, you're not making sense. You know it's not like that."

"Sense, Leander? When did any of this make sense at all? I knew it was dangerous, but you couldn't do it could you? You couldn't let me walk away. And now this..." She raised her hands in frustration. "I promise you, if anything happens to my father—"

She silenced as the queen appeared, then slumped back when Leander's mother began to speak. "I'm sorry to interrupt, but we have to go. Perrine..." She let the name hang between them. "I'll do what I can, I promise. Be strong."

Any hope of affection between Perrine and Leander seemed wildly optimistic. He offered, "I love you," but to this Perrine simply turned away. "I'll see you soon," he added, returning to full height to follow his mother's exit. Guilt knotted his stomach, but Leander knew that he couldn't, wouldn't let Perrine down. He had to make things right lest she be lost to him forever.

At the top of the stairs his mother smothered him in a tight hug. "Things will all work out," she whispered in his ear. "Go with your father. I'll take care of things here."

They parted ways and Leander retraced the steps that led to his chambers. Early sunlight poured into the long corridors, but a darkness hung over him, hampering his every step. Could he really blame Perrine for her reaction? Her life was in tatters and her father's precarious health was, as yet, unknown. No matter how Leander looked at it, he'd let her down. He wasn't angry at Perrine, only at himself.

The sound of jaunty morning birdsong came in through the windows, almost comically at odds with Leander's worsening mood. He forced a smile on his face for the palace guards and staff who crossed his path, moving with swift purpose until raised voices brought him to a sudden halt.

Unbeknownst to the king, the door to his chambers was ajar, leaving his angry voice to echo out for all to hear. "I don't pay for your opinions," he shouted at an unknown victim. "I pay for solutions. So find one or my health will be the very least of your concerns."

"But Your Majesty..." the simpering response came in reply. It was unmistakeably that of the royal surgeon. "I'm sorry but I simply must caution against this. We've discussed it all previously; you're not a well man."

The sound of smashed glass caused Leander to flinch.

"Fuck well!" yelled the king. "I am more than a man."

"Be that as it may, your health is deteriorating. Please, Your Majesty..." the surgeons voice lowered with a tremble of desperation. "If you want to live to see the winter, I urge you to remain in Cadrael where I can observe you."

The room fell quiet. Leander pressed himself to the wall when heavy boots suddenly sounded in his direction. He sighed with relief as the door slammed shut, the conversation now continuing but too muffled to hear.

Alone in the corridor, his heart threatened to burst from his chest. Only then did it dawn on him. His father was dying.

Unsurprisingly, two days in the saddle only worsened Leander's mood. With Cadrael behind them, the group had travelled north, following the Maasmeer River away from the city and into the wide-open plains beyond. After many hours of uneventful riding, they'd come to a crumbling wooden bridge that gave passage across the fast-flowing Bremburg River. They'd then spent their first night under the stars at a temporary camp on the riverbank, near the fishing village of Tillen, where barges bobbed in the shadow of creaky old wooden shacks and a lamentably rowdy tumbledown inn.

Recent events had left Leander sour-faced, and though his travelling companions made every effort to speak with him, the prince had become more removed with every mile. Before long, his attitude earned Leander the space he had so keenly sought, the ministers instead gathering to speak in hushed tones amongst themselves, or, as was typical, toadying to their king.

With guards, chefs and maidservants, they numbered around fifty. Eager to realise his aims, the king rode at the front, with all six ministers hot on his heels. Likely, this was where his father had expected him to ride too, but Leander's path wandered with his thoughts. When they stopped, he'd retired to his tent to dine alone. Honeyed pork was normally one of Leander's favourites, but a full belly made little difference to his blackening mood. Every burst of laughter from the nearby dining tent made Leander imagine himself the butt of the joke. The carrying sound of animated, and in most cases inebriated, voices made it clear that he was not sorely missed.

The following morning began with a chill in the air, one which played havoc with his father's cough. The surgeon's words echoed in Leander's mind and his frustration grew at the futility of their journey. Continuing north, they passed through the Ebenfurt Forest, with giant red-beaked Gorehawks hungrily watching their every step from ancient trees coated in emerald green moss. Ground level was no less dangerous either. Recent rains had turned the earthy pathways to quagmire, with some trails rendered unpassable or left overgrown with razor-sharp thorns. Breaking free from the forest, and with the unnerving screech of the infamous hawks left echoing behind them, peat bogs provided an unwelcome reward. Leander couldn't help but question their luck.

Yet onward they persisted into the foothills of the Walencote Mountains, their first view of the famous jagged peaks that had towered on the horizon through most of their journey. Nature on this scale had previously seemed impossible to Leander, but now, up close, he felt a sense of wonder overcome him as the fledgling sun crept up behind the tall crests, painting the sky a dazzling orange.

Their accommodation for the second night lay in the shadows of these same mountains: an imposing castle belonging to Lennart, made from the same stone towering above it. Saddle-sore and stomach growling, Leander felt some relief as they approached their resting point. At least, that was, until Lennart's horse purposely drew alongside Remi, the minister's expression one of concern.

"You have to speak to him," the minister said, quiet enough to remain out of the king's earshot. "You know this is folly, and you're the only one he'll listen to."

Before Leander could reply, the Minister for Justice rode off to re-join his peers. Despite their best efforts at subtlety, it was obvious they'd been watching. Lennart was merely the messenger, his task now passed to an unwilling Leander. The worst of it was that he knew they were right. They drew to a halt and dismounted as they entered the castle's cobblestone courtyard. They were now only a handful of miles from the Tenevarrean border.

Time was running out.

Darkness descended upon the castle, bringing quiet. It seemed that two days of hard travel had weathered any early enthusiasm. The crackle of torchlight sounded in the hallways, but the mood was sombre and there was a notable absence of drunken revelry from the castle's dining hall. Alone in his chambers, Leander stood then sat, repeating the action again and again before perching on the edge of his bed. A whole evening pacing and fretting and wondering why it had to be him. He had hoped that wine would bring clarity or confidence, but in the end, it only served to worsen his frustration. A prince of Fermantia and heir to the throne, only he could think to challenge the king.

It had to be now.

The guard at the door bowed as he left his room. On his way, he passed two other soldiers drinking and playing dice, laughing without a care in the world. For a moment Leander envied them, wishing to share their freedom, but he knew this was his naivety at play. He continued, passing rooms containing sleeping ministers, finally coming to a halt in view of his father's quarters.

His heart pounded in his chest, but he refused to let it show in the presence of the two remaining sentries who stood in his path. Instead, he lifted his chin, puffed out his chest, then walked toward the doors without ever breaking stride. Now more than ever, he needed to be his father's son. On this night, he wouldn't take no for an answer.

"I wish to see my father," he said to the first guard, a man with long, curly black hair that fell to his shoulders.

The guard's head lowered. "I'm sorry, my prince, but the king has requested quiet at this time."

The perfect excuse to turn and walk away, but Leander held fast.

"Of course," he said smiling, "but it's quite urgent that I see him. Please ensure we're not interrupted."

The guards stepped aside as Leander walked between them. They were, it seemed, otherwise unsure how to react.

Beyond the doors, Yorick's room flickered with golden candlelight. "Son," said the king, from his position behind a desk. "What a pleasant surprise. I was starting to think you were avoiding me."

More than anything, he wanted to confirm his father's suspicions and question the wisdom in imprisoning Perrine.

He opened his mouth, but the words died on his lips. In the end, he simply smiled to mask his nerves.

The king gestured to a seat in front of him. "Sit, you make the place look untidy."

Leander obliged, and his father smiled broadly. The older man placed his quill on the table, pushing some papers aside to make space between them. "So come on then," he said, raising both eyebrows. "I highly doubt you came here to sit in silence."

Leander cleared his throat. "No," he said, "There was something..."

"Tenevarre, I should imagine? It seems my Ministry are not without resourcefulness. Imagine manoeuvring a prince to do your bidding."

Leander's skin reddened under his father's appraising glare. "I think you have misjudged the situation," he said, containing the doubt in his voice. "I speak to you only as a son counselling his father. I have my own concerns regarding our current course of action, and I would petition you to reconsider. It's not too late."

"And what would you have me do?" The king sat back in his chair and took a long mouthful of wine. "Run back to Cadrael with my tail between my legs? Go home and allow my ministers to grow fat and wealthy while our enemies make plans and sharpen their claws?"

"But Father, I think you overestimate our enemies. I can't believe that Orsolina would be so foolish. I don't deny your claims to Tenevarre, but there is no need for all of this. You have nothing to worry about."

The king's hands slammed on the desk, sending a small glass bottle hurtling to the floor where it smashed on impact. "There is always something to worry about!" he shouted, red-faced, veins bulging angrily from his neck. "There's always something to fuck you when you least expect it. I wish I shared your mother's romantic view of the world. Perhaps I would be as optimistic as you are, or maybe I'd be more like The Ministry and simply not give a shit. But that's not the real world, Leander, and I will make you see this even if it's the last thing I do..."

Leander's brow furrowed. "Is this about your health?"

"Fuck my health!" The king grabbed a knife from the table, pointing it at Leander with fire in his eyes. "I am your king, and don't you ever forget that. Never question me, and do not pretend to know the measure of my thoughts." He walked around the desk, bringing the two men toe-to-toe. "Whatever the danger, it is my job to be vigilant. That's why history will remember me, Leander. Even if you are blind to your king's achievements. Orsolina, King Jannick, they are all little more than playing pieces at my table. The girl too," he said with a wolfish smile that left Leander unsettled. "The one from the arena, to whom you were so keen to show mercy. I've hired a man to hunt her like the vermin she is. I will not allow rodents like her to roam the streets, spreading her filth. We will find her, and you'll watch her die so you both learn your lesson. You see, Leander, your time will come, but let me remind you, it's not today."

At that, the king turned and reclaimed his seat. He drained his glass of wine and folded his arms, inviting Leander's reply. A hopeless situation had somehow worsened, yet Leander had come too far to give up so easily. He steeled himself, trying to embody some princely authority.

"So that's it then?" he asked, shrugging his shoulders. "The slightest hint of a threat and your answer is murder. I thought you were a man above all others. Your actions are those of a cut-throat or common butcher."

The king laughed haughtily. "There we are. Finally The Ministry's puppet learns to speak for itself."

"Is this just a game to you?" Leander asked shaking his head.

The king's eyes narrowed. "It's whatever I say it is."

A brief pause in their heated exchange allowed the temperature to cool between them. This type of encounter was sport to King Yorick, like the destructive rutting of two territorial stags. Leander knew his efforts were flailing, but he had to find a way to break through the bravado.

"Your plan then, to be clear, is to destroy everything that stands in your path? Some dangers are better handled more delicately, with patience and understanding. Negotiation..." This time Leander's brows raised, challenging his father. "Or advice from others, like, say...a venerated surgeon?"

The king's face dropped. "Careful, Leander. You've seen what your meddling has done for the servant girl and her rather fragile father."

"Fragile?" snapped Leander. "Father, you're dying!"

"Pah," the king swiped dismissively. "A king dies of old age or heroics on the battlefield. The surgeon cares only for his pocket and self-importance. I'm no normal man, Leander, and I will use my time to make this clear."

Finally, Leander understood the heart of the matter. A king absorbed by his own reputation. A dying man with little to lose.

"But what of your people and their future? Should they throw down their lives to write your legacy?"

"I should think that a considerable honour," said the king. "Remember, Leander, that is the place of the common man."

Leander sneered. "Not in my kingdom. No life is worth more or less than any other. I will not stand by and let you do this. I may be your son, but puppet I am not."

The king's chair flew back as he rushed to stand. "You dare to defy me?"

A cough escaped him, silencing him abruptly. The king's eyes widened as another cough caused him to double over, retching in agony. Leander stood, shocked, as his father fell to his knees, blood spraying from his mouth onto the desktop. Yorick tried to grab the edge of the table as he went down, but the blood caused his grip to fail.

A moment later, the king was on his back.

"Leander, help," he gurgled, his voice now quiet and strained. The veins in his neck seemed fit to burst, not from anger this time, but desperation and fear. His arm shot into the air, reaching helplessly towards his son, but as Leander moved to meet the gesture, a crippling shock overcame him, and then panic set in.

Frantically, he began to gaze around the echoing expanse of the chamber, but for all the trunks of clothes and other baubles, he saw no other sign of the life-preserving vials. Only the remnants of the broken flask remained dashed on the floor, their contents pooled into a wretched puddle. With every second, his father was dying. The bloody cough had shifted to a wheezing retch that shuddered through his body, leaving him shaking as life quickly escaped him.

In a moment of clarity Leander rushed to the king's bedside, where, among papers, sealing wax and other scraps, he was relieved to find the desired remedy. Quickly he removed the stopper from the vial, returning to crouch beside the king's dying form. Their eyes met, but Leander's hand froze in place, his mind a battleground for a thousand conflicting thoughts.

Here was the man who had given him life and a place in the world. A father and a husband. A king who, for better or worse, had made Fermantia the centre of arguably the finest realm in recorded history. A man who, perhaps with the right influence, could still see events to a peaceful conclusion.

Wistful optimism.

Leander stayed his hand.

His father's eyes widened with terror.

King Yorick had imprisoned Perrine and her dying father. He had sent Ferran Veraza into the afterlife in the trail of his two boys, with every intention that his daughter would soon follow. Leander's father had sentenced thousands of young soldiers to meaningless deaths on the battlefield in a campaign that was still just beginning. He'd made Leander's mother suffer over many years, an act that had peaked with the unforgiveable physical attack shortly before their departure from the capital.

By his mother's own words, Leander knew the king would never change. Besides, the man was dying anyway. In this act, Leander had the chance to spare war and suffering.

The chilling voice of Ferran Veraza's daughter echoed in his mind. *The king must die.*

In the end, it was hardly a decision at all.

He replaced the cork in the top of the vial and pushed the tincture into his pocket as heavy tears formed in his eyes.

"Son..." wheezed the king, who had never looked more hopeless than in that moment. A sudden convulsion crashed through his body, and a mouthful of blood showered Leander's shirt. Instinctively, Leander clasped his father's hand in an attempt to comfort the king as he hacked and coughed. Eventually the older man fell still and almost silent. The king's breathing slowed, and his grip began to loosen.

Leander whispered, "I'm sorry, Father..." and by the time of his final word, the king was gone.

Except he wasn't, was he? Leander was king now.

Reality cut through him with the sharpness of a guillotine blade. In one fell swoop, Leander was a killer and a king. He thought of his mother and Oskar and was consumed by a sudden and severe pang of grief. Who was he to decide what was good for them? A king was answerable only to the Goddess, yet Leander had taken it upon himself to play creator. Purgatory would be the uncomfortable seat of his father's throne.

As regret and sadness began to overwhelm him, there came a knock at the door.

"Everything okay in there, Your Majesty?" a guard's voice echoed from the corridor.

Leander cuffed the tears from his eyes. His mind had frozen, and his mouth tasted like sawdust, his throat dry and unresponsive.

For a second time the guard called, "Your Majesties?"

Leander remained silent, wondering how he could ever answer. If nothing else, he hoped to buy himself some time. Would he be accused, or worse, arrested? His father's ill health was well known, but few understood the extent of his ailments. Moreover, the man had been very much alive when Leander had arrived to speak with him only moments before. He thought to run, but there was only one way in and out of the room that now acted both as grave and gaol.

Moments into his reign and Leander already had already become another hapless king inevitably bound for the unforgiving pages of the history books. Had his father really been so bad, and would Leander prove to be any better? Maybe it had all been a terrible lapse in judgement. Justice was closing in on him, more literally than he knew in that instant.

"You must excuse us, Your Majesty, but we're coming in to check you're okay."

Lennart's voice sent chills through Leander. Once more, he scanned the room, this time searching for a means of escape. A secret door. Would he survive a daring jump from the window? He was all out of options, and time was soon to follow. The door crashed open, he startled, and Lennart's face dropped at the bloody scene before him.

He turned to a guard and shouted, "Don't just stand there, go and find a surgeon."

By now, Leander was trembling with fear. The impression of guilt was hard to contain, but he stood looking shocked as Lennart arrived at his side. The Minister for Justice shared a similar expression.

"What happened?" asked Lennart, dropping to his knees and searching unsuccessfully for the king's pulse.

Before he could answer, Emile appeared in the doorway, where Joran, Roel and the remainder of The Ministry, joined him.

"What the fuck happened?" the Minister for War repeated. A different voice, but the same question as before. Even with such chaos before him, the man paused to perfect his hair, sweeping strands away to expose his scar. Unmistakably, this was a significant moment, and Emile, it seemed, was intent on looking his best. The ministers poured into the room, closing the doors behind them, and Roel rushed to kneel at the king's side, whispering prayers to the same almighty power who had done little to spare their king.

"I...he..." Leander stumbled to find an answer.

"It's okay," said Joran, stepping forward to place a hand on the prince's shoulder. He glanced at the king's prostrate, blood-soaked form, and then back to Leander, "I'm sure that there was nothing you could have done."

It was then that the man's eyes flickered to Leander's pocket. His sharp face narrowed in suspicion at the sight of the glass vial protruding guiltily. With this glare, an unspoken sense of doubt seemed to fill the room. Emile, of course, was the first to speak.

"Leander," he asked. "What actually happened?"

"Father had one of his outbursts." Leander's panicked response did little to assert his innocence. "You know about his cough, but this was the worst I've heard it. There was...is blood everywhere, and Father dropped his tincture. There was nothing I could do," he finished, swiftly repurposing Joran's words.

Six sets of eyes scoured the floor, resting on the small mound of broken glass that would corroborate Leander's story.

"Unfortunate," said Lennart. "Even more so that it was his only vial."

Emile cleared his throat. "Or was it?" He nodded in the direction of Leander's pocket.

Leander's instinct to reach and cover the evidence was damning, but the brief silence was interrupted as the surgeon announced himself unseen from the other side of the chamber door.

"One moment," said Lennart. "Please wait in the corridor." The Minister for Justice reached toward his own pocket, and for the first time Leander noticed the ornate sword that hung in a scabbard at the man's side.

He thought to come clean, to admit his sins and try to reason with the ministers. Likely, they would appreciate the greater good and celebrate Leander for his decisive action. Maybe they would sympathise with his situation, burying the sorry affair along with his father. In that desperate moment Leander locked eyes with the late king's vacant expression. A whole lot of "ifs," "buts," and "maybes," he realised, when it was decisive action that had brought him this far. He was his father's son, and it was time to prove it.

He grabbed the king's knife.

"I wouldn't do that if I were you, Lennart. Nothing stupid..." he growled, waving the knifepoint menacingly between them. "Let's all calm down, shall we, then perhaps we can talk?"

The ministers turned to statues. Roel gasped theatrically, but the others stood with jaws hung loose.

Joran was the first to speak. "Come now, Leander, why don't you drop the knife so we can discuss this sensibly?" The Minister for Wealth raised his arms to plead for a peaceful resolution, dropping them abruptly as Leander jabbed his blade in warning.

"He was dying already," Leander said desperately. "I never killed him, I'm not a murderer. It was his cough...ask the royal surgeon, he'll tell you."

Bram spoke softly wearing a funereal expression, a mood as dark as the deep lines beneath his eyes. "We understand, Leander, questions can wait."

"But the vial," said Lennart, pointing accusatorially. "You had the means to save him. He was your father, why didn't you?"

Leander stood stunned. How many reasons did they want? He thought back over his father's countless indiscretions and fresh anger formed within him. How was it that he had become the villain of the story? He'd done what he thought to be right, for Perrine, for his mother and for all within the Cadraelian Realm. He wasn't going to stand by and face these accusations. He was king now, and it was time for his ministers to learn some accountability. The late king wasn't perfect, but he had commanded respect.

"Isn't this what you wanted?" asked Leander, scolding six of Fermantia's most powerful men like naughty children. "You of all people had your chance to influence my father. I watched you fold like silk bedsheets under the king's scrutiny, with little consideration outside of your own best interests."

It was certainly simplifying the situation, but Leander refused to face this alone. To his surprise, he found that many of the ministers seemed to sag with a look of guilt. The reaction gave him cause to continue. For the first time in his life, Leander felt that he was in control.

"You came to me, Lennart, and told me to fix this."

"I told you to speak to him, but this? I never..."

Leander shook his head. "What were you expecting? You knew the man as well as anyone. I tried to make him see sense, but my father was intent on building his legacy. I couldn't undo everything that you've all allowed to develop over the years. His greed and ambition have done much to line your own considerable pockets, but the situation got out of hand, didn't it?"

Silence.

Then, kneeling beside the body, Roel answered in a whimper. "In the end it took something far greater than us to stop him. What you've done is a sin, Leander."

"A sin? Then take your complaints to the Goddess herself. Perhaps I could have done more, but that would only have delayed the inevitable. Would you have had me save him and continue our march to war with Vicentia? Tell me, Emile, what would you have done in my position?"

The Minister for War was quick to avoid eye contact. A rare occasion where he was not vying for attention.

Leander continued, "And you, Joran, how would you have balanced the books? My father wasn't all wrong; you've grown rich and restful under his kingship. So enough of the feigned disappointment; sincerity doesn't suit you. The king is gone, and we need time to mourn. Time, that is, to return home and consider our next steps." He paused. "My next steps. Remember, I am your king now. My father tolerated you, but there's no reason to expect the same from me. Unless, of course, you are willing to pledge your fealty? I expect that I will regularly face...difficult decisions. Can I expect you to aid me in these most challenging moments, to demonstrate unequivocal loyalty and act with the required amount of, shall we say, discretion?"

The threat was obvious, but he raised the blade a little higher to be sure. It took all his resolve to steady his shaking hand. More frightening still were the echoes of his father's voice within his own. This was the first and last time that Leander intended to imitate the man he would succeed. Desperate times called for desperate measures, and Leander couldn't imagine a situation more desperate than this.

"Would I be right to place my faith in you, Roel, and expect your blessing?"

The Minister for the Faith nodded. "It is the will of the Goddess, my king."

"And you, Joran? Would my trust be ill-advised or a wise investment?"

The Minister for Wealth lowered his balding head with similar reverence. His deep-set eyes seemed suddenly kind and understanding. "I live to serve, Your Majesty, and I've no doubt that you'll be most pleased with the returns."

Dumbfounded, Lennart stepped forward to contest his fellow ministers. "Gentlemen, please, you can't be serious. He murdered our king; justice must be served."

"We know it, Lennart," said Emile. "But right now, what we need is togetherness and stability. It's fair to say we had our *reservations* concerning King Yorick's plans. Perhaps this is the greater good or an act of divine intervention. Either way, what's done is done…"

Lennart's eyes darted among them, searching for support that never arrived. Dejectedly, he repeated, "What's done is done," before retreating to join the others, who, in turn, pledged their allegiance to Leander with the same subservience they had shown to his father.

Leander was equal parts relieved and repulsed by their fickle nature. The immediate threat was over, but these were the men who were supposed to help him lead the realm, men whose interests were entirely their own. He wondered how long it would be before one of them would get a better offer and what would happen if, or when, they did.

The surgeon banged at the door to remind them of his presence, and Leander decided to save his concerns for another day. "One moment," he called, further stalling the man to halt his entry. He lowered his voice and surveyed his ministers. "What happened here today we take to our grave."

Staggered and hesitant, six voices replied, "To the grave."

Sadness for his father bubbled just beneath the surface, but nervous energy pulsed through Leander, heightening his senses to something approaching excitement. The sense of exhilaration recalled his younger years and the games of hide-and-seek with his mother about the palace. Now, like then, he would escape capture against the odds. The very thought gave him confidence as he opened the door, inviting the surgeon to enter. Roel moved aside and the man wasted no time tending to the fallen king, who, unbeknownst to him, was already some way beyond saving.

Leander, meanwhile, reclined in the doorway. A guard slipped past him unexpectedly, moving with something between caution and condolence. Leander's intuition immediately told him that something was wrong, a feeling that only heightened when the guard approached Lennart. The two men huddled to speak in hushed tones, briefly pausing as the Minister for Justice raised his head to peer at Leander, whose curiosity finally got the better of him.

"Is something wrong?" he asked, approaching the two men, who straightened to greet him.

Lennart bit his lip in thought. "Maybe, maybe not..."

"Well, could I possibly trouble you for some insight to the situation?"

"Of course, Your Majesty." The apprehension in Lennart's voice did little for Leander's nerves. "The guards on the door," he started slowly. "There were two when you entered, but one has gone missing."

CHAPTER 5

"Your Majesty, the girl is here to see you."

Leander straightened on his throne, fussed his hair and released a deep breath. Two days of travel and the following three buried under a weight of unavoidable formalities. Five days of waiting for this exact moment. He had to make it count.

A fur robe hung elegantly from his shoulders, complementing a black silk waistcoat embroidered with extravagant gold thread and matching breeches. If nothing else, he certainly had the look of a king. He hoped that these details would not be in vain.

For a second time, the bald man in ceremonial dress spoke from the doorway.

"Announcing Miss Perrine Delport," he boomed, sweeping into a low bow. The door opened to reveal Perrine's silhouette, and after some hesitation she began forward. Though the throne room itself was quite some spectacle, the lavish furnishings, imposing portraits and sparkling chandeliers were no match for Perrine.

Almost unrecognisable from the last time he had seen her, Perrine floated into the room, her long, blue silk gown caressing the polished marble floor with each step. A luxurious tunic covered her upper body, embroidered with lace and sparkling gems. Her braided hair was styled in the shape of a crown, and she looked every bit a queen. Leander could scarcely contain his smile.

"My king." Perrine curtsied but her voice was cold and her face remained expressionless. She halted in the middle of the room, reinforcing the distance that Leander suddenly felt between them. He knew her well enough to expect a challenge, and it would take more than indifference to dissuade him.

"Perrine, you look beautiful. I'm sorry it has taken so long to make time for you. A king's responsibilities are seemingly never-ending."

Perrine's face remained blank. "I'm sure you have a number of priorities, my king. It's no surprise to find that I'm not at the top of them."

"Don't be silly," said Leander, rising from his seat. "You know it's not that, it's just everything with my father and..." He paused, walking forward to take Perrine by the hand. "That's not important now. I'm just pleased to see you. You look like a queen, you know?" He smiled, but the gesture was seemingly ill-judged.

"Thank you for the clothes, my king."

"Of course, it's the very least I could do."

Leander's brow furrowed with confusion. Perrine's behaviour was that of a stranger, with none of the affection they'd shared in the past. He followed up, "Is everything all right? You know I never wanted to see you in that cell. It's over now, and we can begin to plan our future. You want that don't you, Perrine?" He squeezed her hand. "That is what you want, isn't it?"

At this, Perrine laughed unexpectedly, and despite his grip, she tore herself away.

"Now all of a sudden it matters what I want, does it?" She bellowed. "We just move on and live our life together happily ever after?"

"Well, I thought that—"

"You thought what, Leander? That everything could go back to the way it was? I warned you about this and told you that it would all end in a mess. It's fine, I suppose. You got your fancy chair, and in a few days, you'll have your golden crown. What about me? Do you think a few nice clothes and some powder can change me? I'm still the common girl who your father despised. The girl you failed to protect despite all your promises. The girl whose father..." She trailed off and began to weep. The sound cut through Leander, but he sensed he needed to be strong. He was a prince no more, and it was important for Perrine to see the change in him.

"Your father?" he enquired, keen to display a suitable level of empathy. "I presume that he has been released. I instructed it upon my return to the city."

Perrine turned and scowled at him. "Really, Leander, you're going to pretend you don't know?"

"Don't know what?" Clearly, he didn't know, and how could he? He'd only been back in Cadrael for three days, and every moment had been filled with meetings and preparations for either the coronation or his father's funeral.

The realisation dawned on him, and his face dropped just as Perrine confirmed the worst.

"He's dead, you idiot."

Leander wanted the ground to open up and swallow him.

Of all the challenges they had faced together, this was the worst of them. Tears streamed down Perrine's face forming lines in the otherwise flawless powder.

"Perrine, I'm so sorry. I did everything I could. I promise."

"Of course, I should be grateful. Thank you, King Leander. Thank you for sharing your bed with me. For filling my ears with false promises." Her voice turned spiteful. "For letting them beat and imprison me, while my innocent father died in a rotten cell."

He made to speak then paused, desperate to find words that would appease her. "My father's actions," he said, and regretted it immediately. His face dropped and Perrine must have noticed. She shook her head and looked at him with pity, as though, of the two of them, she was in the position of authority.

"I expected excuses, but I never thought they'd sound so pitiful. Do you think it matters to me whether you or your father is ultimately responsible?" Her face screwed even tighter. "You knew my father's condition, but you never did enough to prevent this from happening. It's easy to distance yourself isn't it, to blame someone else for your own inaction? Easier still when the accused isn't here to defend themselves."

"Perrine please, you're not alone in your loss." Murderer or otherwise, he knew how ridiculous it must have sounded.

Surely, he couldn't have expected any sympathy. He'd always felt a little out of his depth with Perrine, and never before had this been more obvious.

Perrine exploded with laughter, an obvious expression of disbelief. "Really Leander, that's your angle? You dare compare that murderous tyrant to my blameless father? I thought you were better than that." She turned away with disgust.

However unreasonably, this put him on the defensive. "Careful, Perrine—that talk is treason."

"There it is: a reminder of the worlds that exist between us," she bellowed as she turned, her words echoing from the walls and tall ceilings about them. "I suppose it must have been fun to have me dressed up and delivered to your palace for a bit of light fun among all your important meetings." She clawed at her hair to remove the intricate braids. "I'm hurting, Leander, sorry if this is inconvenient for you. There was a time when you used to love me for my words. If that's no longer the case, then go on—do your worst."

His shoulders slumped at the frustrating trajectory of their conversation. "You know I didn't mean it that way," he said apologetically. "I just want you to be careful. Isn't this situation already bad enough?"

"It's a bit late for your concern, Leander. I've already lost the only man who ever truly loved me. Besides, do you honestly think you can protect me from Lennart and those other thugs? A gold hat doesn't change anything, Your Majesty. The Ministry is a law unto itself, and Lennart de Meiren is the worst among them." She stood up tall and her face reddened with anger. "Don't worry about me," she said with the hint of a threat. "Lennart's the one who needs to watch his back. They all do."

Exasperated, Leander wondered how it had come to this. He'd let his own father die for a chance to make things work with this girl. All the false grief since, the extra responsibility, the countless meetings, he'd suffered it all for Perrine, and this was how things were going to end?

He rushed to take her hand, recoiling as she pushed him away. "Come now, Perrine, you don't mean that. Surely your emotions have gotten the better of you? If you need time, then take it. In fact, I release you from your job so that you needn't ever see Lennart again."

An eye roll accompanied her shaking head this time. "You just don't get it, do you? I'm starting to think you never did, not really. I don't have a royal vault, nor tax money to provide me with warmth and food. I need this job to keep me from the streets, and though it would make my day to tell you to stick your job and walk out of here, honouring my father, principles are a luxury not afforded to commoners. I do what I must. I always have."

The relationship, for what it was, was crumbling down around Leander. A sudden grief struck him, harder than the moment he had lost his father. He supposed that in that moment, Perrine had always been that beacon of hope, a light on the horizon. Now, it seemed that light had faded, and with it, Leander's spirit had all but burned out.

Meekly, he asked, "So you'll stay...at the palace?" Perhaps there was time yet to regain her affection.

"What choice do I have?" There was no longer any anger in her voice, just despondency. She paused, and then seemingly shook her melancholy away, clearing her throat to speak in that tone which Leander found painfully distant and formal. "If you'll allow me, I'll remain here until I can find something new. I only ask you give me distance."

The weight of finality crashed down upon him.

"Of course," he said, with the slightest nod. "I'll do what I can."

This time, he really would have to make sure of it.

In his optimism, he imagined a happier time when things might return to normal. She was staying, for now at least. He'd have to do better.

"Was that all, Your Majesty?" Perrine angled her body toward the door. Clearly, she'd said all that she came for, and Leander did not intend to keep her against her will, only adding to the anger that she already felt toward him.

His lip tugged with a sorry smile that never fully formed. "That's all," he said, gesturing toward the doorway. He followed for the first few steps, but Perrine never slowed, nor turned back to face him as she passed out of the throne room and moved swiftly down the adjoining corridor.

He stood for a moment, thinking of all the things he could have said, and ways he could have handled the situation better. However much he had maligned his father, the start of Leander's kingship had been disastrous with little sign of improvement.

The approach of someone new called him back into the moment, and he turned as Marcel, the Royal Chamberlain, asked "Everything okay, Your Majesty?"

Of all the answers that Leander cared to give, "Of course," was perhaps the least among them, and certainly the most disingenuous. In truth, he had always been a little intimidated by Marcel. The man was precise, prepared, and always pristine. Today he wore a perfectly arranged velvet coat and silk neckerchief, which set off the magnificence of his glossy shoulder-length black hair, interspersed with strands of shimmering grey. He exuded the sort of confidence required of a man in his lofty and typically demanding position. These same qualities often left Leander feeling inadequate or out of his depth in comparison. It hadn't mattered so much as a boy, or a younger prince, but for the king of Fermantia, things had to be different. He pushed his pain away, raised his chin and said, "I'm fine, why wouldn't I be? I presume that plans for my father's funeral are nearing completion?"

"Yes, Your Majesty."

"And the coronation?"

"Why, of course, Your Majesty."

Leander nodded. "Good. There was one thing—the girl, Perrine Delport."

"The maidservant who was imprisoned?"

"Yes," answered Leander, doing all he could to sound unaffected, kingly and stoic. "I'd ask that the girl is assigned to...other areas of the palace. Her presence is unsettling to me." His lip trembled as he forced the words. "I think it best that she is out of sight, for the moment anyway."

"Understandable, Your Majesty. I will look to resolve that right away. With your permission..." He gestured his intention to leave, then halted, pursing his lips in a thoughtful expression. "Would Your Majesty prefer the girl to be removed entirely? I've added a significant number to the staff in preparation for the occasions you have already mentioned. It's no matter to me if you would rather...curtail her employment."

Marcel shrugged, but Leander swiped the notion away with a dismissive wave. "No need for that," he said, in a way that he hoped to appear nonchalant. "A little distance should do it."

At least he hoped so, more than anything.

For now, at least, the ministers seemed good to their word, and Leander began to concern himself less with allegations of any wrongdoing in his father's death. In brighter moments, he even consoled himself with the hopeful promise he had made to do better than the late king.

Thus, it was Perrine who dominated his thoughts in the days leading to his father's funeral. This sadness imbued the occasion with an even greater depth of emotion, and though he forced a grateful smile as well-wishers arrived at the cathedral, this soon turned to tears as King Yorick's casket lowered from sight, disappearing into the crypts below.

It was Perrine's absence rather than her presence that upset Leander the most. His eyes searched for her comforting smile to no avail, and he began to feel loneliness such as he had never known before, a loneliness that fed the dark pit of sorrow that existed within him, bringing grief to the fore. As he left the cathedral in the royal carriage and passed through streets of mourners on his return to the palace, the realisation dawned on him: his father was gone. More sobering still, it was time to make good on his promises, with the eyes of a kingdom watching his every move.

Whether she had her suspicions or not, Leander's mother never questioned him about her husband's death. By the time of the funeral her black eye had faded, taking with it a perceptible weight of worry. She mourned of course, tears of sadness for the end of a marriage that had shaped her adult life. When asked, she told Leander, "If nothing else, he gave me two wonderful sons."

For Oskar, the loss seemed to hit much harder. Leander's brother was not naïve to their father's failings, but he'd idolised the man for his lofty ambitions and commitment to seeing them realised. Oskar's lip trembled throughout the funeral, in what Leander perceived as an unnecessary attempt to stifle his emotions and show strength. His uncharacteristic quiet, however, was notably telling, and it was only back at the palace that the two brothers finally exchanged words.

From the doorway of his chambers. Oskar asked, "May I come in?"

Seated by the window, gazing out mindlessly, Leander was pleased for the company of another who shared his loss. "Of course," he said, gesturing to an accompanying chair. His brother accepted and a timely maidservant arrived to furnish him with a glass of wine.

"To Father," said Leander, and their glasses clinked before they both took a sip.

A smile appeared on Oskar's face, belying the obvious redness of his puffy eyes. "To King Leander," he added spiritedly. This time, Leander did not feel compelled to drink.

"He wasn't perfect, but father certainly made his mark."

Oskar sniggered. "That's one way to put it. Big boots to fill. I don't envy you, Leander."

"Thanks."

They both smiled and then paused to take another drink.

Oskar sat forward, gripping the stem of the crystal wineglass with both hands. "But what type of king will you be, brother?" The question reminded Leander of Oskar's unyielding pragmatism. Any sadness in his brother's eyes had given way to a glint of intrigue, as though the ghost of King Yorick lived within him. Oskar truly was his father's son.

The question was a good one, and Leander's first chance to impart his vision. Oskar's brow furrowed with anticipation, and Leander sensed a suggestion of uncertainty, or perhaps judgement, in his brother's expression. It felt as though Oskar's support for Leander's kingship hinged on the answer.

Above all else, Leander knew he needed to stay true to his ideals. "One of peace," he announced proudly. "A king for the people. All of the people."

"Lofty ambitions," Oskar said, breaking his gaze to wave the maidservant over to refill his drink. "Nice ideas in principle, but perhaps not so easy in practise. There are many who do not consider the Cadraelian Realm a beacon for peace. Conquered peoples have long memories, and the peace you seek is often hard fought."

"Be that as it may, I must begin my kingship in the hope that results can be achieved through…different means."

"Hope?" Oskar recoiled with an exaggerated look of wide-eyed shock. "Brother, I trust you have more in mind than the fanciful notions of peace and hope. Father assembled a kingdom, the like of which has never been known, but it's folly to think our walls impenetrable. There are always plenty of wolves waiting at the door."

It was as though King Yorick himself sat opposite. "You sound just like Father," said Leander. "With all his ambition and watchfulness."

"Qualities befitting a king, at least to my mind anyway. I mean to help you, Leander; I only fear that you have underestimated the task before you. The people are one challenge, but The Ministry—well, that's a different story. You know how they pecked at Father, hindering progress. Will you allow them to shape your reign? Or will you do what Father couldn't and abolish their titles and influence?"

Leander began to wonder if he had underestimated his brother. In the cold light of day, Oskar seemed somehow even more ruthless than their father had been. It was all just words, though, he reasoned. Far easier in the saying than the doing. He grinned at his brother's youthful enthusiasm.

"You'd have me remove them? Think of the consequences."

"Kill them if you must," Oskar responded flatly. "Of all a king's worries, consequences should not feature among them."

Leander almost choked on his drink. He knew his brother to be indelicate, but it began to dawn on him that Oskar might be truly dangerous; his words alone were deeply controversial.

Playing it down, Leander responded, "Come now, Oskar, I know you know your history. The Ministry has provided Fermantia with governance for as long as records have existed. I'm not blind to their failings, but it's important to have leadership and diversity of opinion. I know this will irk you, but those six families are as important to the kingdom as you or I."

"The words of a defeated man." Oskar's words were cold, and he swiped the air in a gesture intended to dismiss Leander's sentiment. "Six noble families, with title and power as their birthright. We both know what fools they are, yet you sit there unprepared to do anything about it. It's—"

Leander finished his sentence. "No different to the privilege we've both inherited?"

He raised his eyebrows at the silence that followed, enjoying his brother's sudden loss of words. "I feel your frustration, brother, but Father's kingdom wasn't built overnight, and wholesale change rarely happens with haste. Forgive me, but Father's throne is still warm, and a king is most kingly when decorated with his crown. Your fervour is appreciated, but I would ask you to trust me." He extended his glass in an attempted peace offering, returning his brother's smile as the crystal gave a satisfyingly tuneful clink.

"So, peace then?" said Oskar, looking wistfully beyond Leander and out of the window where the sun was shining. "Work to be done with our friend Queen Orsolina, I should imagine. Before that, I suppose your first concern is a little closer to home. I hear things are less than peaceful with that servant girl, what's her name Pernel? Or is it Paulina?"

"Perrine," snapped Leander. "Her name is Perrine."

Oskar smiled as if he'd known this all along. "That's right. I hear that things are far from perfect between the two of you. I assume you've heard by now, but her father died in the cells while you were off gallivanting. A tragic incident," he added as an afterthought, though from the casual tone of his voice, Leander doubted he meant it. "And that's before we mention Perrine's own imprisonment. I gather that King Jannick will attend your coronation, and from what I hear he's unlikely to be alone. How does Princess Sanne feature in your harmonious future? If she's anything like I've seen in portraits, she's rather ravishing."

It occurred to Leander that in all the upheaval, he'd hardly given the Elurian princess a thought. Naturally, she would be there, if only to explore the betrothal that King Yorick had promised. How could Leander appease King Jannick without upsetting Perrine? His thoughts turned to Oskar, who sat with a smirk on his face, taking great humour in Leander's suffering. Perhaps there was an alternative match to make? The echoes of his father's decisions continued to shackle Leander in the present. He was a new king with new ideas, but a fresh start would not come easily.

Oskar, on the other hand, didn't need to know that. "All in hand," Leander answered with a confident smile. "I'm under no illusion that kingship will be easy, but we must learn to be adaptable, I think. I've certainly no intention of making an enemy of Jannick."

"Naturally," said Oskar, his voice betraying his dwindling interest. Evidently, he had hoped to provoke a more panic-stricken reaction, and his look of disappointment was a small victory for Leander.

"Well, I'm sure you're busy," Oskar stood to leave. "Much to plan for, I would think. I wish you the very best for a happy and healthy reign, brother. May your luck be better than Father's, in the end so horribly betrayed when he least expected it."

"Betrayed?" Leander's heart beat a little faster. What was it that his brother knew? More importantly, who had told him?

"By his own body, brother. Isn't it always those closest to us?"

A sigh of relief, before the lingering hint of a threat caught up with him. "Quite," he said gingerly, and then raised his empty wine glass for attention. "I suppose I shall have to learn a little restraint, brother. Father was many things, but he was certainly indulgent. An appetite for all things that was difficult to satisfy."

Oskar's frown softened. "You're not wrong there. Well, let us hope that he now rests in peace."

"Rest in peace," agreed Leander, and he watched as Oskar made to exit before pausing in the doorway.

"King Leander, eh? You finally have your moment. You know what this means, brother. Now I'm first in line for the throne."

He snickered and left without saying another word. Maybe it was just the heightened emotion of their father's funeral, but Leander already sensed a none-too-subtle shift in their relationship. No longer was Oskar that impudent little brother; he was heir to the throne of Fermantia, an unnerving presence, like a beast chomping at Leander's heels.

Leander wondered if his father had felt the same about him.

Cadrael Cathedral, two days later. The same venue, but the occasion very different. Gone were the tears, black clothing and sombre expressions. Instead, enthusiastic revellers lined the capital's wide thoroughfares dressed in their finest embroidered surcoats or colourful linen gowns with floral headdresses. Leander passed by atop his regal horse Remi, both bedecked in dazzling ceremonial wear. Cheers, smiles and an explosion of colour greeted them as they passed through the city for coronation day.

With every step, Leander found it increasingly difficult not to enjoy himself. This was his moment after all, and whatever had gone before, he owed it to these people to be the best version of a king that he could possibly be. It occurred to him that Cadrael's city folk knew little of the man who would become King Leander I, but today was a day for hope and new beginnings. Leander appreciated the faith they had shown him and silently swore to see it repaid.

The ceremony itself was a blur of music and pomp, with no shortage of Roel and his insistence on religion. Finally, Leander took to his knee with the golden crown lowered to its rightful place—the weight of a nation and with it, the power. As Leander returned to his feet, he did so feeling somehow a little taller. The known world watched on through the eyes of the foreign dignitaries. Leander's mother cried tears of joy, and even Oskar applauded as his new king passed by to make an exit, showing no indication of the friction that had underlined their noteworthy prior encounter.

At the palace, Leander met with similar, considerable fanfare. The Master of Ceremonies marked his arrival,

"Welcoming King Leander I," and the company of armed guards that had escorted him throughout the day led Leander to his seat at the head of the table in the banquet hall. With his mother to one side and Oskar at the other, Leander found himself enjoying a perfect evening in cherished company. He told himself that he had been wrong to feel suspicious of his brother, and the two shared drinks and laughter with the same amity they had once known as children, an affection Leander had long thought lost.

"The greater good" was a phrase that had always troubled Leander, but with the prospect of peace and a renewed sense of hope for the people of Fermantia, he finally saw the sense in it. His guilt had already started to fade.

However, the actions of a king are often second to his words, and Leander's tenure, it seemed, would be no different. As maidservants arrived to clear evidence of a sumptuous course of spiced pheasant decorated with gold leaf, his mother gave him a nudge that stirred him into action. The room silenced as he took to his feet. He cleared his throat and fought to steady any remaining nerves not already quelled by his considerable intake of potent Elurian wine.

"Ladies and gentlemen," he began, surprised by the booming authority of his voice. "Nobles of Fermantia and honoured guests from lands abroad. I thank you for your presence at this most special occasion. A new beginning for our tremendous realm, and a juncture in our shared history."

Here he took pause, taking a moment to survey his audience. It held a vibrant array of race and culture. Olive-skinned representatives from Verasca and Sagan in the far reaches of Leander's realm ornamented in brightly coloured, full-length ceremonial dress, and the darker complexions and muted tones of envoys from Selendor marking his eastern borders. Darting about the room, his eyes quickly discerned his six most prestigious ministers arrayed among the assembly. Most notably, Bruno had situated himself among the delegates from Salmanus, and though his body portrayed full attention to Leander, the man's eyes flickered to the sparkling bangles of gold and precious gemstones that adorned the forearms of his new associates. Elsewhere, Bram was being characteristically amorous with a young, dark-haired maidservant who had made the mistake of arriving to fill his wine glass. Though she had her back turned to Leander, he lamented the poor girl's discomfort, and it came as some surprise when she leant forward to touch the lecherous man's arm with unexpected fondness.

The others were being far less conspicuous. Emile held a tall tankard of ale aloft, while Roel clasped a religious text to his chest with similar conviction. As always, Lennart's eyes surveyed the room with professional caution, and the same went for Joran, who appeared deep in thought. On this of all days, there was no masking the man's deliberation. The sight amused Leander, who was here to enjoy his moment and happy to let the Minister for Wealth count the related cost.

With all accounted for, Leander made to continue his monologue. It was only then that he noticed her.

He cleared his throat to buy time as he tried to find the words her vision had stolen, but an all-important question consumed his thoughts: who is she? Had they met already? Surely, he would remember...

The girl was of a similar age to him, perhaps a little younger. She had white-blonde hair styled in a perfect fishtail braid that gleamed like silver when she moved. Even at distance, her lips were soft and inviting, pastel pink against the alabaster of her perfect skin. When she smiled her angular cheekbones drew attention to dimples that snatched Leander's breath away, prolonging his silence.

Impatient coughs began to sound around the room, and he wondered how long he had lingered on his unknown but exceedingly beautiful, and thus welcome, guest. Just then, their eyes met in an instant that set Leander's heart racing. He felt a smile develop, then fall away just as quickly, when from the corner of his eye, he noted the startling and somewhat less welcome sight of Perrine. Why was she here, and why did her presence provoke the singular feeling of guilt?

"To new beginnings," he said, raising his glass, feeling, more than anything that he had to say something.

The sentiment echoed back at him, and Leander berated himself as he returned to his seat, bemoaning the rather unfortunate double meaning of his chosen toast. Around him the feast and celebration redoubled, but Leander sat a little less comfortably with Perrine's scowl upon him. If looks could kill, Oskar's wait for the throne would be a short one after all.

As he sat swirling his wine, he couldn't help but wonder—was his brother responsible for Perrine's surprise appearance?

"Marcel, why the fuck is Perrine here?" Leander had left his seat and stepped away from the table, forcing a conclave with the Royal Chamberlain to keep their conversation private. The venom in his voice was making this difficult, but this was more than an angry outburst. He was intent on answers. "I specifically told you to keep her away from me. Was my request too difficult or perhaps unclear?"

The Royal Chamberlain recoiled. "I'm sorry, Your Majesty. Your instructions were irrefutable, but in the end, the decision was taken out of my hands."

Leander made to reply, then took pause, giving thought to those who might have challenged him. Oskar remained the most obvious choice, but Leander's brother showed no interest in the unfolding drama. His mother then? Perhaps an ill-judged gesture intended to warm her son's aching heart. Again, she spoke animatedly with Oskar, seemingly unaware of Perrine's presence and the fluster it had caused.

As Leander considered his audience, it dawned on him that there were many in attendance who might harbour ill intentions. Natives of conquered nations, ambassadors from those seen as rivals to Fermantia, the whole room was teeming with people who were just as likely to stab him in the back as they were to smile upon his coronation. A swell of trepidation spiralled within him, curtailed only by a timely and rather humbling spike of common sense. Whatever pernicious thoughts existed in the room, there were few among them with knowledge of Leander and Perrine's involvement, and fewer still who could have overridden Marcel's orders.

The list was a short one, but Leander's patience was wearing thin. "Who?" he asked, fixing Marcel with a glare that was eerily close to the one he had suffered from Perrine only minutes before.

Marcel's eyes twitched as he turned to look over his shoulder, then back at Leander to whisper, "It was Lennart, Your Majesty."

"Lennart?" said Leander, sharply. "That prying fucking idiot. Presumably, you told him about my orders. What reason did he give you?"

"I made your views very clear, Your Majesty. The minister was adamant on keeping the girl nearby where he could…" He cleared his throat in a way that made his incredulity abundantly clear. "Monitor her behaviour."

Leander shook his head, "Is that what he told you?"

"I'm sorry, Your Majesty, but those were his orders. He said to keep her close in the best interests of your safety. But if you ask me," he said, lowering his voice conspiratorially, "I hear the girl wasn't especially compliant during her imprisonment. It seems that Lennart took quite a disliking to Miss Delport, and it would be fair to describe their relationship as hostile."

As Marcel spoke, Leander's eyes wandered to where Lennart was sitting. The man had that self-satisfied grin on his face that so infuriated Leander. To make matters worse, the Minister for Justice was ogling a maidservant as she cleared silver platters and discarded remnants of food from the table. Not just any maidservant, though. Perrine.

"You know what Lennart is like," Marcel continued. "A man of fine breeding, but not without conceit and his fair share of prejudice. Perrine is, after all, of common stock. I fear he may have objected to the prospect of her elevation during your brief…" He selected his final word carefully, "Entanglement."

Leander's teeth gritted with anger and frustration. The insinuation should have left him embarrassed, but the red mist had descended, and Lennart was the cause. A traditional Cadraelian lute filled the hall with music, but the unmistakably jaunty sound felt suddenly at odds with his worsening mood. Lennart's laughter seemed somehow aimed in Leander's direction, and it was all he could do to prevent himself from reacting.

He steadied himself and apologised for addressing Marcel so sharply. "Please see to it that Perrine is relieved of her duties for the rest of the evening."

"Right away, my king," Marcel smiled and bowed.

"Oh, and Marcel, see if you can't free that other poor maidservant from Bram's clutches."

"They seem to have taken rather a liking to one another."

"For Bram's part, I find that hardly surprising."

A well-timed swell of laughter drew his attention to where the Minister for Land sat. The man's eyeglasses had fallen from their perch on the end of his large nose, and as he raised the frames to inspect for damage, it was clear the glass had shattered.

Nevertheless, and with much drunken amusement, Bram restored the empty frames to his face, and continued his pursuit of the maidservant in question.

"Be that as it may, I'm sure she'll thank us eventually," said Leander. "If nothing else, she can help cover Perrine's absence. I'm sure you'll work it out. Father always told me you're the very best."

Marcel blushed. "You honour me, Your Majesty. Your wish is my command. I shall see to it immediately."

Marcel swept away in the direction of Perrine. Leander returned to his seat but only very briefly, straightening himself at the sight of new company.

"King Leander, I do hope that I'm not interrupting."

"Of course not," he said, steadying the excitement in his voice to welcome the silver-haired girl he had noticed earlier. "I would ask your name, though," he said, now smiling.

A smile of her own sent Leander's heart racing. "How rude of me," she said, fixing him with ocean blue eyes. She extended a delicate hand for Leander to kiss. "I'm Princess Sanne of Eluria. Pleased to finally meet you."

CHAPTER 6

⚬❧⚬

Portraits of the princess had not done her justice. Sanne was an inimitable masterpiece.

"Princess Sanne, what a pleasure..." he fumbled. "Of course, I've heard much about you, but nothing that does justice to your beauty."

He sat back in satisfaction, before noticing that a large man stood behind her. There was every likelihood that he'd had been there all along, eclipsed by the princess's dazzling beauty.

"I see the two of you have met then?" he said, speaking in a tongue that was common with Leander's but with rising intonation typical of the Elurian dialect. The large man had a healthy paunch that spoke of a lavish diet and unruly grey hair that suggested the confidence or position not to dwell on appearance. "It has been some years, King Leander. I'd venture to say that you don't remember me."

By now, the pieces had fallen into place. "King Jannick," said Leander, adding warmth to his voice and extending a welcoming hand to his Elurian counterpart. "Much time has passed, but I'm not one to forget a friend. You've hardly changed," he added, not entirely truthfully. "It is a pleasure to find you back in Cadrael. I know my father would have loved to share a drink in your company."

In truth, King Yorick never needed company to enjoy a drink, but despite Leander's inexperience, he was not naive to the merits of an amiable relationship with these western neighbours. He remembered meeting a younger Jannick when he was yet a boy prince. Though the memory had faded with the passing of years, the prevailing recollection was of a gentle man who had made Leander laugh by pulling silly faces and telling jokes. The greying hair and scraggly beard did little to obscure Jannick's unquestionably kind face, and as Sanne turned to look fondly upon the Elurian king, Leander wondered how it might have been to share that level of affection with his own father.

In the moment, however, all thoughts of past and future gave way to Leander's most immediate concern: Princess Sanne.

"I trust you will stay with us," he said to the king. "Remain in Cadrael and enjoy a few days of Fermantian hospitality."

Jannick placed a meaty hand to his chest, indicating a suitable level of gratitude. "I'm afraid not, young king. Sadly, this will be a rather fleeting visit. My wife, the queen, is suffering with illness, hence her absence from today's proceedings."

"Nothing serious, I hope?"

"No, I wouldn't have thought so. She's in the hands of our very best physicians who have, so far, shown little concern. I should just like to be by her side at this time, I'm sure you understand. In my absence, Princess Sanne shall act as my proxy." He paused with a wry smile, which Leander fought all his instincts not to reciprocate. "Your late father had indicated some interest in a union between yourself and the princess. It is of course, an honour to see you after so many years, but I must confess that our visit is not entirely innocent or without agenda. If you'll excuse my impertinence, I would ask that my daughter remains in Cadrael to explore the possibility. No commitments of course, simply a chance to get to know one another a little better. Sanne has always been an enthusiastic traveller, and Cadrael is beautiful this time of year, I'm sure you'll agree."

To Leander's mind, Cadrael was no match for Sanne. He began to wonder why he had ever challenged the union, flinching with guilt as thoughts of Perrine surfaced unwittingly. He wondered what it could hurt to explore a friendship with the princess. At its core, the act was one of basic diplomacy. It would be good to have company while Perrine was intent on spurning him, and there was always the prospect of a marriage between Oskar and Sanne.

No, he pushed the thought away firmly.

Oskar possessed none of the poise and stature befitting a princess of Sanne's quality. He was a boy; she was a woman. A princess, but one destined to be a queen.

"Of course," he said, answering his counterpart. "The princess is most welcome in Cadrael. I will see to the arrangements."

"Thank you, King Leander, you are most hospitable. Sanne has travelled with her lady in waiting; I trust that she will provide minimal imposition."

The princess curtsied in affirmation, and Leander raised his glass to toast the renewed friendship.

"To a long and successful reign," Jannick added, clinking glasses with Leander. "May you remain in good health and find luck in peace and love."

Leander smiled then echoed, "Peace and love," before taking a drink. Throughout the exchange, his eyes never wandered from Sanne, who appeared to regard him with similar interest. It might have been the wine, but the life of a king, it seemed, was full of gifts and pleasing temptations. A warm fuzz consumed him. Could it be that kingship wasn't so difficult after all?

"You remind me so much of your father," said Jannick, unexpectedly. "I look forward to seeing the sort of king you'll become."

Though Leander gave a gracious nod, he wasn't sure if this was a compliment. The comparison provoked his fear of replicating his father's mistakes. Fortunately, the thought was to be short-lived. The music slowed as he made to speak, and Sanne reached forward, offering her hand.

"Care to dance, King Leander?"

There was nothing in the world he wanted more.

Together they made their way to the centre of the room, people parting and watching on with interest. Among them Leander's mother looked on approvingly, and even Oskar gave a playful wink that screamed, "I told you so," a reminder of their discussion concerning Leander's predicament.

Perrine still played on his mind, but she was out of sight, presumably thanks to Marcel's efforts. Leander was clear to enjoy the moment, and he intended to do so.

It didn't even matter that he wasn't a particularly skilled dancer. He was a king now, with few brave or foolish enough to ridicule him. Besides, he was dancing with the most beautiful girl in the room. She moved with a level of balance and finesse befitting her royal status, and as she pulled him close to guide him through each twist and step, Leander couldn't help but wonder how this perfect evening might end. As they moved together, turning as one, he noticed she smelled like roses, a perfect scent for someone who embodied all the elegance and vibrancy associated with the most romantic of flowers. Savouring the moment, Leander let his eyes close, and all too soon, the music ended.

"You can open your eyes now," Sanne whispered, laughter tingeing her words. "You dance well, King Leander, but there's always room for improvement with a little practice."

He began to answer, but something stole his attention. Over Sanne's shoulder, Bram and Joran were locked in an intense argument.

Eventually he responded with an uninspiring, "Thank you," instantly kicking himself for falling short in the moment. Briefly, at least, he concurred with Oskar: the ministers were often an unwelcome distraction. However, this was certainly no time for blame or sorry excuses, and his concerns soon passed when Sanne stepped forward to kiss his cheek.

"Thank you, King Leander, for a wonderful evening. I look forward to spending time together in the days to come. For now, I must say farewell to my father; a more caring and attentive man you couldn't hope to find. I suspect I will also benefit from some rest. I find travelling to be quite draining and wish to be at my best for the remainder of my stay."

With that she floated away to re-join her father, who gave a gracious farewell wave as the two of them departed the banquet hall. The party continued all around Leander, but Sanne left him feeling like the only person in the room.

What a night. What a hangover.

Leander groaned as he turned over, casting silk bedsheets away from his clammy skin and covering his eyes to protect them from orange shards of morning sunlight.

His head was a pulsing legacy of the wine he had consumed, yet this couldn't dampen his mood, nor overshadow the brightening thought of his time spent with the Elurian princess.

Above all else, it enthused him to recall King Jannick's suggestion that his daughter remain in the capital. Right now, Sanne, beautiful, talented Sanne, was somewhere in the palace sleeping. She was probably only a short walk from Leander in his own royal chambers. He wondered whether she had dreamt of him or even awoken with the same excitement that had Leander enraptured.

The familiar melody of Cadraelian songbirds sounded from beyond his window. It was, in every sense, a beautiful day. A new dawn, Leander thought to himself, a bright new future for King Leander and the people of Fermantia and the wider Cadraelian Realm. His mind hummed and raced with a thousand aims for his time in power. Already it made him restless, the possibility that there might not be enough time to realise his many grand plans. This tangent prompted thoughts of King Yorick and a lifetime of achievements realised during half a life. Yet every vision of the former king's achievements conjured images of another—Leander's mother, the woman who had guided him. What might he achieve with a woman like Sanne by his side?

It was no good simply thinking about the princess. He sprang from his bed at dizzying speed, making for his desk where he began to construct a letter.

Dearest Sanne, he began, considering each word carefully as he scratched them into parchment with his quill. *It was a pleasure to meet you yesterday evening, and it would be my honour to help you explore our glorious capital as King Jannick suggested. I wonder therefore if you might join me this afternoon for a leisurely stroll around the palace's celebrated gardens. Long-distance travel can be disquieting, but perhaps my company will help you to feel at ease. It is my intention to ensure that your time here in Cadrael is thoroughly enjoyable, and you are certainly a very welcome guest, for as long as you should choose to remain.*

He signed his name and reread the letter. He wondered if it was too keen, gripping the page and considering whether to dispose of his first effort and start again. In the end, he struggled to see how his next attempt would be any different. He wanted to make her feel at home and welcome, but Sanne was more than just another foreign dignitary. He imagined she would be more than smart enough to perceive his intentions, and he folded the letter at the risk of further procrastination.

With it, an immediate feeling of guilt consumed him. His skin turned hot with shame, no longer able to avoid the unpleasant truth of his mistreatment of Perrine. Did she really deserve to be humiliated so publicly, especially after all that Leander's family had already done to hurt her? This was no example of the chivalrous man that Leander had hoped to become. He considered what his mother would think of his actions and cringed at the prospect of falling short of her expectations.

Nevertheless, Perrine had already made her intentions clear. She wanted distance and had spoken of a new job that would take her away from the palace. Perhaps a change of scenery would improve their relationship, but Leander knew Perrine better than to assume so. Certainly, she would not so easily forget the lamentable circumstances surrounding the death of her father.

Another pang, this time for his own father, but Leander shook the thought away, refusing to add to his growing problems. The situation with Perrine was immediate and finely poised. Distance probably was the best course of action. He stamped his letter closed with a royal seal and sat back. In Sanne's case, he'd keep her close. A stroll through the palace gardens was entirely innocent, albeit something his father would never have sanctioned with Perrine for company.

A weary sigh escaped him as he thought ahead to the morning's less stimulating endeavours. His first time as king, hosting the meeting of The Ministry.

To make matters worse, his headache was back.

Bloodshot eyes, untended stubble and a fug of ale and wine—the ministers really were a picture. If Leander had been nervous, the feeling soon faded. He took some comfort from the shared suffering in the room.

"I don't suppose anyone has word from Bram?" Leander looked to the minister's empty seat then raised his eyebrows questioningly, immediately regretting the stabbing pain that it sent through his skull.

Emile smoothed his dishevelled hair. "No, my king. Perhaps he ate something that has left him feeling under the weather."

The other ministers laughed briefly, but each of them remained slouched in their chairs, supporting weary heads with hands propped up by elbows on the table.

"Very funny," Leander's tone showed no humour. "But that doesn't answer my question. Is this something that happens regularly?"

As he waited for their answer, Leander considered The Ministry through fresh eyes. Clearly, there were some things that money couldn't buy: a hangover cure for one, probity for another. Preconceived notions notwithstanding, he had hoped they would surprise him, proving themselves equal to the lofty titles and largely self-supported reputations, that they might be more than the average man. Evidently, he was set to be disappointed.

"I'll ask again," he said, when nobody answered. "Is this normal, and more importantly do any of you think it acceptable?"

He spoke with a confident authority he never knew existed. Apparently, his father's tutelage had been more effective than he had credited.

Like a scolded child, Roel raised his hand to speak. "Apologies, my king, but it is quite unusual. Bram is often the first in attendance. I'm sure his absence is not without a valid reason."

"Is that so?" said Leander, giving voice to doubt. "Joran, you were the last person I saw with him. Anything at all that you wish to add?"

A momentary pause, then Joran cleared his throat loudly. "A brief conversation, my king, nothing of any note."

"Looked rather heated if you ask me," added Bruno. "I've known wars started with less hostility."

Joran's face reddened as he fixed Bruno with a fierce glare. "I can assure you there was nothing to it, my king. A simple disagreement that we were able to resolve quickly."

"Quite," said Leander whose head was throbbing. "Well, I don't fully know how things used to work with my father, but I intend to conduct these meetings at the same time each week. If it isn't already crystal clear, your attendance is mandatory. As for today, I'll keep it brief. I'm quite sure we've all got places we'd rather be. From my side, I want to make it known that things are going to change a little moving forward. My father was a great man, but he and I are very different, with very different aims. I am fortunate to have inherited a vast and enviable realm, but even a novice king can see the many challenges we face to sustain our position."

He paused for a moment to appreciate their silent attention. Not wanting to get ahead of himself, Leander was quite relieved with the start he had made. Thoughts of Sanne had him in high spirits, if impatient. There were a thousand places he'd have rather been in that moment. Almost all of them, in the company of the Elurian princess.

"Peace," he said, emphasising the importance of the word. "Peace within and without our borders, a time free from war and persecution. A time to realise the grand aims with which my father began. But none of this will be easy..." He watched as appreciative smiles wilted with the prospect of hard work. "I will need your full support and best efforts in your respective fields. I have some tasks for each of you to begin with, and I would ask that you apply your fullest attention. I'll be expecting progress reports in time for next week's meeting. Joran..." He looked to the Minister for Wealth, who was already suitably poised to take notes. "From you, I would appreciate a full account of our treasury and contributions from taxation. There are many within our borders living in poverty, and a realm is only as strong as its weakest subject. I would see conditions improved and trade flourish. I had hoped to discuss the development of roads and shipping lanes with Bram, but this of course will have to wait."

Joran nodded. "Yes, Your Majesty."

"Roel and Bruno, there is much work to be done to knit the many cultures of our patchwork dominion. From you, I want efforts to build and share cultural understanding. Meet with the religious leaders in The Clanlands and try to cultivate a more tolerant environment."

"But these people are heathens," Roel replied, doing little to mask his outrage. "The Goddess is one and absolute; we cannot be seen to entertain these false prophets."

Leander raised a calming hand. "Be that as it may, belief is like a diamond—I find it only hardens under pressure. We've already taken independence from these people; let us try a little harder to appreciate their way of life. There will be time to circulate books and introduce Fermantian education. Until then, your task is to improve the flow of more compassionate communication. I presume this is clear?"

"Yes, Your Majesty," both men answered in unison.

Leander turned to Lennart, still harbouring frustration about the previous evening and the incident with Perrine. "From you, Lennart, a similar mindset. Let us try to be less heavy-handed when implementing our law, particularly in the far-flung regions of the realm. My father always felt that the conquered peoples were most fortunate to benefit from Fermantian stewardship. Allow them the chance to perceive these benefits; no longer would I have us seen as tyrants or aggressors."

"Of course, my king," answered Lennart, "but do remember that effective leadership requires the occasional show of strength."

The answer confirmed the full extent of the challenges that Leander was facing. He sighed and said, "You're not wrong, Lennart, but perhaps real strength is in knowing when to show clemency. My father had the unfortunate habit of comparing people to animals, dogs in particular. It's true that a threatened dog will demonstrate unacceptably aggressive behaviour, but care for a dog and you will earn its loyalty. I don't expect you to bring every lawbreaker home with you, but perhaps there is room for leniency within your methods?"

Lennart nodded reluctantly before scratching at the wiry grey hair about his ears in regretful silence.

"Moreover," Leander continued, undeterred, "we will no longer host the mass executions that have passed for entertainment. We must learn to value life and instil a more optimistic view of the future. Which leads me to my final point, and your involvement, Emile."

The Minister for War crossed his arms and sat back in his seat, expectedly defensive.

"At the last meeting, you mentioned that the army was overstretched and tired. No doubt they miss their families and the memory of Fermantia, which will likely have faded during years in foreign lands."

Emile's body language relaxed, and his arms unfolded. "It's true, Your Majesty. The campaign has been long and hard, you know this yourself."

"Well, perhaps it's time to bring the men home," said Leander. "Let them witness the fruits of their labours first-hand and remember what they fought for."

Emile's expression turned to a frown. "Full withdrawal, my king? It's a charming idea, but I fear the decision would leave us exposed."

"An insight which is highly valued, Emile. I yield to your judgement on what would constitute a suitable presence at the borders and in The Clanlands where things are still settling. In time, it is my aim to visit the people, all of the people, and when I do I want to arrive not as conqueror, but as king."

"A fine aim, Your Majesty, but experience has taught me to expect the worst. I worry that you may have overlooked one pressing concern beyond the bright horizon."

Leander grinned knowingly. "Let me guess, Vicentia?"

"Well, yes, my king, but more specifically Queen Orsolina. Though your father's..." He paused for a moment, searching for the right word. "*Regrettable* demise left the queen unaware of our intentions for Tenevarre, she's no fool. She has scouts throughout the realm, and I doubt our initial efforts to mobilise troops at the northern border went unnoticed. If there's one thing we know about her, it's that she'll be planning the next move."

Lennart chimed in. "He's right, my king. Orsolina is no slouch, and you're something of an unknown quantity."

"A young king with limited experience on the battlefield," said Emile rather jarringly. "Orsolina will probably view this as vulnerability. Whether her eyes are on Tenevarre only time will tell, but it would make sense to target some of the gains your father made during his reign."

Leander scratched at the stubble on his chin, giving due consideration to the opinions of his ministers. This verbal sparring felt like a battlefield in its own right, but this was the time and place for change to begin. If Leander were to make a difference, he'd need these men to play their part.

"It seems to me that our biggest enemy is fear." He stood as he spoke, resting a hand on the tall, decorative back of his chair, commanding attention as he'd seen his father do so many times before. "Fear of religion, of lawlessness. Fear of Orsolina and her armies. Fear of the unknown. Fear is not strength, nor will it make us stronger. Trust is the quality that will drive us toward a peaceful and productive future. Trust is the answer, gentlemen, and trust starts with independence for Tenevarre."

A pronounced gasp echoed about the room. The nation status of Tenevarre was a question unanswered by many former kings of Fermantia. The dilemma had troubled generations of Leander's forebears and created an impasse that Leander was keen to overcome.

"Excuse me, Your Majesty," Bruno spoke, looking troubled. "Do you mean to say that you will surrender Fermantia's longstanding claim to the land?"

"The word 'surrender' suggests defeat, Bruno," said Leander. "Peace is a victory, and one we shall pursue. Emile, please arrange an invite for Orsolina's envoy. I would speak with the man and gauge the measure of his queen's thoughts."

Emile's eyes darted between his counterparts, but nobody spoke their objections. The Minister for War eventually uttered, "As you wish, my king."

"Good," said Leander, enjoying the weight that a crown had added to his voice. "Together we will build a better Fermantia. The work begins today. You have my leave to make start."

The five men rose from their chairs with reverent bows, muttering among themselves as they made for the door. As Lennart was leaving, Leander called to halt the man's departure. The Minister for Justice turned back with some reluctance. "Was there something more, my king?"

Now it was just the two of them, Leander could no longer contain his frustration. "In fact, there is. The simple matter of Perrine Delport. I'd be keen to know why you thought to undermine my authority. I expressly asked to keep the girl at distance during the coronation, but Marcel tells me that you had better ideas."

"Yes, my king. I simply thought it was the safest option."

"Ah, that's it. Presumably, I should thank you. Of course, you were simply looking after the best interests of your king, who you serve unquestioningly. It couldn't possibly be the matter of a personal vendetta against the poor girl." He paused to let the inference hang heavy between them. "I forget that you're such an advocate of safety, Lennart, like the safety afforded to Perrine's father, who died in a cell while in your custody."

"I'm sorry, my king, but I don't really see what—"

"What?" snarled Leander, banging his fists on the table. "There's much that you don't see, isn't there, Lennart? Perhaps you need to reconsider your focus, lest I be forced to reconsider your contributions."

Anger alone was carrying Leander forward now, masking his inexperience. Though it was highly unlikely that Lennart considered himself in the wrong, Leander was gratified to see that the man glistened with a fresh sheen of nervous sweat as he fussed with his hands to avoid eye contact.

"Do better Lennart, and make this the last such conversation we have. You will drop any animosity towards Perrine and pay reparations for her untimely loss."

"Yes, Your Majesty."

"Good," said Leander. "I appreciate your understanding. Things are going to change quickly. Run with me or risk being left behind."

The Minister for Justice bowed once more then began for the doorway.

"Oh, and just one other thing," called Leander, causing Lennart to hesitate with apparent frustration. "Find Bram and have him explain himself, or his safety will be your next concern."

The afternoon was pleasantly warm and bright, and as Leander stepped out into his verdant gardens, he let any remaining worries fall away. Sanne had accepted his invite; this was no time for other distractions.

All told, he had every reason to feel good about his morning. It was still early days, but he had imparted his vision and set very clear expectations. The ministers were lazy and self-interested but by no means stupid. They had fallen into a rut, the same complacency that Leander's father had observed, albeit in different circumstances. In the end, Leander believed that they might prove useful with clear guidance and the opportunity to make a real difference. This was, of course, Leander's objective, and on reflection, he had rather enjoyed the work to get things underway.

He strode through the palace grounds, seeking Sanne, and he found her sat on a stone bench under an arch of colourful flowers. Pink and red roses, yellow honeysuckle and purple shades from the aptly named passionflower. The display was testament to the craft of Leander's royal gardeners, yet no match for Sanne, whose presence made the picture a work of art.

With her head buried in a book, she never noticed Leander's approach. The afternoon sunlight shimmered through her hair and her flowing, sapphire blue dress somehow both stood out from and blended in with her surroundings, making her part of the nature around her.

The gardens had always been Leander's favourite place, even as a boy. So many nooks in which to hide, seek and discover. Towering trees, soaring birds, skittering insects and other creatures. This was his world, the gardens within his own palace, yet out here, he had no real authority. The gardeners did a fine job arranging plants and manicuring lawns, but this was largely a wild place beholden only to its own needs and desires. Like Fermantia itself, these gardens would be here long after Leander. He was little more than a steward, here to preserve, to maintain balance, and ensure that things remain both peaceful and beautiful.

For now, he had more immediate desires. He smoothed his hair and tentatively walked towards Sanne.

"Princess Sanne," he said, "what a pleasure to see you."

She folded her book and looked up with a smile, covering her eyes against the sunlight. "Greetings, King Leander. Your invite was a welcome one. I've been so keen to see your gardens and to learn more about this young king I've heard so much about."

Leander blushed, wondering what she might have heard. This was his chance to tell his own story. He offered a hand, helping Sanne to her feet, then gestured to a pathway that skirted the lawns, in the direction of the lily pond his mother had created.

"Only good things, I hope?" he asked, eventually. "My father's achievements are widely known, but I did not consider myself to be of great interest."

"A new king is always of interest, Your Majesty. People speak; surely you know this by now? I look forward to seeing if there is any truth in the rumours."

Sanne ended with a smile, pausing to enjoy the scent of some vivid orange peonies. A large honeybee loitered in the air as if inspecting the princess, then buzzed away to leave them in a moment of perfect quiet.

"Well, I do hope that you will not be disappointed," said Leander. "I'd heard tell of your beauty, but words do you no justice."

To his surprise, Sanne laughed, and Leander's skin prickled with embarrassment.

At length, the princess silenced, then turned to face him and said, "That's very kind, King Leander. Would that these accounts of my appearance had been conveyed by one as articulate as you."

"I'm sorry," said Leander. "I do hope you weren't offended by the compliment?"

"Of course not. We both know the reason I'm here, the arrangement made by our fathers. I had heard that you were...averse to the union."

The conversation had taken a swift and unexpected turn that had Leander floundering.

"No, of course not," he stuttered, "I've just been preoccupied is all. What with father's ill health and all the responsibilities of a growing realm."

"I understand," said Sanne, evidently convinced by Leander's excuses. "I see how the burden of rule weighs upon my father. As for marriage, well, it is a matter of unavoidable necessity. A prospect that I trust has become more appealing in person. Until yesterday we'd never even met before, had we? I could well have been ugly, unintelligent or worst of all boring."

Sanne grinned, and then continued down the path once more, leaving Leander to follow alongside smiling. Surprised by the princess's forthright and confident manner, Leander was beginning to relax, especially now the uncomfortable formalities of the conversation were behind him.

"Well, there's no fear of that," he said, "Though I can't speak for you. Perhaps you think *me* ugly or boring, or whatever the third word was that you used. It was a little long for me, I'm afraid."

At this, Sanne gave his arm a nudge, her infectious laugh causing Leander to smile too.

"I see the king is not without humour. Perhaps this match may yet surprise me."

"So, ugly and boring, that's what you were expecting?"

Sanne shrugged. "You never know what to expect, King Leander. It's some relief to find you so agreeable. My father wanted an alliance with King Yorick, and as the only eligible princess of Eluria, this was always going to be my destiny."

"Destiny." Leander shook his head at the word and all that went with it. "Don't you just hate that feeling that life is out of your hands, like your path is predetermined?"

"That is the life of a king or indeed a princess. Would you trade it all to live among the common folk? The Goddess blessed our families with the privilege and power of rule. A position to determine and influence change. That, in itself, is not something to complain of."

Leander tilted his head in agreement. He'd known romance to soften the sharpest of minds, and even kings, it seemed, were not immune to the influence. She was right, his birthright was truly a blessing. Sanne came across erudite, pragmatic and ambitious. He only hoped that some of these qualities would brush off on him, and wondered what great changes she might have in mind. "Even when it means moving away from your home," he asked. "To live with a king you've never met?"

"Now King Leander, I fear you're getting ahead of yourself. I am but a guest in your humble palace. What happens next is yet to be seen." She smiled, giving a playful wink. "Again," she said, more seriously. "Things could have been far worse. There aren't too many suitable young, unmarried kings from which I can choose. No," she said smiling, as Leander's cheeks turned hot pink. "You'll do, just fine. You have all your hair and teeth, and you aren't old enough to be my father."

"Thanks." Leander grinned back.

"You're welcome," said Sanne, as they arrived at the lily pond. At Leander's gesturing hand, she lowered herself elegantly onto another bench, a perfect position from which to enjoy the view.

The pond was teeming with wildlife. The reed-beds rustled with a family of swans, bright blue and orange kingfishers skimmed the water's surface and dragonflies hovered above large, indigo water lilies, noteworthy for both for their eye-catching colour and aromatic vanilla fragrance, making them a popular ingredient in rich Fermantian perfumes.

"It's beautiful," said Sanne. "It seems to me that there are far worse places to be sent."

"It's all I've really known, other than time away with my father's armies. It's not perfect, but it's home to me and I wouldn't change it."

"Perfect is such a strange word, isn't it? I've known many to question whether it even exists, outside of a notion to prevent us from appreciating the good in things. Is there something in that, King Leander, or would you consider this a poor excuse for those prone to settling?"

Leander pursed his lips in thought. Did Sanne view him as perfection, or was their proposed union something she would consider good, or worryingly, an example of settling? "It's a fair and perplexing question, I'll grant you. I don't know about settling, but in his entire life, I'm not sure if my father was ever truly satisfied."

"And your mother," said Sanne. "I'm sure they shared some good times together?"

Leander sighed. "So she tells me. If nothing else, I know mother is proud to have raised two princes."

"Well, one prince and a king. An enviable achievement for any queen. I'm sure her life has been full of happiness, King Leander. Remember that we are just players in a game far bigger than we are. All we can do is perform our part."

Leander nodded, considering Sanne's wisdom. It was clear that the princess possessed maturity far beyond her years and a rational mind that reminded him of his own mother. Moreover, Sanne was both interesting and funny. Funnier perhaps than Perrine, and in so many ways less challenging. He reflected on this past love affair and the "us against the world" attitude that had excited him and brought them together. In a way, it had him in mind of the siege of Ardalan, yet this time he and Perrine were defending their castle against the odds. An unwinnable battle made even more difficult now that he was fighting alone.

Could King Yorick have been right? A relationship with Sanne would be much easier. In addition to her obvious, visible qualities, the princess was of the right social stock, raised to live in this world of kings, queens and often-troublesome nobility.

Leander had fallen for Perrine's coarse charm and unfaltering directness, but he was king now and everything was changing. Perhaps his queen would need to be somewhat more refined.

As if reading his mind, Sanne continued. "Tell me about Miss Delport. From what I hear, the two of you had grown rather fond of each other."

Blindsided, Leander took a moment to consider his answer. Clearly, his relationship with Perrine was not as clandestine as he might have hoped. That or someone had mentioned to it to Sanne in an attempt to thwart him. Oskar, maybe? He didn't dare think about it. This was a faultless moment, and Leander wasn't prepared to let it go to waste.

"Perrine is," he corrected himself, "*was* someone very special to me. We've both been through a lot of change of late, the sort of change that has underlined our differences. In the end, we simply grew apart," he added, saddened, but feeling a little bit sick at his own imaginative interpretation of their relationship. "That chapter has ended now. No cause for concern."

Sanne nodded, but the gesture couldn't spare Leander's inner turmoil. Though relieved to have articulated a convincing explanation, his guilt toward Perrine was gut-wrenching. He had, in his own way, accepted defeat in his pursuit of their connection. In the end, it had only taken the interest of another woman. Was it weakness, common sense, or realism? Only time would tell.

After a moment, Sanne said, "That's good to know."

"It doesn't bother you then?"

"Bother me?" Her lips pursed. "I must say it's not ideal, but it's something I must learn to live with. Clearly Miss Delport is not of appropriate stock, nor are you the first king to surrender your standards in pursuit of male pleasures. I shall only concern myself with happenings from this day forward. My mother and father have been successfully married for many years, and I am expecting a similarly exclusive union. I trust you have outgrown servant girls and other unsuitable distractions. Love is desirable, King Leander, but respect in a marriage is absolute."

Leander sensed the threat underscoring Sanne's tone but couldn't help but feel that her comments about Perrine were a little unsavoury. *Was she wrong though?* he wondered, edging a little closer, irresistibly drawn to the princess. In her defence, Sanne had not met Perrine in person, and the latter was, in all intents and purposes, socially beneath him. Furthermore, this wasn't the first time he'd heard such comments. On the other hand, Sanne's ambitions for their union were refreshing to hear. On that, at least, they were closely aligned. "Now who's getting ahead of themselves?" he asked, in jest. "Anyone would think us engaged to be married."

Sanne grinned. "Let them. I'm sure the news would prove most welcome."

"Marriage though," he said. "It's quite the commitment. Of course, I'm pleased you aren't already running for the hills, but I must tell you, there is much to be done. Things aren't likely to be easy."

Sanne took his hand. "Nothing good ever is, King Leander. Remember, we have a duty to secure the future of two kingdoms. I don't need to tell you that a king is most vulnerable when without an heir. I will give you the stability you surely seek. Anything more… well, we shall consider that fortuitous."

This woman was beyond even his most optimistic imaginings. Her potential to be queen, mother, partner and steadying influence filled him with excitement, and her candour left him silent, lost in the depths of her ocean blue eyes.

After some moments he added, "Then let the people speak of marriage."

Once more, he found himself struck with an overwhelming sense of desire. His gaze shifted to the softness of her pink lips, and he leaned in to close their remaining distance...

"My king!" The booming voice of a new arrival brought Leander's advances to an abrupt halt. Sanne smiled, but Leander was far from happy. Could a king ever expect the indulgence of privacy?

"Yes, Lennart, tell me. What's so important that you've chosen to disturb us?"

Breathing heavily from his exertions, Lennart apologised. "It's Bram, Your Majesty," he said, doubled over, and with thick dark hair plastered to his forehead. "We've found him, but it's bad news. He's dead."

CHAPTER 7

"**I** know you," said Leander, sitting forward in his throne to eye the new arrival.

The man had thick, curly dark hair that flowed down his neck to gather at his shoulders and a heavy moustache that curled upwards at the tips. Beside him stood the even more familiar Lennart de Meiren. No longer did the Minister for Justice appear dishevelled and out of breath. He'd arrived in an ornately embroidered ensemble of coat, waistcoat and breeches. His shirt bore decorative cuffs, and a white silk cravat solidified the formal nature of his appearance, an impression reinforced by his steely-eyed expression.

The other man spoke first. "You honour me, Your Majesty. My name is Ciel Huertroop, and I served under your command during the conflict with Tenesca."

A flood of memories hit Leander in an instant. "That's right. And one of the first to scale the city walls at Ardalan?"

"Indeed." The recollection brought a short laugh from Ciel. He raised the walking cane he had used when entering the throne room. "Rare that I am first to anything these days, but war is known to change even the best of us. I'm sure you have your own scars to show for it."

Leander mumbled a sound of affirmation, but in truth, he'd survived the campaign entirely unscathed. He supposed his wounds were in the mind and the memory, but victorious armies could not exist without men like Ciel, the type of warrior that King Yorick had sacrificed to achieve his ambitions. Though Leander sat in the seat of power, he found himself in admiration of the man before him.

"Emile's loss has been my gain, Your Majesty," said Lennart. "Ciel's injuries have forced him to leave the army and seek alternative employment. Meanwhile, I have found him to be a most useful asset."

Ciel bowed as much as his injured leg would allow him. "You flatter me, Minister. I only do what I can to support your efforts."

"Ciel is being modest," Lennart continued. "Nobody knows Cadrael as well as this man. There are times where it is necessary for my investigations to be a little more surreptitious. On those occasions, Ciel offers eyes and ears in parts of the city that are otherwise cloaked in shadowy silence."

"A man of many skills," said Leander, suitably impressed. "I presume then that you have news of Bram Hoste's sudden and unexpected demise."

Lennart stepped forward. "One of many lines of investigation, Your Majesty. Before his own end, your father commissioned Ciel to pursue Ferran Veraza's daughter, the girl you encountered and chose to spare following her father's execution. More recently, he has also been helping us to find the guard who fled my castle the night of King Yorick's passing. I thought it wise to make introduction. I'm sure that Ciel would like to share his findings."

"Thank you, Minister. It is my honour to serve you. I hope that my labours will help in some small way." Ciel turned to face Leander before continuing, "The death of Bram Hoste is certainly a troubling one. His body was discovered in the slums of Lower Cadrael, left to decay in a filthy backstreet."

Leander's face pinched with confusion. "Lower Cadrael? Whatever was he doing in that part of the city?"

"My investigations on that point are ongoing," Ciel answered. "All I know is that he died from a wound sustained to the chest."

"Murder then?"

"It seems that way. I'm sorry, my king, but it appears that Minister Hoste met a gruesome end not befitting a man of his stature."

Lennart was next to speak. "Was there any sign of motive? The minister was not without his critics, but I can't imagine why anyone would want to see him dead."

"Nor me, Minister de Meiren. But take comfort in knowing the attack was unlikely to have been premeditated. We found his body in one of the capital's most dangerous neighbourhoods. More than half the city's taverns, brothels and drug dens are within walking distance. It pains me to say it, but this is likely a case of wrong time, wrong place."

Leander's head shook with a combination of shock and frustration. "Evidence?" he said instinctively. "Is there no indication of what happened to him, or who may have done it?"

"Very little that can be considered useful, my king." said Ciel. "A knife or a dagger, to tell from the wound. As to Bram's person, he appears to have been pickpocketed. Whether this was the motive for the attack remains to be seen, but by the time I got to him, literally everything had been taken."

"You mean to say—"

"Yes, my king. When we found the minister, he was entirely..." He paused to grimace. "Shall we say, unadorned? Everything was gone, even his eyeglasses."

"It's a mess," added Lennart. "And one that we will clean up quickly. I don't know why Bram was there, but it does little good for the reputation of The Ministry. Ciel is a man with many connections; rest assured his investigations will continue in earnest."

During Lennart's assurances, Ciel never flinched. "Someone must have seen something," he stated confidently. "I beg your patience, King Leander. I will get to the bottom of this, I promise."

Leander had no reason to doubt it either. He'd witnessed Ciel's steadfast determination first-hand. A man prepared to storm a walled and heavily defended city, Ciel was an honourable warrior, sworn to the ceaseless service of his king.

"Thank you, Ciel, your commitment is highly appreciated. In the meantime, Lennart, I trust you will handle the delicate issue of notifying Bram's wife and family. Of course, this means that his son Esra will have to take up the mantel of minister."

"Yes, my king, and I will see to it that arrangements are made. I understand that Esra is currently in the Clanlands for the purposes of business, but I will send word immediately and ensure his swift return. I've no doubt that news of his father will help in this regard."

Leander only hoped that Esra would avoid the details. "Thank you, Lennart," he said, his mind turning to other items in a growing list of concerns. "And what of the guard who fled your castle? Has he vanished into thin air, or do you have good news for me?"

He sat back and tried to appear as nonchalant as he could muster, but inside his stomach was turning over with a mixture of fear and guilt. Was the guard aware of what had happened in the room between Leander and his father? If so, what plans did the man have for this information? No longer did Leander sit comfortably upon his throne. He only knew that he would need to maintain an innocent outward appearance and trust in Ciel to see the deserter brought to justice.

His heart sank as the injured warrior announced, "No news as yet, my king. I have some leads that I am following up with my informants, and I hope to have information on the man's whereabouts very soon."

"And the girl?" asked Lennart. "We have a name, and a very public account of her recent whereabouts."

"That's true, but the girl is careful to be seen only when she wants to be, and the last report has her heading toward The Clanlands. With each moment, our search becomes ever more difficult, but rest assured that my spies are continuing to track her. Any threat she once posed has since been removed."

Leander blew out his cheeks. "A wild goose chase. The girl is gone and no harm done. The only victim here was my father's ego, and for better or worse, that's no longer a concern, for me or indeed for the girl. Ciel, I'd ask you to focus your efforts elsewhere. Find the absentee guard and determine the underlying cause of Bram's murder. Above all, I trust that you and Minister de Meiren will keep me updated."

Ciel nodded, turning to make for the doorway before pausing. "Make sure to let me know if you think of anything that might be relevant, my king. In particular, if you remember anyone with ill will toward Minister Hoste."

"Of course," said Leander, but a memory flashed through his mind as Ciel completed his exit. A vision from the night of his coronation since overlooked. "Lennart," he said. "Please summon Joran; I would have words with him. I think it best that you're present when I do."

Joran entered the throne room with his usual assuredness.

"My king, I gather you wanted to see me? Fortuitous timing, since I am keen to share some updates from our recent meeting."

Leander inclined his head. "Thank you, Joran. All in good time. There was, however, something that I wanted to discuss with you."

Beyond Joran, the doors snapped shut. Lennart completed their company, stepping forward to stand at the shoulder of his fellow minister.

Leander reconvened, "I'm sorry to start with bad news. I'm afraid to say it concerns your colleague Bram."

Unexpectedly Joran laughed. "You found the old fool then? Which gutter did you have to fish him out of?"

The lack of reaction caused Joran's smile to fade. The room fell silent, and the minister's sunken eyes began to twitch nervously.

"King Leander," he continued. "Is everything okay? I'm sorry I didn't mean to...I just thought..." he fumbled to find the words.

Unconvinced, Leander had plenty of questions he wanted to ask. "Bram was found dead this morning in Lower Cadrael. His body was stripped of all possessions, and he died from a stab wound sustained to the chest."

"Dead?" Joran repeated eventually, eyes wide with shock. "But who, and why, and..." He paused suddenly, as though an idea had hit him. He turned to Lennart, then back to Leander and said, "Your Majesty, you don't think that I had anything to do with this, do you?"

Leander raised a palm to slow Joran's gathering concern. "It's early to be jumping to conclusions, Joran. Just know that our investigations are underway. I thought a man of your standing should be allowed to answer to his innocence in suitable surroundings."

"Answer to my innocence." Joran's wide nose wrinkled with outrage. "I tirelessly served your father for decades. I'm sorry, Your Majesty, but never before have I heard such madness."

"Never before has a minister been murdered in such unusual circumstances. If you've nothing to hide, then there's nothing to fear, Minister."

Once again, the room fell silent. Joran, it seemed, was intent on maintaining a look of total surprise. If he was guilty, the act was fairly convincing, but there was something in his defensive behaviour that irked Leander, who watched on closely.

"The night of the coronation," he started. "I understand you left the celebrations early?"

Joran laughed nervously. "I'm a busy man, Your Majesty. I was keen to rest and make a quick start on your ambitious plans for the realm." He twisted to Lennart. "I presume you'll be dragging Emile here for similar reasons? I know things are changing, but is diligence unlawful now?"

"Now, now, Joran," said Leander. "I know this is uncomfortable, but let's not be facetious. What we know is that Bram is dead. We also know that on the night he went missing, the two of you were seen arguing."

"So that's what this is about, a silly little disagreement?"

"Maybe," said Leander, "But only one of us knows the cause of your quarrel. Enlighten us, Joran, and put my mind at ease. Believe me; I would much prefer to pursue other possibilities."

Joran sighed heavily, while Lennart watched on through narrowed eyes. "Women," said the Minister for Wealth, firmly. "If you must know, the conversation was about women."

"An unusual subject on which to disagree so fervently," said Lennart. "We all know what Bram's like. I've never seen you take umbrage on the matter before."

Joran's head shook dismissively. "This was different. We were speaking about the servant, the girl who kept filling his wineglass. It's one thing to behave a particular way in familiar company, but I didn't think it appropriate to fraternise with staff in the presence of esteemed guests. Unlike some of the others, I still believe in the sanctity of The Ministry."

"So, you argued then left, presumably finding your words to be fruitless?"

"Yes, my king. In the end I had to remove myself."

"And you went where?"

"Home, my king."

"Straight home? We can, of course, corroborate the timeline with your household staff."

Joran began to scratch the bald top of his head with revealing vigour. "Not exactly," he said, slowly and reluctantly. "My journey home was broken by a brief diversion."

"To where?" asked Leander. "I must say, this isn't looking very good, Joran."

"My king, the matter is, well, a little sensitive. I wonder if we could perhaps continue our conversation alone?"

Leander shared a glance with Lennart, whose brow raised questioningly. Leander wanted answers, but he knew better than to leave himself alone in the sole company of a potential killer. "I'm afraid that won't be possible," he said officiously. "Of all people, you know the importance of Lennart's role in establishing guilt and dispensing punishment. Tell me, Joran, where did you go?"

This time, the silence between them was deafening. Joran picked at his nails, deep in thought. Eventually he looked to Lennart and said, "What I'm about to tell you must stay in this room. Promise me."

Lennart looked to Leander, who nodded his approval. Joran wiped sweat from his brow, cleared his throat, and then continued with an unfamiliar tremble in his voice.

"Bruno's wife, Annelise Bekaert. She and I have been…" he paused. "Involved for some time. I don't know how, but Bram came to know of it. He began to speak too freely during the coronation, making threats. You know what he's like, or what he *was* like with wine inside him."

Though Lennart made to speak, Leander beat him to it. "So, you argued and then what? A scandal like this could destroy The Ministry. Presumably you decided you had to silence him?"

"No," snapped Joran. "Of course not, nothing like that. "He told me that he was going to tell Bruno if I didn't end it or tell him myself. I didn't want our hostility to overshadow the occasion, so I left and decided to discuss the matter with Annelise while Bruno was still busy at the coronation."

The explanation was thorough, if surprising to Leander. "You mean to say that you went to Bruno's estate, discussed the situation then returned to your own?"

"Correct," said Joran. "My carriage returned me no more than an hour after I left the palace. Annelise agreed that we should come clean and tell Bruno. I decided that I would tell him in the coming days but was careful to leave before he returned home to discover us."

Lennart scowled at Joran. "You might not have killed Bram, but the actions you describe are hardly more honourable."

Leander paced in front of his throne, mind reeling. Only days into his tenure and he was already dealing with murder and deceit. He had hoped to find support and guidance from his ministry but felt more like a parent minding difficult children. He feared that this information would soon become a new problem altogether.

"That's enough, Lennart," he said, hoping to douse the flames before they had opportunity to spread. "This is a rather unfortunate complication, but one I trust that Joran will soon resolve. My biggest concern is that I have been lied to, and these underhanded pursuits hardly fill me with confidence."

Joran let his head drop and began breathing heavily. "I'm sorry for the lies, my king, but my relationship with Annelise is nothing to be ashamed of. We love each other—you must believe me."

Lennart's head shook. "A sordid liaison with another man's wife. Take a long, hard look at yourself, Joran. Ashamed is the very least of what you should be feeling."

Finally, Joran cracked. "Should I, Lennart?" he shouted. "Should I really? You act as though you are without your vices. It's fine for you, Emile, or any of the others, so why should I face different judgement? Reliable old Joran," he continued mockingly. "*The moneyman*, whose interests only extend as far as protecting the king's coffers…Two decades,

Lennart, two decades I've served our wondrous realm. Tell me, what do I have to show for my efforts? No wife, nor children, just pages of ledgers mine to nurture."

"But Annelise!"

"What about her?" asked Joran. "Don't pretend that Bruno has any romantic interest in the woman. You're hardly the sharpest arrow in the quiver, Lennart, but don't begin to insult *my* intelligence. I love Bruno like a brother, but the man spends most of his time in front of the mirror or inside his young rent boys. We preserve his secret, all in the best interests of The Ministry, but does Annelise not deserve to experience true love? Do I not deserve my own share of happiness?"

Mouth agape, Lennart was visibly lost for words, and Leander began to wonder how the situation had unravelled so rapidly. Bruno's sexual interests were hardly Cadrael's best kept secret, but Leander's primary concern was managing the repercussions of Joran's more surprising revelation.

"So, what next?" he asked. "With Bram gone I presume you plan to keep your secret?"

Joran's face dropped. "I won't lie. When you told me his fate, I had hoped to continue with Annelise as before. I wish things were different, and I do not intend to harm Bruno. We'll have to tell him. I can't see another way."

"A public scandal could well be the death of him," said Lennart. "Not least with all the uproar that is likely to surround Bram's murder."

"But," said Leander, "Bruno does deserve to know the truth, as Joran himself has acknowledged. Joran, I propose you distance yourself from Annelise while we corroborate the story you've given us. Worry not, I'll ensure that the matter is handled with the utmost care until the time is right to discuss the matter with Bruno in person."

It was, at this moment, a case of damage limitation as much as anything. Though Bruno was a man of gentle demeanour, his occasional spiteful temper had earned him a reputation. It was also widely known that he had an uncanny ability to hold a grudge that was foolish to incite. Simply, it was best for Leander to try to bury the situation until calmer times. Perhaps the two men could resolve the situation amicably. His priority was to avoid a scandal, for Bruno's sake if nothing else.

"Our next step is to notify the others about Bram's murder," said Leander. "For now, I'd ask that you keep all of this to yourself and return home to continue your work. Comply with Lennart as he continues his investigations, try to keep things normal, but remain vigilant and don't leave Cadrael."

Lennart looked frustrated by Leander's inaction, but Joran rolled his eyes and said, "Yes, my king. I live to serve."

With that, the man backed away and Lennart escorted him to the door, leaving Leander alone with his thoughts.

He was exhausted, head spinning, but the baptism of fire was surely over. He'd earned his rest and tomorrow would be a new day.

A new day with Sanne.

He rediscovered his smile.

The royal carriage trundled through the heart of Cadrael, big wheels turning over on the cobbled streets. At either side of the carriage, the reassuring clip-clop of horse-bound guards and the sound of well-wishers, chasing their procession. The day was warm and bright, but a refreshing breeze passed through the body of the carriage where Leander sat with Sanne beside him. It was an ideal morning in ideal company, but as Leander gazed through the window blankly, he couldn't disguise that his mind was distracted.

"Is everything okay?" asked Sanne, after an extended silence. "It seems that something is playing on your mind, perhaps the minister they found dead? Bram wasn't it?"

Leander grimaced and placed his head in his hands. News had spread fast. He already feared the repercussions. He only hoped that the scandal with Joran could be contained.

"Sorry," he said. "I'm not much company, am I?"

Sanne shrugged. "No need for apology. If I'm to be your wife, then you must learn to share your problems."

"Thank you," he said. "The responsibilities of rule already weigh heavy upon me."

"Which is why it is best to let me shoulder some of the burden," said Sanne. "But most importantly, never let it show. Common folk will always ask for more money, better education or improved conditions, but what they really *want* is a ruler who inspires them, someone to look up to. When you smile, a whole nation smiles with you, no matter the circumstances. So, whatever is happening beneath the surface, try to keep it there. A king is supposed to be more than a man; never give them any reason to doubt you."

Leander laughed. "No pressure then." He looked out of the window once more, observing a band of children chasing the carriage calling his name. With Sanne's insight, he smiled and waved, and his smile only widened as the children slowed, cheering and congratulating one another. A priceless moment for children born into hardship. A memory for a lifetime, and it hadn't cost Leander a single bronze piece. He now saw the truth in Sanne's words.

Sanne's hand rested gently on Leander's leg. "I imagine we are going to make quite the partnership, King Leander. Remember, there are some things we can change, but there are others that simply aren't worth worrying about. Try not to let your worries spoil the occasion. You promised to make my time here *thoroughly enjoyable*. Is my company not suitably distracting?"

"Well..." said Leander, taken a little off-guard.

"I'll take that as yes." Sanne's grip tightened. "I certainly hope so anyway, for I intend to be your carriage company for some time."

Already, the princess had done wonders to improve his mood. The usual associated thought of Perrine floated to the surface of his mind and tried to force a feeling of guilt, purgatory for the way things had fallen apart, but nothing surfaced. Was he really going to sabotage this opportunity because of the past? His skin tingled at Sanne's touch, giving him his answer.

"Look." He pointed, and Sanne leaned across him to peer out the window. "It's our famous bell tower, constructed more than a thousand years ago by my ancestors. Of course, it was originally a wooden frame, since restored in stone. The structure was one of the very first in Cadrael, and it marks the centre of the city. The bells can be heard all over the capital."

He gazed at Sanne and was delighted to find her expression equal to the enthusiasm found in his voice. "Impressive," she said, "just as I imagined it. I'd read about the tower in books, but it is an honour to finally bear witness in person. Classical architecture isn't typically to my taste, but you certainly seem to know your history."

"Thanks." His shoulders relaxed, both relieved and encouraged. "If you're going to remain here, then it's in your best interest to become acquainted with the city. Take this," he said. "The Bridge of Waves, over the River Halven. The river itself is the reason my people settled here, and the parapet of the bridge has curved stones to imitate the flow of water. At its conception, the early Fermantians honoured the river by naming the capital Halven. That was, at least, until my ancestor King Cadrael thought to change it. Is it not interesting to know the origins of a nation?"

"It certainly is, but what of the future? Your enthusiasm for the past is admirable, but what will you build for your descendants to speak of?"

Leander fell silent, giving it thought. He knew the answer, but Sanne had him on his guard. For obvious reasons, he wanted to impress her. He already knew that she would bring out the best in him.

"Well, for starters, I shall rename the capital, Leander…" He grinned as Sanne laughed, but when he continued his tone was more serious. "I suppose I plan to lay building blocks on the foundations of the new world my father imagined. The realm is no longer about Cadrael or the borders of Fermantia.

King Yorick conquered nations with bold promises, which I intend to see realised so that we all might prosper."

"Leander the Liberal. I imagine that history would remember you fondly."

"Perhaps, but I would rather be judged by those who have lived alongside me. My father placed too much stock in his legacy. The man died with unfinished business. I intend to live in the moment."

"Well, that's every bit as ambitious as it is compassionate. I must say, I'm somewhat relieved. When I came here, I didn't know what to expect, but I had hoped to escape the clutches of a bloodthirsty tyrant." They shared a smile. "You say you want to live in the moment, so go ahead, King Leander. Tell me, what is your heart telling you to do in *this* moment?"

The puckering of her lips left Leander enchanted. King of half the world, but in that instant, he was merely a puppet with Princess Sanne holding the strings. Before he knew it their lips were touching, and he lost himself, focusing on the gentle touch of her skin, the scent of her hair. His hand brushed her cheek, exploring the hollow of her dimples and savouring every moment as the carriage continued down the uneven road. Eventually they broke apart and shared a knowing grin. That special exciting moment found in every new connection.

A world of possibility that Leander never wanted to leave.

"You read my mind," he admitted, somewhat bashfully. "But look," he said quickly, "We almost missed the bathhouses, and just up ahead are the famous libraries. I've spent my entire life in this city, but there is still so much I am yet to explore."

The carriage rattled onward, with Sanne now sat a little closer. Tall, forward-leaning, wood and brick residences shadowed the wide thoroughfare, casting dark shapes along the cobbles. Leander noticed that the princess's grip had tightened on his leg, and he found his mind wandering back to the palace and his chambers.

"The cathedral is up ahead, but you knew that anyway," he stuttered.

"It *has* been a few days, but I find myself recalling the vaguest memories."

Leander shook his head, trying to suppress an awkward grin. "All right," he said, a little bit embarrassed. "I just want to make sure you feel at home, that's all."

"I know, King Leander, your efforts are appreciated. I wonder though, is this jaunt really just for my benefit?" She raised an eyebrow.

"It has been some time since I was able to venture out and be among the city folk. Indulge me though; there was one last landmark that I wanted to show you."

"Last one, promise?"

"Promise. And better still, I've saved the best for last."

"Is that right? Pray tell, King Leander, where are you taking me?

"The statue of The Goddess," he answered, full of confidence. Of all things, surely this would impress her. "Twenty feet tall and crafted from the finest Saganese marble, the statue attracts people from across the known world with its beautiful craftsmanship and imposing appearance. My great-grandfather King Nicolas II commissioned it many years ago, but it still shines like the day it was unveiled. I don't share Minister Dubeck's enthusiasm for religion, but the statue is not of this world. I challenge you not to feel something."

"I fear *feeling something* is not the issue, King Leander. In fact, it's quite the opposite. I've had a fine time, but I find myself tired from my exertions. One more, then back to the palace?"

Leander offered his hand, which Sanne gently shook to seal their deal. "One more," he agreed, before an eruption of crowd noise sounded outside of the carriage. He narrowed his eyes as he felt the carriage's progress slow to a halt. Outside the window, the horse-bound guards were circling on high alert. This new sound was someway from the outpour of applause and affection that had accompanied them throughout their journey.

Sanne asked, "Is everything all right?"

Leander held his answer, not entirely sure himself. He instinctively reached for the sword at his side, pricking his ears to try and discern what the raised voices were all about. He unlocked the carriage door, preparing to step out into the hubbub.

Sanne's face drained immediately. "Where are you going?"

"To find out what's happening," he answered assertively. He was no stranger to precarious situations, but if the princess was to be his wife, she had to know he could protect her. He might have failed Perrine, but he swore that mistake was not for repeating. He pushed open the door and hopped down to land beside the carriage, where two guards rounded to cover him immediately.

"Your Majesty," said the first, a young man with sweeping chestnut hair and a light dusting of stubble. "I think it best you return to the carriage. There seems to be something of a disturbance."

Before them a crowd had gathered in frenzied speculation. Approaching from behind, Leander remained largely unnoticed, but peering back over his shoulder he noticed that Princess Sanne was at the carriage window watching with interest. Her presence sparked a moment of bravado that carried him forward toward the crowd.

"Make way," said another guard, this one on foot, halberd raised to force the throng away from them. Leander's entourage had grown to at least five that he could see, and the crowd parted with little fuss, sounds of surprise and of Leander's name rippling among them.

The concern in his men's eyes made the seriousness of the situation clear. He'd come too far to turn back now and saw this decision to march into the crowds for what it was: an act of reckless curiosity and bluster. The behaviour of a young prince, not of a king—he'd endangered himself, and with it, his men.

When they reached the front of the gathered people, the cause of the commotion became evident. Leander's jaw dropped, and the world fell silent around him. Silent, that was, but for the sound of creaking rope, and the gentle sway of a lifeless body in the breeze.

Tight at the neck, the rope had caused nasty lacerations, but these scrapes were no match for the deep cuts in the man's chest. A diamond shape, the sign of the Goddess, and with it one word, scribed in blood: *Perjurer.*

A woman's voice said, "Leander," and he was suddenly aware of Princess Sanne at his side. "Is that...?" she asked, taking his hand hesitantly.

"It is," said Leander, squeezing it tight.

With the statue of The Goddess looming in the distance, they stood together, hand-in-hand, watching as flies feasted on the body of Roel Dubeck.

CHAPTER 8

———⚜———

"Just the two men I wanted to see, and not a minute too soon. You'd better have good news for me."

Outside of custom and largely through impatience, Leander stood as the two men entered the throne room, causing him to leer down at them with unrestrained impatience.

"My king," said Lennart, while Ciel bowed deeply, wincing as he did. "I'm sorry; we came as soon as possible. The incident with Roel took some time to clear up and that was after we'd been able to disperse the crowds. There's a nervous energy about the city, Your Majesty. None of this makes our job any easier."

Leander could hardly contain his disbelief. "Well, sorry if I haven't shown you enough sympathy, Lennart, but another minister is dead, and your problems are simply the peak of a mountain that I have to overcome. Roel was an endlessly frustrating religious crackpot, but he was one of us and an attack on The Ministry is tantamount to an attack on the throne. So, I ask you. What news do you have for me?"

"Yes, my king," said Lennart. "But you must understand this situation is quite unprecedented."

Leander rubbed at his eyes with frustration. "I know, Lennart. I used to be quite the student of history. Two hundred years since a minister died of anything other than natural causes, injuries sustained at war, or in Arjen Roos's case, a rather public execution. If we're talking two underhanded murders, well, this would be the first, and what fine timing too."

His entry in the annals of history were fast becoming farcical. Forget Leander the Liberal; at this rate, they'd call him Leander the Liability. He had to get the situation under control quickly so that he could focus on making his changes. More immediately, he had to stop people from dying. Against all indications, he yet hoped that Lennart would have the answers.

Sadly, these hopes soon faded, taking with them Leander's patience.

"Sorry, my king," said Lennart, "But our investigations have been somewhat challenging."

Ciel intervened. "In the case of Minister Hoste, we are yet to find any reliable witnesses, only drunks and chancers. Since the manner of death is different from that of Minister Dubeck, it is possible that the first murder was an isolated, if regretful incident."

"We will of course continue the search," added Lennart. "An attack on one is an attack on all, as you say..."

Excuses and procrastination. Leander felt his annoyance rising. "And what of Roel?" he asked them, sharply. "Who did it, and how is it that I was first to discover the body?"

"A sorry incident," answered Lennart. "I hope the princess was not too badly shaken. And in view of The Goddess, that most holy of places. I can't believe—"

Leander interrupted. "Lennart, you're stalling."

Once more, Ciel stepped into line of questioning. "Investigations into the Minister for the Faith's murder are especially delicate. I started my enquiries immediately but have faced a series of obstacles along the way."

"Obstacles?" Leander's face tightened with displeasure.

This time, Ciel took a moment to consider his words. "Cardinal Schellet," he started, slowly. "He considers the incident a churchly matter. Though unwilling to provide any further insight, the cardinal speculated as to the involvement of a radical movement recently renounced by Minister Dubeck and the other senior members of his congregation."

"A churchly matter?" By now, Leander was incensed. "I appreciate your efforts, and indeed your candour, but surely anything within the borders of the Cadraelian Realm can be considered a matter for its king?"

Ciel nodded. "I've never been one for religion myself, Your Majesty. The horrors of war make you question the existence of The Goddess, or any other deity for that matter."

"Heathen," snapped Lennart, but he silenced as his king raised a hand. Shooting a sharp look towards the minister, Leander encouraged Ciel to continue without further interruption.

"What I mean to say is that no matter what I think, faith is a dangerous virtue, which can, in certain conditions, make people do very dangerous things. I intend to get to the very bottom of Minister Dubeck's murder, but in the meantime, I think it prudent to work alongside the church and support their own investigations."

"Well," said Lennart, "I can't say I fully agree with him. However, one thing is for certain: you don't want to start your reign in conflict with a deity. Civil war, holy war, whatever you call it, the outcome is certainly undesirable. If I remember rightly, it was the undoing of your ancestor King Quinten?"

Reluctantly, Leander agreed, though somewhat pleased for a chance to demonstrate the depth of his knowledge. "They stormed the palace and removed him from power," he said. "His brother, Pieter the Pious succeeded him. Since then, Fermantia has always been beholden to The Goddess."

"And not without reward," Lennart said, as though his point were proven. Leander couldn't remember such reverent behaviour when the minister was beheading and terrorising innocent people, but he supposed that death caused strange and unexpected reactions, and apparently, Lennart was no different. Worse still, the man was probably right. Had Leander really thought to challenge the church and risk a possible conflict? Surely, his place was to bring calm and peace to a country that had been at war for as long as Leander's memory extended.

Eventually he conceded. "Understood, so what plans do we have?"

"If you're asking my opinion, I'd say do nothing or as little as possible," said Ciel. "To my mind there are two possibilities, and neither will benefit from our intervention. One..." He raised his index finger. "The attack was the religious faction; I believe they call themselves The Sworn. In this case, best not to get involved. Let the cardinal keep his house in order. Two, and perhaps more unsettling..." He raised another finger. "The attack came from outside the church, perhaps targeting the institution. I need not remind you that you're a new king, not especially well known to the cardinal and his peers. You're perceived to have fairly liberal views, King Leander, not as devout as many of your forebears nor as Schellet would like. There's enough wariness already without adding fuel to the fire by infiltrating their inquisition. Roel Dubeck was a minister, on that we agree, but he was also head of the church, and thus, one of their own."

Ciel's arguments had Lennart convinced. He put his hand on Ciel's shoulder to reaffirm his support and spoke as Leander returned to his seat in frustration. "Though it pains me to say, he's right, Your Majesty. Remember your father's relationship with the cardinals was often fractious. An unfortunate situation no doubt, but no less an opportunity to build bridges with the brotherhood of the faith."

No action—could that truly be the solution? Leander wanted to stomp and shout, to gather his men and rush the cathedral. In the end, he slowed himself, seeing the truth in Ciel's words and the patience that is oft required of a king.

"It seems you have things all worked out between you," he said, dejectedly. "Lennart, maintain contact with High Cardinal Schellet. Extend our deepest sympathies and remind him that the full extent of our judicial resources is at his disposal if required. Meanwhile, Ciel, I must ask you to do something very sensitive. I suspect that Minister Rensen might hold some clues to help with our investigations. Please use this time to monitor and consider our Minister for Wealth fully. The minister is under strict instruction to remain in Cadrael until our investigations reach their conclusion. With any luck, his actions will lead us to the killer, or at the very least, set us in the right direction."

Ciel's eyes tightened. "Is there something you aren't telling me, Your Majesty?"

"Plenty," said Leander. "But sadly for you, that's my prerogative. Nevertheless, your orders stand, and I will require regular updates. I'm sure you'll have plenty to tell me, and that's without mentioning our elusive guard. Am I foolish to expect some new information?" He ended with a churlish shrug.

In truth, it was unnecessarily pompous and confrontational, but to Leander's surprise, Ciel's confidence never faltered.

"I expect to have news for you by the end of the day, Your Majesty. My informants believe they have located the man. It's a simple case of verifying his identity."

"Good," said Leander. At last, some good news to ease his mounting nerves. "You both know your business, and with any luck we'll have the killer in chains before the day is through. Go," he said, "and bring this sorry situation to a close. For now, I have other business. Please excuse me; the envoy from Vicentia is waiting."

The royal solar had always been King Yorick's favourite room—a sanctuary within which he could read, drink wine and avoid the day-to-day rigours of kingship. A sizeable living space centred around an imposing hearth, the solar was richly decorated with colourful tapestries, portraits of former kings and queens, ornamental weaponry, and armour. This splendour was brightened by a large window affording unrivalled views out onto the palace gardens.

In many ways it could be considered the heart of the palace, and though Leander was still in the infancy of his own time in power, he was already coming to appreciate the refuge the room afforded.

For now, however, solitude was no option, and the location of his next meeting was not by happenstance. The envoy from Vicentia had every reason to attend with suspicion, and Leander was keen to establish a hospitable overtone. He hoped that the informal setting would go some way to easing any tension. He reasoned that by inviting the emissary into the inner sanctity of his palace, he would be welcomed into the bosom of Vicentian trust.

He sat upright and pulled his chair to the table. A knock sounded, and the doors opened to reveal Marcel accompanied by the Vicentian envoy and one of Leander's own royal guards. The envoy paused to remove an opulent knife from a scabbard, which he handed to his escort without contention, handle sparkling in the afternoon light. Marcel proceeded to introduce Leander's guest as Spano Rizzuti.

A tall and wiry character, Spano had bronze skin and dark features. His mid-length, raven hair glimmered in the sunlight, falling in waves that somehow appeared both disordered and meticulous. His traditional ensemble consisted of a long, black velvet jacket with gold thread embroidery, soft leather slippers with complementary patterning and contrasting white stockings. He was every bit the quintessential Vicentian, down to the haughty swagger of his walk—a feature for which his people were known and often ridiculed. However, as the man paused to bow, Leander forced aside any remaining preconceptions. If things were to change, he would have to think differently. All being well, this meeting could change the course of history.

"Welcome, Consul Rizzuti," he said warmly. "It is my pleasure to host you. Please, make yourself comfortable."

Honoured, Spano placed a hand to his heart to express appreciation. He smiled and then moved to take the seat Leander had proffered. "The honour is all mine, King Leander," he said, in flawless Fermantian with no discernible accent. Evidently, the man was sharp and well-educated. Leander knew he would need to be at his best.

"Wine?" he asked, offering the bottle. He took a sip from his own glass to assuage any fears of tampering, but to his dismay, Spano declined.

"Thank you, King Leander, but where I'm from we have a saying: a man with a clear mind is a man with clear thinking."

"Of course," Leander smiled, and then pushed his own glass aside, somewhat embarrassed. For all his pomp, it seemed that Consul Rizzuti was unlikely to be a source of fun. Nevertheless, Leander reminded himself that fun had never been the purpose of their discussion. With the weight of two dead ministers bearing down on him, he was keen to move the conversation forward and, in turn, achieve the positive outcome that would see an upturn in his ongoing poor luck.

"I'm sure you're a busy man, so I'll get to the heart of the issue, Consul. It is my view that our two nations have spent far too long in a game of stalemate. Trade has suffered, movement has been limited, and the people have been forced to live in a state of perpetual uncertainty under threat of war."

If the consul was surprised by Leander's directness, he didn't let it show. Instead, he nodded with approval. "Some very reasonable points, King Leander, but we must first ask ourselves the origin of this uncertainty. It is my understanding that only recently, your own father, King Yorick III, mobilised troops with ambitions for Tenevarre."

"I regret to say that you're correct, Consul Rizzuti. I fear that, by the end, my father was not himself."

The consul seemed unconvinced, conceding, "Illness can play havoc on even the greatest among us. And yet." He paused. "This was not the first sign of Fermantian aggression. Queen Orsolina has long sought to cultivate amiable relations, but King Yorick was a somewhat...unpredictable character. The only undeniable truth was the man's ambition. It need not be said that decades of war are a poor foundation for peace." He ended, looking very pleased with himself.

Leander was no stranger to King Yorick's shortcomings, but it took all his self-control not to react to the consul's righteousness. It was one thing to think ill of his father, but something very different to hear it from another, and a rival at that. In the end he took a deep breath and tried to focus on what was at stake. Change occurs when someone gives life to a new way of thinking, and in this case, Leander sensed it would have to be him.

"In his defence, my father was not the first to fail in improving the bond between our two great nations. There is much that either side could have done better over the years, though I accept that King Yorick's reign must have appeared somewhat unsettling for your queen and her people."

Spano smiled, as if celebrating a small victory. "Thank you, King Leander, I think that a very reasonable assessment. I know that my queen is an advocate for order and stability. I've no doubt your words will come as music to her ears."

"I'm glad to hear we're all singing the same tune," said Leander. "Tenevarre is the tension that stands between us. An age-old dispute that even today rumbles beneath the surface of all our issues. Our discourse is the very barrier to Tenevarre's nation status, and while these arguments persist, we are the enemy of progress. As you know, there are many within Tenevarre who already call for autonomy, arguing that it has become a country in its own right—a nation deserving of a brighter future. Maybe it is time to entertain this very notion, no longer considering Tenevarre as property for Fermantia or Vicentia to squabble over. I propose an end to these enduring disputes. I propose Tenevarrean independence."

It gave Leander great pleasure to see the consul left speechless. He sat back and watched the man's eyes narrow in deep thought. Perhaps now Spano Rizzuti would realise the type of man he was dealing with. Perhaps now the consul had started to believe a new king's ambition.

He muttered, "Interesting. It seems you have grand plans, King Leander."

"What use is a king, if not to imagine the unimaginable? Yet, good ideas are little use when confined to the mind's eye, Consul. It seems to me that the world is changing whether we like it or not. The question now is whether your queen is ready to embrace it?"

Once more, Spano took a moment to consider his response. The momentum had shifted in Leander's favour, but he remained calm and expressionless, as yet unwilling to celebrate success.

"An interesting idea," said the consul, eventually. "But one that overlooks our historical claim to the land you mention."

Disappointed but not fully surprised, Leander forced a smile onto his face. "Come now, Consul, we both know those claims to be debatable. Have we not spent enough time living in the past discussing imaginary borders? I intend to spend my tenure looking to the future. An independent Tenevarre ends these tired arguments. Better still, it delivers the peace and harmony Queen Orsolina so clearly seeks."

The consul sat back in his chair, and for a moment Leander began to hope that his passionate entreaty was making a difference. In spite of Spano's endlessly smug countenance, Leander had to believe that the man could see sense and relay his good intentions to the queen accordingly.

"Thank you, King Leander. You raise some fascinating points that I will certainly share with Queen Orsolina. I appreciate the enthusiasm of youth, and your keenness to make change, but I would temper your enthusiasm with the unfortunate events of recent years, events that have, shall we say diminished trust. You see, your father—"

"I'm not my father."

"Yes, but your father—"

Leander slammed his hands on the desk. "I'm not my fucking father!"

The consul flinched. Leander instantly felt a wave of remorse. A stupid move, especially in the circumstances, but the consul didn't seem to have been listening. Did Leander, a king of all people, not deserve to be heard? Though regrettable, his actions were not entirely without provocation. Did the consul not know the pressure Leander was facing? Two dead ministers and decades of King Yorick's bloodthirsty rule hanging over him. Finally, he braced himself, smiled, then apologised.

"You see, Consul Rizzuti, I'm a passionate man, true to his convictions."

"That much is obvious, King Leander, and I am sorry if my words were poorly chosen. You certainly possess King Yorick's single-mindedness, and if turned to peace, then perhaps there is hope for your vision. What you propose is twofold then: a new charter granting independent nation status to Tenevarre, and a revised treaty for peace between our two great nations?"

Progress finally. "Exactly," said Leander. "Papers that we will ultimately sign on a momentous occasion befitting such an historic agreement. Imagine it: the King of Fermantia and Queen of Vicentia, joined by a third, the newly elected leader of Tenevarre. A shared commitment to a brighter future. A mend for the rift that has long existed between us."

A slow smile crept across the consul's face with every word. "A fine notion, King Leander. Let's see what Queen Orsolina makes of it."

The meeting with the consul left Leander feeling buoyant but exhausted. Never before had he so clearly appreciated the charmed life he'd been living as a prince free from responsibility. He'd quickly learned that it took a huge amount of energy to learn new skills, or at least to act as though he knew what he was doing. Though satisfied with his efforts, his vigour waned as soon as he and Consul Rizzuti amicably parted ways. By now, he was ready to return to his chambers for a quick nap; the last thing he expected or wanted was the sight of Oskar, waiting to greet him.

"Brother," said Oskar, unfolding his legs, but choosing not to rise from his spot in an armchair beside the window. "I hear the consul from Vicentia has left already. I must say, you do move quickly, don't you?'

"A king's work is varied and never-ending," said Leander. "Remind me, what is it that a prince does these days, brother?"

Oskar rose from his seat with an exaggerated show of mock offense. "Oh! How you've changed, Leander. A few days on the throne and already so distant from your underlings. I had hoped to catch you in a better mood," he said, pouting. "Two down already, that's worthy of congratulations. I thought myself a man of action, but I must say you've surprised me."

Leander's face pulled into a scowl. He was tired and his patience was wearing thin for his brother's goading. "What are you talking about?" he asked angrily. "Oskar, I'm sorry, but I really don't have the time for this right now, and—"

"Bram and Roel," answered Oskar. "I've never cared much for them myself, but two murders. You really are ruthless."

Leander was lost for words. "Excuse me?" he uttered, then waited expectantly.

"You killed them, didn't you, just as I said you should? I was joking at the time, but that's not to say I disagree. Modern Fermantia has no need for those corrupt old fucks. You've done us all a favour in the end. You always said you were going to change things."

Leander's face was one of total disbelief. "Are you out of your mind or just entirely stupid?" he growled. "Two men dead and you think it a laughing matter. What's more, and with everything going on, you try to place the blame at my feet?"

Oskar seemed shocked by the ferocity of his answer, though as always, his defence was to hide behind a characteristic smirk. "Calm down, Leander, it's just a joke," he said with a half-laugh. "There was a time when we always used to laugh together, back when we were children. When did you start taking life so seriously?"

"Fuck you, Oskar." The aggression of his words seemed to surprise them both. He walked across the room to stand at eye-level with his brother. Leander's patience had reached an end. "*You* used to laugh," he continued angrily. "Not me. Not with father's eyes always upon me. You never had to deal with his displeasure and impossible expectations. The requirement to become a man you can hardly stand, and from whom you couldn't possibly be more different. Life is serious, Oskar, at least for me anyway..."

Years of resentment bubbled to the surface, Oskar the unfortunate recipient of feelings that Leander knew he could not bottle up any longer. It seemed that everyone was intent on adding to his problems. "It might have escaped your notice, Oskar, but I'm your king now, and will be addressed accordingly."

"But, brother, I—"

"No, Oskar, I've heard more than enough from you. I'm tired, pressured and have enough to deal with without entertaining your nonsense. You dare accuse me of murder. To my mind that sounds a lot like treason; a very dangerous joke indeed, don't you agree?"

He paused as a new idea occurred to him. The guilt of their father's murder was certainly stoking the fires of his anger, but Oskar himself was not without fault, and as Leander looked at his brother, a regrettable thought began to take hold.

"You accuse me of murdering them," he said, more calmly now. "But if I remember rightly, it was you who wished for the end of The Ministry. You wanted to kill them all, I believe. Those 'useless old fucks' or whatever it was that you chose to call them. So, I ask you, brother, where we you yesterday when Roel was murdered? I know you were there the night of the coronation, so there's no reason you couldn't have followed Bram to Lower Cadrael where he met his end."

It was Oskar's turn to look flabbergasted, and any ghost of a smile had now faded. "You can't think...but surely..." he stuttered. "This is ridiculous. You know I was joking. A poor joke, admittedly, but you can't think I killed them. Leander—"

"King Leander."

"King Leander, you must see the sense in this."

"I asked you a question," said Leander, firmly. "Where were you at the time of Roel's murder, or do I have to ask Lennart and his inquisitors to question you? I think you'll find that a lot less comfortable."

"You wouldn't."

"I would. Now answer the question."

At this stage, Oskar was visibly uncomfortable. His face was red and glistening with sweat and his eyes danced about the room, as if searching for an escape that never presented itself. Eventually, he huffed a reluctant sigh and his shoulders sagged. He dragged himself back to the chair, sat, and slumped his lowered chin into a hand for support. "It hasn't been easy you know." His voice was softer now, sincere. "I know you never saw eye-to-eye with our father, but I loved him, adored him even. While you were being prepared for kingship I was being mollycoddled by mother, always reminded of my place: the spare. I was never any match for my big brother, everyone's favourite, Fermantia's golden boy, Prince Leander." He laughed briefly, but there was no hint of joy in it. "I never saw or heard much from Father, but it didn't matter. I idolised the man from a distance. Likely, some of it was my own imagination, but I envisaged getting to know him one day as a man. Dreamed of gaining his respect, earning his attention."

This unexpected turn had Leander confused, but he didn't doubt the tears that glistened in his brother eyes as he spoke. "It was hard on both of us," he offered, trying to console Oskar.

His brother didn't react other than to wipe his eyes with the cuff of his shirt and continue. "If you must know, I was passed out in a gutter somewhere in Lower Cadrael when Roel was murdered. You've been busy, Mother's been grieving, and me, well it seems I share Father's penchant for a drink when times get difficult. I couldn't tell you exactly where I was or what I was doing. I spend most nights in the brothels, taverns and the gambling dens. In most cases I'm home by sunrise, but that part of the city is nothing if not unpredictable."

"Oskar..."

His brother brushed him away. "If you're looking for proof, then speak with Lennart. I don't know how, but he found me and brought me back to the palace, promising not to say anything. I suppose that's why he wasn't there when Roel was murdered; neither of us were. I swore him to secrecy but never expected to face this scrutiny. Perhaps it's best you know. You aren't the only one that's suffering, King Leander..."

He turned to face the window, and an uncomfortable silence settled between them. If Leander's guilt wasn't bad enough already, he now realised the full repercussions of the decision to let their father die. In doing so, he'd deprived Oskar the chance to build that relationship, and to make matters worse, Leander had failed in his duties as an older brother. He'd spared little thought for Oskar's suffering, and while he thought of it, he also hadn't been to see their mother in days.

"I'm sorry, Oskar," he said. "I hadn't realised. I'll try to be more observant."

"It's fine, you're king now. You can't be chasing around after your errant little brother, can you?"

Exhausted, and deeply disappointed in himself, every word hit Leander like a knife to the heart. He wasn't himself, but it would have been lazy to hold tiredness accountable for his uncharacteristic behaviour. He yielded, "Perhaps not, but I can do better."

A heartfelt promise, but one followed with another moment of quiet. Eventually, Oskar turned and said, "You've changed, you know."

Leander answered, "I fear we all must."

For him, it seemed the change was even bigger than he had anticipated.

Leander's head had scarcely hit the pillow when a knock at the door roused him from his much-needed slumber.

A thousand profanities passed through his mind, but these were silenced as a voice beyond the door informed him that Lennart was in the throne room awaiting audience. It seemed the minister had arrived with an important update, so the previously unwelcome news of his arrival now filled Leander with a renewed sense of optimism. The guilt of his conversation with Oskar still hung over him like a heavy cloud, but there was no time for self-pity—this new life would never allow it. If nothing else, he could solve the murders. From there, he could focus on rebuilding his family.

He jumped from the bed, arranged his hair and rushed to the throne room, where Lennart and Ciel were already waiting.

"Gentlemen," he said, taking a seat in his gilded throne. "You promised updates. I knew you wouldn't let me down."

His jovial tone was a false reflection of his mood, and his spirits dropped further on seeing the minister looking unexpectedly dismayed.

"It's Joran," said Lennart. "I'm sorry, my king, but Joran's been murdered."

Forget clouds, it felt like the sky was falling down around him. "He's what?" said Leander. "I beg you Lennart; please tell me this is some sort of sick fucking joke."

"No joke." The sombre tone of Lennart's voice was equal to his subdued posture. "This morning, Ciel visited Joran's estate to keep an eye on the minister—"

"But he never emerged," Ciel interrupted, confirming the obvious. "I waited long into the afternoon before I started to sense that something wasn't right. The guards at the gate said they hadn't seen hide nor hair of him all day. It was then that I knew I had to involve Minister de Meiren."

Lennart nodded. "And a good thing he did too. Sadly, we were too late to save Joran." His lip trembled before he steadied himself. "We found the minister sprawled in his office covered in blood. Poison, we think. Ciel noticed a suspicious wine bottle at the house."

"Poison," said Leander, hardly able to believe what he was hearing. "Who sent it?" he asked in desperation. "And more importantly, why?"

Less confidently than on previous occasions, Ciel cleared his throat to pick up the mantle. "Whoever it was, they arrived before I did. I was there all morning, and nobody came or left. From what I can tell, his staff were all well-paid and perfectly treated. No reason to suspect an inside job."

"But the bottle of wine," muttered Leander. "If that is the offending item, then surely it must hold some clues?"

Sadly, it seemed that Lennart thought otherwise. The minister shook his head with a frown. "It's not unusual for local producers to curry favour, and no great surprise for a bottle or bottles to turn up unannounced. The vintners use it as an enticement for investment or future orders. There was little reason for Joran to be suspicious. At least, that is, until it was too late."

"But the bottle." The desperation persisted in Leander's voice. "Presumably it is marked with the name of the vineyard. Is this not cause for investigation?"

Ciel considered the thought before answering, "Perhaps, my king, but that's much too easily unravelled. It's more likely to be the ill-judged action of a rival vintner, but even then, poisoned wine is bad for business. For all business. I'll follow up to ensure nothing is overlooked, but I think our killer is, as of yet, evading our attention."

Lennart's foot stomped loudly. "When I catch the scum, there'll be hell to pay, of that I can promise you. Three ministers dead, but they don't scare me. I'll get them in the end, I always do."

"Well, I admire your commitment, Lennart, but so far, we're being made to look fools. Three ministers, three murders and three very different methods," said Leander. "We had a couple of suspects; is it wrong to hope for good news? The guard who deserted, the night of my father's passing, for one. Three murders since and no sign of the elusive bastard. Surely you aren't going to pass this off as coincidence?"

Ciel's head shook. "I'm sorry, my king, but this I can answer. The man you mention is one Morgan Vandaele, and on the night of King Yorick's passing, he made the strange decision to leave his post to head, not for Cadrael, but for home. His house, you see, is only a handful of miles from Lennart's castle, and from my enquiries, it seems it had been some time since he had last seen his wife and children. I should say that Vandaele was a member of your father's armies for some years before he eventually joined the Royal Guard."

The story did little to reassure Leander. "So he deserted and went home? That leaves plenty of time to commit the murders."

"It would," said Ciel. "Except his homecoming was not straightforward. It appears that in his absence, Vandaele had been, shall we say, out of sight, out of mind." He winced. "On his return, Vandaele discovered his wife and brother in *intimate* relations. The revelation led to a rather violent exchange for which Vandaele has remained incarcerated ever since. Put simply—"

"There's no way that Cornelis could have committed the murders." Leander's heart sank.

"No, my king," Ciel responded. "Absconder and malcontent maybe, but Morgan Vandaele is not your murderer."

The wind emptied from Leander's sails. Three ministers dead, and scarcely a clue to work with. He wondered how his father might have dealt with this situation, a pointless act that only added to his frustration. He'd chosen to put himself in the seat of power with all its responsibility. It was his job to solve the mystery. What were they missing?

"The maidservant," he said, hopefully. "The one fraternising with Bram during the coronation banquet. Any news on her movements?"

Again, Ciel was quick to answer. "I've spoken to the Royal Chamberlain about this already. He assures me the girl remained at the palace long after Minister Hoste's departure. I understand that her inappropriate, amorous behaviour earned her a warning, but no reason to consider her a suspect. The same goes for the other murders."

An audible sigh escaped Leander, who began chewing his nails with painful zeal. "So that's that then, we've got nothing more than a half-empty bottle of wine, and no other discernible suspects? I ask you, how many must die before we start to make some progress? I'm sorry, Lennart, but I really must start to question your credentials."

On closer inspection, Leander realised that Lennart now cut a rather troubled figure. His eyes were heavy with tiredness and framed by deep lines, while his patchy stubble was unusually disordered. If Leander hadn't been under similar pressure, he might have found some sympathy for the suffering minister.

"Fear not," said Ciel. "We won't stop searching. Until now, we might have been looking in all the wrong places, but the net will continue to tighten with each new piece of information. In the end," he said, poignantly, "we might just have to learn to think a little differently."

The former soldier bowed, but his words made an immediate impression. Absentmindedly, Leander uttered, "Looking in all the wrong places..." stopping Ciel in his tracks as a new idea gathered pace. When it all fell into place, disbelieving laughter escaped him. "Of course, it was never Joran. How could I have been so stupid?"

"No, Your Majesty?" Curiosity surpassed the minister's weariness.

"No, Lennart," said Leander. "Think. Who had the most to lose with Joran alive?"

A look of realisation appeared on Lennart's face almost immediately. A solution that had been there before them all along.

"Prepare your men, Minister," said Leander firmly. "We ride for Bruno Bekaert's estate. And this time, I'm coming with you."

CHAPTER 9

The royal carriage bounced along the cobblestones with purposeful urgency as it careened though the heart of Cadrael. From beyond the window, the city was a blur, but this journey was not for the scenery; Leander had only justice in mind.

Beside him sat Lennart, quiet in his contemplation. The man chewed his lip in thought, then broke the silence by turning to his king to ask, "Bram I understand, but why kill Roel?"

The question still puzzled Leander too. "Perhaps he also knew about Joran's dalliances," he speculated. "I assume it was a means of tying off any loose ends, silencing any who might disclose the information and bring Bruno's marriage into disrepute."

"Imagine the scandal," said Lennart, under his breath.

Leander nodded. "But perhaps it was more than that. We all have our...thoughts, on Bruno, but that's little more than conjecture at this point. If nothing else, Annelise is Bruno's wife of many years. Love, affection, companionship, whatever you'd call it. These emotions can make a man do unexpected and terrible things. I know it's too late for the others, but we're ahead of him now, and finally in a position to stop him before any further damage is done."

Just saying it brought a cautious smile to Leander's face. He'd felt so clueless, hopeless, but now, for the first time, they had the advantage and were rapidly closing in on the murderer.

"And not a minute too soon," said Lennart, letting out a deep breath. "I suppose it could have been us next with what we know. Let's just hope that Bruno isn't expecting us. We cannot let him slip through the net again."

The thought had also occurred to Leander, but the killer had so far shown himself to be brazen. Some would say that the murderer was perhaps a little too confident, a trait which had aroused the imagination of the common folk, causing them to label the fiend as the Cadrael Killer. "Always so sullen, Lennart. Where's the faith which you were, only recently, so keen to demonstrate? Trust that we are about to end this sorry chapter. We've much work to do if the Cadraelian Realm is to achieve its full potential." He paused to look out the window; already they were nearing their destination. "Our first job, of course, will be to rebuild The Ministry," he continued. "Perhaps the fresh impetus will help to drive my many aims for peace and prosperity. A refresh in personnel, and an opportunity to usher in new ways of thinking. Things haven't been easy of late," he said, optimistically voicing this huge understatement. "But perhaps things are about to change. And underpinning all of this," he turned to Lennart. "Trust."

The lump in the minister's throat shifted with an uneasy gulp. It seemed Leander's inference had hit the mark just as intended. "I'm sorry, Your Majesty," he started apologetically. "I only meant to help Prince Oskar, and in doing so, take any worry away from you."

"A well-intentioned lie is still a lie, Lennart. You know that better than anyone." Leander's face was firm and humourless, leaving the minister in no doubt as to the seriousness of the matter at hand. In time, Lennart let his head drop and quietly apologised.

"Say no more of it," answered Leander. "Watch out for my brother but keep nothing from me."

The carriage drew to a halt, punctuating his sentence. Leander heard the scuff of boots echoing against the ground as their accompanying horse-bound guards dismounted before one arrived to open the carriage door.

"Thank you," said Leander, stepping down into the shadow of Bruno's opulent mansion. Beyond him, Ciel, in the company of two armoured guards, was already making efforts to gain access to the estate. Outnumbered by Bruno's men guarding the set of imposing golden gates, Ciel's endeavours were stalling when sight of Leander forced their opposition to their knees.

"I'm sorry, Your Majesty," said one of them, an older man with thinning white hair and a neat white beard that framed his jaw and mouth. He returned to his feet and added, "The minister had specified no further guests today. Is it perhaps possible to return at another time?"

Concerned at the prospect of losing their killer, or indeed risking another murder, Leander was not prepared to take no for an answer. "I must insist on seeing the minister immediately," he said, "I trust that this will not be an issue."

With his final word, both sets of men raised their weapons, their brief standoff interrupted only when the guard with the white hair called for calm. "Of course, my king," he answered amiably. "I would be happy to escort you. My name is Cedric Verhelst. Antoine, Theo, see to the gates..."

Within moments the gates were open, and Leander strolled purposefully into the grounds of Bruno's home. As expected, the estate was pristine, a first impression compounded by a lush, manicured lawn and an extravagant, cascading water fountain. As Leander walked closer, he saw that the fountain was adorned by a cast of gilded warriors depicting the last famous battle between Fermantia and Vicentia during the reign of Leander's great-grandfather.

To the other side of the property stood a small walled garden that instantly caught Ciel's attention. "Can you smell that?" he said, inhaling the air, then summoning the group for closer inspection.

Leander obliged, following behind the former soldier until they came to an abrupt halt where Ciel slowly dropped to his knees to inspect a patch of striking, cerulean flowers, which were responsible for the sweet scent in the air. After a moment, he turned to Leander and said, "Just as I thought."

"Blue Meadow Lilies?" asked Leander.

Lennart answered hesitantly. "It appears so, Your Majesty."

Leander turned back to the house and noticed a brief flash of movement in an upstairs window. It was obvious they had no time to waste; he just hoped they were not already too late.

He turned to run and called the others to follow him. In his wake, Ciel, Lennart and the guards hurried to keep up, but Cedric kept pace, before advancing to speak with the guard at the door, who permitted their entry with less difficulty than they had experienced at the gates.

Inside, the house was predictably lavish. A long hallway greeted them, lined with glittering chandeliers, rich tapestries, and assorted artworks and trinkets from the breadth of the Cadraelian Realm. Together, they passed reception rooms, banquet halls, a music room, and a strange space where every wall glittered with mirrors. The impression was one of never-ending space, and Leander became disoriented by the search until they eventually arrived at the foot of a vast marble staircase with ostentatious oak handrails. Here, another of Bruno's men met them.

"The minister is upstairs, Your Majesty," he said, kneeling to display the shiny crown of his bald head. "I imagine he's in the library, but I can't be sure. I'm sorry; it has been some hours since I last saw him."

Just then, a sudden noise filled the air. The guard's eyes widened with Leander's, both of them startled by the now undeniable sound of a crying woman reverberating from a room above.

Was Bruno's wife, Annelise, in danger?

Leander and Cedric leapt to ascend the staircase, the others racing to keep up behind them. Ciel's walking cane tapped on the marble steps.

"Where's the library?" Ciel asked breathlessly as he hobbled to catch up.

"Up ahead," answered the bald guard who had joined them. They rushed down another long hallway as one, their boots echoing as the woman's cries grew louder with every step.

At the end of the corridor, a large set of double doors— the only thing that now stood between them and their quarry. Leander tried to force them open, but they were locked from the inside. With every moment, they were running out of time. Already, the woman's cries had fallen silent.

He turned to his men and screamed, "Get these fucking doors open now!" Three of the guards braced themselves and rushed the doors shoulder-first. The door shook, but stood firm, and Leander stepped back in frustration. "Bruno, this is your king. Don't do anything stupid, you hear me? We know what you've done, but we can still make things right. If you just open up, we can talk things through. Whatever you do, just don't hurt Annelise."

The guards regrouped for a second assault on the door, Cedric, the bald guard and more of Bruno's own men joining the effort. The door began to buckle against their combined strength, hinges creaking under pressure to give the first sign of hope. Encouraged, the men rallied, and a final concerted effort sent the door crashing inward, to reveal a scene in the library which was most unexpected.

Bruno's prone form sprawled on the floor.

Leander blinked in disbelief.

Tear tracks glistened upon Annelise's cheeks as she cradled her husband, weeping inconsolably. A trail of red stained Bruno's beard and the upper body of his robe. His figure was pale and motionless, yet Cedric rushed forward undeterred, calling Bruno's name and separating Annelise from her lifeless husband in a futile, if admirable attempt to revive his master.

Frozen with shock, Leander scoured the room until his eyes fell upon another suspicious wine bottle on a table that Ciel had already moved to investigate. Could it be that Bruno was not the murderer? The thought brought a flood of emotions that threatened to drown Leander. Guilt and shame at the wrongful accusation. Fear that they were no closer to catching their murderer.

Worst of all was the sense of frustration—anger that they had arrived too late to save Bruno, despondency knowing they'd been on the wrong path all along. Plainly, this was about more than adulterous behaviour. Someone was systematically murdering the ministers.

Arriving at Leander's side, Ciel sniffed the mouth of the wine bottle before presenting it and saying, "Poison, but not Blue Meadow Lily. There's a slight staleness to the wine, and a hint of acrid celery consistent with hemlock. It's barely perceptible, unless you know what you're looking for. I'm sorry, but there's really no doubt about it."

Beyond them, Cedric lowered Bruno's body and gently closed his eyes, comforting Annelise as she continued to cry hysterically. Seeking space to think, Leander moved to sit in a velvet armchair, but the sound of Lennart's maddened voice stopped him from gathering his thoughts. The minister, of course, was not alone in his outrage. Leander held some sympathy for the man, whose peers were slowly dying all around him.

"Poison," said Lennart. "A woman's weapon. How dare the coward..."

The minister hung his head, but the words piqued Leander's curiosity unexpectedly.

A woman's weapon...he thought to himself, mind exploding with new possibilities.

It couldn't be, could it? There was only one way to find out...

"Lennart, be sure to question Annelise. I want to know everything about that bottle of wine."

"But Your Majesty—"

"Enough, Lennart. Just do as I ask. It's too early to begin apportioning blame, but I'd like to ensure we're not missing anything. Speak with Annelise when she's in suitable condition. I must leave to conduct investigations of my own."

He'd get his answers, one way or another. Leander stood, then hastened out of the room.

Leander looked out of the window and saw something most unexpected: crows circling ominously above the palace gardens. The portentous sight caused him to swallow deeply. One thing was certain—there was murder in the air.

He turned as the solar door opened to reveal Marcel, the Royal Chamberlain, resplendent as always.

"Presenting Miss Perrine Delport, Your Majesty," he said, before stepping aside to reveal Leander's somewhat reluctant-seeming company.

Dressed in a simple maidservant's uniform consisting of a blue linen smock and an ankle-length tunic, Perrine bore none of the elegant trimmings from their last meeting but seemed to have retained all the resentment. After days of not seeing each other and all that had gone between, Leander's prevailing feeling was one of distance. Though she was undoubtedly beautiful as always, Perrine, to him, felt even more of a stranger than before.

He stood and said, "Please sit," gesturing Perrine to the chair at the opposite side of the table. The same spot where he had welcomed the Vicentian consul.

Once more, he trusted that the location might have some bearing on the outcome. That it might disarm Perrine or see her warm to Leander as she had done in the past. He reasoned that his chambers were too familiar, presumptuous even, while the throne room was cold and the banquet hall would have seen them speaking at great distance.

This was the right choice. The best chance of success. The rest, of course, was up to Leander.

With a head full of questions and a plan that he had formulated in his mind and tested ten times over, Leander, at first, found himself speechless. Time and distance had done little to weather his inescapable attraction. Perrine's characteristic frown still beguiled him. In spite of all that had happened between them, all the worries keeping Leander awake at night, notwithstanding the hard questions that had prompted this very meeting, he still wanted her to like him.

Love him maybe. With her arrival, Sanne had stolen Leander's attention, but Perrine's company prompted old thoughts and feelings. Was there any hope for them after all that had happened, and was it the challenge or the girl that really excited him?

He shook the notion away, reminding himself why he had summoned her to join him.

"Wine?" he asked, moving to fill her glass. "It's Elurian White from my father's cellar. I know Elurian was always your favourite."

Perrine gave a half-smile but declined politely by covering the glass with her hand. "I shouldn't, I'm working," she added, flatly. "Besides, I find my tastes have changed."

"So soon?" asked Leander, "You used to enjoy it."

"People change, sometimes quite unexpectedly." Perrine was more spirited than before, and predictably scathing. "It's a kind offer, but one I shall have to decline. Tell me, King Leander." She scanned the room impatiently. "How can I help you?"

Clearly, Perrine was in no mood for small talk, and while thoughts of romance were but a distant memory, Leander had questions which needed answering.

"To business then," he said, straightening in his chair. "I've no doubt you've heard the news about The Ministry."

"The deaths, you mean?"

Leander winced. "Indeed. We've been investigating each murder. I have eyes and ears all over the city. I can assure you that the killer won't escape punishment."

"Well, that's good," said Perrine. "And somewhat reassuring. I'd hate to live in a city where murders occur needlessly and without repercussions. It seems a little strange that you brought me here to share that, though. Tell me, King Leander, why am I here?"

The insinuation was not lost on Leander, who chose to ignore the jibe and cut to the matter at hand. "Okay then," he said purposefully, "where were you this morning at the time of Bruno's murder?" The question seemed to take Perrine by surprise. "And for that matter, the murder of Roel and Joran too."

Perrine made to answer then paused. After a moment's consideration, she said, "I'm sorry, King Leander, but what exactly am I being accused of?"

Leander never flinched. "Nothing yet. Please just answer the question. As I said, we're investigating every possibility. I'm sure your answers will help us to move forward."

"Every possibility?" said Perrine, scowling. "And these enquiries, are they normally the business of the king, or should I consider myself lucky?"

"Perrine, please don't make this any more difficult than it needs to be."

"Difficult?" Perrine's eyes widened, and Leander found himself sinking into the plush cushioning of his armchair. "I'm sorry that these questions are making you uncomfortable, King Leander. No doubt, I'm already taking up far more time than you can afford, but once again, I'd ask the nature of your accusations. It seems to me that you're suggesting I killed the ministers, but the Leander I knew would never sink so low."

Frustrated, Leander's grip tightened around his armrest. "I'm not accusing you of anything," he said, desperately trying to maintain control. "Please, Perrine, just answer the question."

At this, Perrine's eyes threatened to roll from her head. She sat forward, "If you must know, I spent this morning at my father's grave."

"And do you have any witnesses?" Leander hated himself, but he had to ask.

"It's a busy cemetery," said Perrine dismissively. "I'm sorry to say that people die every day in your perfect capital, King Leander. Ask around and I'm sure you'll find plenty who will have seen me there. What you won't find, on the other hand, is anything to connect me with the murder of Minister Bekaert. Which has me wondering why you ever thought to bring me here for interrogation."

"Now, Perrine, I—"

"No, Leander. I'm tired of your excuses. How dare you accuse me of something like this, or even think it possible. What are you thinking?"

"I understand your frustration, but my question is not entirely without reason. You told me yourself that, given the chance, you'd do away with the ministers, and that was before everything that happened between us."

Perrine shook her head and began to laugh wildly. "Empty words again, King Leander. As for our relationship, remember not everything is about you. We had fun, you let me down and my father suffered the consequences. Do I hate you for it? Yes. Would I kill for you?" She paused, to look him up and down. "Don't flatter yourself."

The ferocity of her attack made Leander retreat further into his chair. Every word was an arrow, and his pride was no armour against the sharp edge of the truth. It had all made such perfect sense back at Bruno's estate. The motive, the opportunity, the method. At least in his mind, and in the heat of the moment, it had all seemed to point towards Perrine. He now saw his foolishness laid bare before him. In a list of those Perrine might care to murder, Leander himself would be at the top. Once more, he'd managed to hurt an innocent woman he cared for. To make matters worse, his efforts left him no closer to finding the Cadrael Killer.

"Perrine, I'm sorry. I shouldn't have asked, I just thought—"

Perrine snapped to interrupt. "I know what you thought, Leander. You've made that very clear. I can't imagine how disappointed you must be, realising that I'm not your killer. No doubt that would have tied things up for you very nicely. The mistakes of your past permanently removed. Why, this was your chance to finish the job you started with my poor old father. To excise our...*association* and any unwanted memories that might hinder your new life with Princess Sanne." She stopped and breathed deeply; her face was red.

Leander had never felt so stupid. More than anything he wanted to move on and make peace, but his recent record was not particularly heartening, and every word he spoke to Perrine seemed to make matters worse.

"I'm sorry," he said, keen to avoid any further conflict. "I had to ask. It's this business with the ministers—it's a lot at the moment, and I'm not myself."

Perrine scoffed. "Don't kid yourself. You're the way you've always been, unable to just let things go. You have all these big ideas, but no idea how to handle them. You think every situation is better for having you in it. Like I wouldn't have been fine without you. Like I couldn't get by and deal with my own business without you forcing Lennart to pay reparations for my father, money given through a clenched fist. Money that has only increased the size of the target on my back. Don't bring me here to tell me how tough your life is, King Leander. If it's sympathy you're seeking, you won't find it here."

The silence that followed was deafening and miserable, causing Leander to consider what he had really hoped to achieve with his questioning. Did he truly suspect Perrine, or was it a veiled excuse to spend time with her? Most troubling of all was the thought they'd grown so far apart so quickly. If he hadn't been certain before, he now knew their time together was truly over. The thought brought him a sickening feeling, and in the cold light of day, Sanne, for all her beauty, was no consolation.

He stood and said, "I'm sorry, Perrine. I should have known."

"I'm sure you're under great pressures in your new role, and I'm happy that I've been able to help with your investigations. I wonder," she added, "if I might be able to return to my duties?" Her words were cold and officious once more.

Reluctantly, Leander nodded, Perrine stood, curtsied, and then walked beyond him, before, at the last moment, Leander called her to a halt.

"I didn't ask if you've had any success finding work outside of the palace..."

She turned and smiled. "Not yet, King Leander. It may have escaped you, but your capital is short on opportunities, and that's being generous. Step outside and you'll find that there are far bigger issues than the death of a few nobles. Don't worry though." Her false smile widened. "I'm sure I'll be out of your way before long."

Pottage, rabbit, chunks of venison in a red wine sauce. Leander sighed and pushed the rich foods about his plate distractedly. Each course was more extravagant than the last, but it may well have been pigswill for all that he was interested.

"You seem distracted, my dear," said Sanne, from across the table. It wasn't the first time she'd mentioned it. She looked no less than spectacular in her deep-red velvet dress and matching ruby necklace, but even that couldn't shake the thoughts from Leander's head. It was a beautiful evening too, the sky a palette of otherworldly pink and purple hues. An idyllic moment, if only he could allow himself to enjoy it. Instead, his mind buzzed with thoughts of the dead ministers and the identity of their murderer. More troubling still were the aching thoughts of Perrine.

He forced a smile and said, "Sorry, my lady, just a little preoccupied is all. You will have noticed that things have become a little complicated of late, what with the ministers..."

"Awful business," Sanne agreed with a nod, before taking a long mouthful of red wine. "I know you've been working hard to find the culprit. Tell me, are you any closer to finding them, and is it one killer that you seek?"

It was an interesting question that had been lingering in his thoughts. Though it was clear that ministers had been targeted, something about their murders felt different, but for the poisoning of Joran and Bruno. It was possible that these events were entirely unconnected, but this seemed unlikely and far too coincidental. In the end, there was no shortage of resentment toward The Ministry. Perhaps the murderer saw Leander as a soft touch, less able than his father to unravel and punish an incident of this magnitude. Maybe the murderer's intention was to frighten Leander and force his hand into a particular course of action, though he knew not what. Either way, the fact remained: the murderer was still out there somewhere, and time was running out. Leander imagined these frustrations were all too evident upon his face and had to work to contain any anger in his voice.

"The specifics are still a little unclear at this juncture, my dear," he started, confidently. "Meanwhile, Minister de Meiren is continuing his search in earnest. I've no doubt that better news is only just around the corner."

Sanne raised her wineglass. "Well, I'll drink to that; Goddess knows you need a bit of luck, my darling. I know you had such grand plans in mind, and these murders are depriving you of both time and resources. Let's hope this is all resolved as quickly as you suggest. The people will soon see your vision for their future."

"To grand plans," said Leander, and he raised his own drink out of politeness as much as anything. Above all, he wanted time alone to consider the situation and uncover whatever it was that they'd been missing. Every moment seemed to bring new problems or responsibilities, and he found himself retreating into his own headspace, as much to Sanne's disquiet as his own. Nagging thoughts of Perrine continued to trouble him. Despite Sanne's persistence, he was noticeably withdrawn.

"What of the ministers?" she asked. "Will they be replaced, and if so, by whom?"

Another headache, but there was no escaping it. "Traditionally, the son, or next-in-line assumes the role immediately. This can be a brother, or any other male family member. In Bram's case, we have summoned his son from his travels, but Bruno was without children, so that's another quandary. For now, I've taken the decision to halt succession. I fear our murderer has enough targets as is."

Sanne nodded. "A shrewd move, in the circumstances. You've enough on your plate without adding to it. I presume, though, that this will further halt your progress. There's only so much that one man can do alone."

"You're not wrong," said Leander, and it took all his strength to stop his mood from plummeting. "Emile and Lennart are doing all they can to enact my orders, but both men are on high alert with limited movements until the killer is found. Meanwhile, all other areas are at a standstill. The city folk are impoverished and impatient, while the cardinals are rife with in-fighting and distrust. We've made no progress on roads or other developments, which leaves our armies scattered and a long way from home."

"And Vicentia?" asked Sanne, "What news on your plans for peace with Orsolina? I gather the consul was quite taken with your thoughts for Tenevarre?"

Quite how she knew that Leander was unsure, but it didn't hurt to focus on something a little more positive, if only briefly. "I'm expecting to hear the queen's thoughts any day now," he started. "Emile's teams are already working on documents to establish peace with Vicentia, while Lennart is drawing up plans for Tenevarre's independent nation status. The hope is to welcome Queen Orsolina here in Cadrael, and all being well, the new leader of Tenevarre will join us. The beginning of a new world, Princess Sanne. A momentous day that will not soon be forgotten."

Sanne's eyebrows raised. "Very impressive, King Leander, but the plans seem to place little emphasis on your own personal interests. I had hoped to discuss our...union at greater length. A royal wedding could provide much needed distraction for the city folk, while I would be very happy to help in other areas as needed. Take Orsolina, for example. I believe that situation would benefit from a woman's touch. I've no doubt I could be quite the resource, but this is all conjecture until we set a date."

Leander rubbed at tired eyes, pressure mounting and threatening to boil over. In light of all that had happened, was the wedding a priority?

When Leander failed to answer, Sanne asked, "You do want this, don't you?"

"Of course," said Leander, less confident that his words would sound convincing. Why was it that his first thoughts turned to Perrine? "I've just been busy," he added quickly.

"You're right, we should decide a date and move things forward. I want Cadrael to feel like home for you. For us." He ended with a reassuring smile.

His efforts earned the desired response, causing Sanne to beam from ear to ear. "Excellent," she said, "I'll make a start on plans then. The spring festival is one month from today; perhaps a royal wedding would add to the occasion. No doubt this nasty business will all be over by then. Something to look forward to, unless you have other thoughts?"

"No," said Leander, though he was hardly listening. "Spring festival..." he muttered, "Nice time of the year. Perfect."

Sanne reached for his hand. "Knowing your luck, it will rain. But that's a concern for another day," she said with a mischievous grin. "Let's hope that clearer skies are just around the corner. I'll send word to my father to let him know of our plans."

She broke away as a handful of maidservants entered the banquet hall to join them. Within moments, the plates were cleared and replaced with an assortment of sweet pies, exotic fruits, sugared almonds and jelly. An alluring offering, but one that failed to capture Leander's imagination; preoccupied and disinterested, he couldn't help thinking the same of Sanne.

"I had a lovely morning by the way," said the princess, using a silk napkin to wipe powdered sugar from her mouth. "This necklace is from the jewellery market, and it was very reasonably priced too. This city is certainly full of treasures."

Leander agreed, "There's much to discover."

"And what of you?" she asked. "Anything else to tell me? I know you spent much of the morning at Minister Bekaert's estate, but you returned to the palace around lunch from what I hear. I know you've been busy, but I had expected to see you sooner. What kept you those hours, or should I not ask?"

Leander nearly choked on his almond. Did she know about Perrine, and would it bother her if she did? "Again, busy..." he said, "Just following up on our investigations. Nothing noteworthy, I'd hate to bore you with the details—"

To his pleasure, a sharp knock on the banquet hall doors spared him.

He bid them to enter without hesitation, wondering if Sanne had discerned the relief in his voice. She certainly didn't look impressed.

Lennart appeared in the doorway, and Leander's spirits rose with the prospect of better news. "Well, you're here so I suppose you haven't been murdered," he said brightly. "You've interrupted our supper, for good reason, I hope?"

Sadly, Lennart had arrived without humour. He bowed and said, "Apologies, my king. I wonder if we can perhaps speak privately."

In his hunger for answers, Leander needed little encouragement. "Excuse me, princess," he said pushing his chair back to stand. "I just need a moment with the minister. Please continue without me."

"Of course," said Sanne, though her expression told a different story. She topped up her glass and said, "Who needs company when one has wine?"

Leander followed Lennart into the corridor, ensuring the doors closed behind them.

"You have news?" he asked, with the eagerness of a small child. "I've been very patient, Lennart. I hope you have answers."

Without pause, the minister reached into his jacket pocket. "This arrived today," he said, presenting a piece of paper. "It's addressed to you, my king, but we are still working to understand it..."

"Understand it?" asked Leander, unable to contain his obvious frustration. He snatched the letter and unfolded it eagerly. His eyes scoured the page, and his expression softened. "What is this?" he asked, unable to discern a single word. The page had but two lines of text, the language unidentifiable.

Lennart sighed. "It's quite the puzzle, my king. We think it's a Clan language, but we can't be sure. I imagine Bruno would have known had he..." He paused. "Well, what I'm saying is that we need a linguist, perhaps someone from the translator's guild. The dowager queen has quite the proclivity for languages; I wonder if she might enjoy the challenge and the chance to help speed things along. Either way, we will get to the bottom of this and quickly too. Rest assured, my king."

"I'm sure," said Leander, though more in hope than expectation. "So that's it then, a letter, which we can't read and may be harmless. I must say, Lennart, I had hoped for better."

At this, Lennart gulped. "There was one more thing worth mentioning, Your Majesty."

"Go on..."

"Ciel has been continuing his investigations into Bruno's murder. The last person to see him before he died was Emile. According to Annelise, it was he who brought the bottle of wine."

CHAPTER 10

In the expanse of the throne room, and with Leander staring back at him, Emile looked small and concerned, a shadow of his habitually haughty presence.

"You summoned me, Your Majesty. Is everything all right?" he asked laughing nervously. "I suspect you'll want an update on the revised peace treaty with Vicentia? My men have been working tirelessly to compile the agreement. It should be ready any day now, and I've no doubt you'll be very happy with the results."

He stopped to take a breath and found Leander expressionless. A smile only caused his king's eyes to narrow, and it was then he must have realised that things were surely not all right.

Leander wasted no time. "Where were you the morning of Bruno's murder?"

"I'm sorry, Your Majesty?" Emile's jaw dropped a little, either confused or stalling. "On the morning of Bruno's murder? Well...I suppose I was meeting with our generals. Yes, that's right. Plans to extract the troops from the

Clanlands, as instructed, Your Majesty," he spoke frantically. "At our garrison on the outskirts of the city. I remember now, I was there until noon."

Leander's brows raised. "At the garrison, is that right? Very good, that means there will be plenty of witnesses. I imagine you'll have no problem with me verifying this information. That is, unless you might have been mistaken?"

He crossed his arms, pursed his lips and watched the lump in Emile's throat shift with an audible gulp. The minister's brow glistened with a sheen of fresh sweat, and his eyes twitched nervously about the room.

Eventually Emile said, "Yesterday morning you mean? Sorry, my king, I think I *am* mistaken. The visit to the garrison was the previous day, which you can certainly corroborate. Yesterday morning, well, I was at home, Your Majesty. Truth be told, I was tired, and a little worried, what with everything that has been happening with Bram, Joran and the others, I'm sure you understand."

"Of course." Leander smiled. "These are dangerous times, and it's hard to know who to trust. The thing is," he said, fixing Emile with a stare. "I know that what you just told me is far from the truth, and I'm wondering what reason you may have to lie to me..."

"Your Majesty—"

"No, Emile, I've heard enough of your shit for one lifetime," Leander snapped. "I suggest you think very long and hard about your next words, and when you open your mouth, make sure to do so wisely. I know you were with Bruno the morning of his murder. So, tell me, why did you kill him, and was he the first?"

Emile's eyes widened. "Kill him?" he exclaimed. "No, of course not, Your Majesty." A deep sigh escaped him. "You're right, I was with Bruno the morning you mention, but the visit was social. I never...I could never have..." He trailed off.

Unconvinced, Leander sat forward for further questions. "A murderer on the loose and you're making social visits? Excuse my cynicism, Emile, but it is a little unusual. What's more, you brought a bottle of wine, didn't you? Wine that was used to poison Bruno."

"No," cried Emile, red-faced with panic. "You're wrong, Your Majesty, it wasn't like that. I just went to speak with him..."

"Speak with him?" asked Leander, "I've known you to be boring, Emile, but never fatally so." He let loose a dismissive laugh. "Conversation doesn't kill people, you know that. A well-chosen poison, though—well, that can produce excellent results, can't it? You'd know of course, having tested the same method on Joran."

Somehow, Emile's jaw seemed to fall further. A performance of innocence that might have had Leander convinced if the man's guilt wasn't already so obvious.

"It wasn't like that, Your Majesty. You have it all wrong. The wine was Bruno's favourite, nothing more. I never poisoned it. You must believe me!"

"But you don't deny you went to visit him that morning? The last person to visit him in fact. Tell me, Emile, what am I supposed to think?"

Nervously, Emile scratched at his long, dark hair. "I did visit him, yes, but our conversation was short. I had no reason to kill him. Surely you can see that?"

"Truth be told, I'm struggling to see sense in anything these days, Emile. What was so important that you left your house with a murderer on the loose? So important that you felt the need to lie about your whereabouts."

The question seemed to take Emile by surprise. He made to speak then stopped himself abruptly. "I just..." he muttered, nervously fussing with his beard. "I'm sorry, my king, but it's rather a delicate subject."

Leander's jaw tightened with frustration. "Speak, Emile, my patience is wearing very thin. I'll give you one chance to explain yourself fully, or you'll end up in a cell just as your father did."

Unsurprisingly, the threat caused Emile to act immediately. Panic gripped his face as he said, "No, my king, please don't do that. If you must know, I went to speak with Bruno about your orders from the last meeting. I'm worried that the withdrawal of our troops will leave us vulnerable to attack from the Vicentians and that protracted discussions of peace are giving their armies time to prepare and mobilise with the same advantage that your father had hoped for."

"And your first thought was to discuss this with Bruno? Do I need to remind you of the hierarchy around here, or am I foolish to even dignify this nonsense with my attention?"

"It's the truth, I promise you," Emile said pleadingly. "I only thought to gain endorsement ahead of our next meeting. I know you don't want to hear this, but these discussions are quite normal. Your father, well, he was occasionally quite erratic in his decision-making. It was important to arrive at the meetings united in our thinking. Without that we would never have been able to influence him."

Leander felt his temperature rising. "So, you conspired against him, and now you do the same to me? You know what I think, Emile? I think you're trying to cover your tracks. You went to see Bruno to discuss your strategy, and when the minister disagreed, you had to take care of him, just like the others."

"No, Your Majesty, I—"

Leander was in no mood for interruptions. "This war with Vicentia has nothing to do with safeguarding borders or protecting the people, does it? It's all about you, isn't it Emile? Your family's reputation and the damage done by your father's actions."

"Your Majesty, I must object—"

"Object as you wish, Emile. I finally see what was in front of me all along. A man so desperate for redemption that he would put an end to anyone or anything that would stand in his way. I presume that Bram and the others were not agreeable, so you had to kill them, didn't you? If nothing else, a mysterious set of murders would distract from the peace treaty. Better still, the blame might fall on Vicentia. It all leads to one place, doesn't it, Emile? A war for the ages, with you leading the charge!"

Emile's teeth clenched, and his mask of innocence suddenly slipped. "Are you fucking stupid? I told your father to delay the war," he said angrily. "You accuse me of murder, yet it is you who has the most to gain from seeing us gone. Fermantia without The Ministry is a kingdom where your power knows no opposition, a kingdom where nobody knows your ugly little secret, King Leander. 'To the grave,' that's what you said, isn't it? We should have seen it coming. Lest we forget, you are your father's son, after all."

The unexpected outburst caused Leander's grip to tighten about the arm of his throne. "Oh, I'm my father's son, all right." he said, threateningly. "Not the walkover you may have been hoping for. Meanwhile, your words sound a lot like treason, Minister. Perhaps I'm not the only one to take a walk in his father's boots. What was her name again; ah yes...Queen Hamida, of Badria, wasn't it? The most beautiful woman in all of the Clanlands, if I remember rightly. The queen who would not surrender to my father. A woman who opposed Fermantia and watched as her people were slaughtered by our troops." Leander paused, and Emile watched on in silence, fists shaking with anger. "The woman who your father was ordered to execute," Leander added slowly. "The woman your father fell in love with and decided to spare."

"How dare you," said Emile. "Has my family not suffered enough?"

Leander laughed. "Don't play the victim with me, Emile. Your father was a traitor and a cheat. He got what he deserved—we both know that. More than anyone, we know how it is to live in our father's shadow, but you couldn't do it, could you? You couldn't step out of the darkness and forge your own path? No," he said with a smirk, relieved as the pieces finally fell into place. "You had to seek retribution, vengeance even. You threaten me with what happened to my father, but I now see what I've been missing all along. That night at Lennart's castle, my father's cough was far worse than it had ever been. Perhaps his condition had worsened—

maybe it was the travel, or the climate or whatever else you choose to blame. Perhaps his tincture could have saved him, perhaps I could have saved him, or perhaps…" He let the word hang between them. "Perhaps my father was already beyond saving. He always did enjoy a nice bottle of wine, didn't he, Emile?"

This latest accusation left Emile speechless. Any sign of the minister's anger long gone, the man now stood defeated, broken and guilty.

"My king, surely you can't think…" His head dropped. "I'm not my father. None of this was me, you must see that."

A look of regret was all Leander could see in that moment. Regret, not for his actions, but for the fact that Leander had uncovered his secret. "You'll have plenty of time to plead your innocence," Leander said flatly. "In spite of everything, you are a minister and will receive a trial befitting your station."

Emile's arms flailed in protest. "No, Your Majesty, not that please."

"For now," said Leander, undeterred. "You will be detained in the royal prisons pending sentencing. I suggest you go with suitable dignity; there is no need to further tarnish your family name."

He called for guards and the doors opened immediately. Four men approached, and Emile sank to his knees. The minister's face was pale, and his cheeks already glistened with the first sign of tears.

"Please, Your Majesty. I beg you, don't do this."

The time for begging was over, and Emile jerked violently as the guards dragged him to his feet.

"Take him away," said Leander, sitting back in his throne with an overwhelming sense of relief. The case was solved—he'd found his man. The Cadrael Killer would kill no more.

"Ah Ciel, good…please come and join me." Leander stood and gestured the former soldier to the other of two large, silk embroidered chairs before the crackling fire. He hoped to make his company feel welcome and stoke the warmth that is common in timeworn acquaintance. Where better then, he thought, than in the comfort of his own royal chambers?

Of course, the two men were hardly friends at all. Not really. Born unto different circumstances, Leander and Ciel had lived very separate lives with paths that only ever seemed to cross in the most regrettable of circumstances. Their bond, for what it was, had been forged in battle and dowsed with blood. Yet, in Perrine's absence, Ciel had started to feel like the closest thing that Leander had to a friend, or at the very least a dependable ally. If nothing else, the man was honest and faithful. Ciel had played his part in apprehending Emile and seemed an obvious choice of company to Leander, who was keen to celebrate their shared success.

They weren't friends yet, but Leander was keen to explore the possibility.

"Take a seat, and please help yourself to a glass of red if it pleases you."

Leander returned to his seat and Ciel hobbled apprehensively to join him. It took a further nod from

Leander before the former soldier eventually filled his own glass.

"You honour me, Your Majesty. Will Minister De Meiren be joining us?"

"Not on this occasion; it's you I wanted to speak with. I hope that's not a problem? With the case solved, I fear you'll not be long for the palace. Tell me, what are your plans now things are resolved? I trust that Lennart has paid you handsomely?"

The question made Ciel shuffle uncomfortably. He hesitated, taking a long swig of his drink. "The reward was more than generous, Your Majesty. It is my honour and one I would have been only too happy to fulfil with or without payment. It is my duty."

"I believe you. You are a good man, Ciel Huertroop, far better, I must say, than many in my employ. I don't suppose you could be tempted to join us in the palace, or do you have a mind toward other arrangements?"

Ciel inclined his head. "Another undue honour, Your Majesty. Your offer is not one that I turn from lightly. Forgive me, but I have been planning to travel for some time; it is my intention to explore The Clanlands in more peaceable circumstances than those faced during our previous excursion."

"I understand," said Leander, shoulders sagging in defeat. He only hoped his disappointment wasn't too obvious. "I must say I don't blame you. I'd likely do the same in your position. For all my wealth, I can't help but envy your freedom. But tell me." He grinned. "Is there perhaps a woman in all of this? A Cadraelian girl who could tempt you to stay in the capital, or maybe something rather more exotic awaiting you in The Clanlands?"

Ciel's skin turned pink in response to the gentle jibe. He lowered his eyes and said, "I wish I had better news, Your Majesty. There is a girl about whom I care greatly, but her feelings for me are confined to friendship."

Leander thought to his own struggles with Perrine, and he wished there was a way to aid Ciel's cause. "Have you told her your feelings?" he asked with interest. "Perhaps the girl is naïve to your intentions?"

"If only things were so simple." Ciel sighed. "She's more than clever enough to deduce my affection, and while she knows that I would do anything for her, she is the sister of an old friend and almost like family. I fear she struggles to see me romantically, or maybe she is simply unwilling to jeopardise our friendship. Whatever the reason, she has a vision for the future, and I'm sorry to say that I'm not part of it."

Leander blew out his cheeks. "Yes, that is quite the dilemma. I've experienced my share of difficult or forbidden relationships. Perhaps you are better pursuing new interests; a longstanding friendship is a valuable thing."

"Of course, and please excuse me, Your Majesty. I'm sure you have plenty of worries without humouring mine."

"Worries yes, but friendship is not quite as plentiful. The position of king is as lonely as it is stifling. I find myself with no shortage of company, but there are few with whom to share decent conversation. It's not like our days on campaign, Ciel." He smiled wistfully. "Honest men sharing stories about a blazing campfire; the laughs, the camaraderie, there's nothing quite like it."

"You make war sound romantic, my king." Ciel's eyebrows raised in playful accusation. "If I didn't know better, I'd say you even miss it?"

Leander swiped the notion away. "Of course not, but well, you know how it is, you more than anyone. War is brutal, frightening but at the root of things, war is real. In war, trust is your strongest armour and your sharpest weapon. Trust in yourself, trust in the man who stands beside you. The oath is one thing, of course, but in the end, it is little more than ceremony for that innate, indescribable kinship shared between warriors."

He took a sip of his drink then laughed to himself humourlessly.

"You know, it's funny really; in war you fight for the people back home: the children, loved ones, family, and friends. You make villains of the enemy and fight them to the bloody end, only to return home and find that you have more in common with the enemy than those who welcome you."

"Cadrael is not all you had hoped for, Your Majesty?"

Leander scoffed. "Come now, Ciel, you've seen it with your own eyes. The capital is not without charm, but it's full of crime and corruption, and nowhere is this more obvious than The Ministry itself."

"Good news then, that we have a king like you to make a difference."

Leander raised his glass. "A fine notion, but kingship and war are not so different…"

"Your Majesty?"

"Strategy and planning." Leander's head shook as he spoke. "Morals, ideals, and visions of success. It's all well and good, Ciel, but what happens when the arrows start flying? What happens when everything is going to shit around you? That is when you find out who you really are as a man…as a king. That is when you really get to know the true character of the men sent to fight beside you. I've no shortage of grand plans, but you know what?" A rueful smile crossed his face and he scratched uncomfortably at the stubble upon his chin. "I've spent most of my kingship simply stumbling around trying to find the enemy, swinging my sword and hoping it strikes the right place."

Ciel's face softened with sympathy. "Remember that things have been exceptionally difficult, Your Majesty. As you know, the greatest generals are those whose plans are constantly evolving. It takes great strength to recognise your shortcomings, and I have every faith that you will make things right."

Leander raised his glass, an act that Ciel mirrored before the two clinked together. "To making things right then," he said smiling broadly. "And to your bright future, Ciel Huertroop. May The Clanlands deliver you better luck, both in life and in love."

"So, in principle," said the consul. "My queen finds your plans for peace agreeable."

Leander smiled. "Excellent. I will have my men complete the paperwork for you to share with your queen in full. We've had one or two complications that have slowed progress in recent days, but I hope to have this with you very shortly. You are, of course, welcome to remain in the palace until this time."

"Thank you, King Leander." Consul Rizzuti lowered his head as he spoke. "Queen Orsolina is excited to attend your great capital in person and begin this exciting new era of peace. She was but a small girl during her last visit, and much has changed in the time since."

The mood in the solar was almost unrecognisable from their previous meeting. The consul was warm, optimistic and respectful. For his part, Leander was relaxed and focused, untroubled by the issues that had thus marred his reign. It had been two days since Emile's arrest, and with no murders since, the man's guilt seemed in little doubt. Work was underway to replace the departed ministers, and Leander's vision was no longer a distant dream but an immediate priority.

This very thought had put Leander in a good mood from the moment he had opened his eyes that morning. A successful meeting with the consul in advance of time with Sanne. After that, the commencement of Emile's trial and curtains for the Cadrael Killer. The sun was shining on Fermantia's young king. He should have foreseen how quickly things could change.

"Thank you, Consul. I'll call for you as soon as the treaty is completed and ready."

He stood and gestured Spano toward the doorway. The man bowed then left, and in his place, Lennart appeared.

"My king," he said, "I trust your meeting with the consul was productive?"

Leander sat. "It was. And with Minister Roos's inquiry this afternoon, I dare to dream that better days are on the horizon."

"Indeed, my king, but about that…" Lennart trailed off. His mouth hung open with a puzzled look that filled Leander with immediate concern. He seemed lost for words, at least the right ones anyway. "About this afternoon," he continued, gingerly. "There has been, shall we say, a change of circumstances."

Leander's brow furrowed. "Lennart, what are you not telling me?"

"I'm sorry, my king, but perhaps it's better you see for yourself."

Lennart turned and Leander followed him without exchanging another word. The palace flashed by as they passed through myriad corridors, descending stairways until they arrived at the foot of the grand staircase. From here, Leander knew, only too well, their next destination.

"Brace yourself, Your Majesty," said Lennart, filling Leander's heart with dread.

Guards stood aside, and they descended into the royal dungeons, taking the same path that Leander had travelled with his mother to visit Perrine. He hoped that this visit would not be so unsettling, but every instinct told him otherwise.

Darkness greeted them as they swiftly but steadily tackled the twisting stairway. At the bottom, three prison guards were huddled in the shadows. They were joined by two maidservants, one with dark hair, and the other a blonde-haired woman who spoke quietly but urgently, heightening Leander's sense of foreboding. It was the unexpected sight of a familiar face, however, which, above all compounded his concern. The sound of Ciel's walking cane echoed against the flagstones as he approached.

"Your Majesty," he said, curling the tips of his impressive moustache in the flickering torchlight. "You might want to come this way. I'm sorry to say, it's not good news."

Once more, Leander followed close behind, thoughts filled with a web of possibilities, only one of which he believed to be true.

It was no less shocking to be proven right.

"What the fuck?" he exclaimed, raising his hand to cover his mouth. The minister was slumped on the floor in a pool of his own blood, his expression vacant. "But how?" Leander's hand muffled his own words. Even in poor light, deep cuts in the minister's wrists and forearms were obvious. Less evident in that moment was how they had occurred.

Lennart appeared at his side. "Self-sacrifice, my king. An admission of guilt, and escape from the ignominy of the trial. A sorry outcome, but one that is easily explained."

"If that's the case, then how was he able to do this?" asked Leander. "The man is expected at a high-profile trial this afternoon. After all that has happened with all the other ministers, do either you realise how this is going to look?"

"It cannot be connected to the other murders, Your Majesty," said Lennart. "Fear not, no blame will fall at your feet."

"Be that as it may, none of this will play well with the Vicentian consul. How can I be expected to maintain a peace treaty when I can't even protect those in my care?"

Leander had seen it in Emile's eyes, the fear of the trial, and further shame upon his family. Self-sacrifice made perfect sense in lieu of the humiliating, public ending that Emile's own father had experienced. Maybe Leander should have seen this coming, yet in spite of the evidence sprawled before him, something about it didn't feel quite right.

As if reading his thoughts, Ciel turned to Lennart and asked, "Aren't prisoners limited to soft foods like bread and broth. Foods chosen for their own safety and that of the guards?"

"Correct," answered Lennart, a little defensively. "The situation with Emile was no different, I can assure you."

"So, no knives or other cutlery?"

"Absolutely not."

"That's strange," said Ciel, "when I searched the cell, I found this." He raised a small, bloodstained knife with an ornate crosspiece inlaid with gemstones.

Leander took the knife and began to inspect it. After a moment, he turned to Lennart and asked, "Who discovered the body?"

"One of the guards, Your Majesty. However, I, myself, was fortunate to be nearby at the time. I had hoped to speak with Minister Roos before his trial, to ensure he was of a *rational* mind-set, if you catch my meaning. Of all things, I know you could do without any further scandal. As you can see, my arrival was sadly too late."

Leander handed back the knife, turned away and tried to gather his thoughts. At first glance, Emile's actions seemed to confirm his guilt. It was a swift and conclusive ending to Leander's own investigations. A tidy ending to the mystery, so why did it all feel a little too convenient?

"Lennart, when prisoners arrive, I presume they are searched for any weapons or items that might aid escape?"

"Yes, Your Majesty. A full and thorough search by our prison guards. Nothing gets in, nothing gets out."

A confident answer, but one that belied the truth. "In which case," said Leander. "I suggest thorough questioning of the guards on duty. I want to know who did the search and anyone else who might have visited the minister since."

Murder or self-sacrifice, Leander couldn't be sure. One question was clear in everyone's mind: who brought the knife?

Tired or rejuvenated? Afraid or relieved?

For Leander, Emile's death had raised more questions than it had answered. His head throbbed with that same dull ache he'd come to know intimately, and in that moment, more than anything else, he wanted to be alone. Instead, he found himself pacing through the palace grounds to meet Sanne.

He arrived at the lily pond, where the princess greeted him. "You're late."

The same grin, and the same playful derision, yet Leander's reaction was certainly different. Sure, Sanne had no lack of character, but was she also a little annoying?

He pushed the thought away, attributing the feeling to his own bad mood. "I'm sorry," he said, taking a seat on the bench beside her. "Another busy morning, I'm sure you understand."

Unexpectedly, Sanne scoffed. "So you keep saying. I might understand better if you took the time to speak with me occasionally. I told you I would here to support you, Leander, but that's not so easy when you keep cutting me out."

Was she joking? Leander had to stop himself from responding angrily. After all that he had been through in recent days, surely Sanne wasn't so foolish as to consider her feelings a priority. He waited a moment for his temper to cool, and then said, "I'm sorry for that, and I will try to do better. You know things have been extraordinarily complicated lately. I only hoped to spare you the details."

Sadly, and despite his best efforts, Sanne, it seemed, was not assuaged. She looked out at the water and said, "Tell me, will things ever be anything other than complicated? I wonder if, in some way, you might rather enjoy the excitement of all this. I'm not sure that a simple life is really your style, is it, King Leander?"

She paused and raised her eyebrows, and Leander felt his temper rising. Returning to his feet, he snapped, "You think I'm enjoying this, all of this bloodshed?"

"Maybe, maybe not," said Sanne. "But either way, you can't help but involve yourself, can you? All your grand plans, yet here you are dragged through the muck with all this. It's not becoming of a king, Leander, if nothing else it places us both at unnecessary risk."

Leander could hardly believe what he was hearing. Five men dead, did she expect him to simply stand by and do nothing? "Are you serious?" he asked fiercely. "All these ministers murdered, what do you expect from me? You know what I think?" he asked, a new thought emerging through his annoyance. "I think this attitude has nothing to do with me or the ministers. I think you're a long way from home and you're bored. I understand that. You're used to being the centre of attention and your father sent you here expecting the same to happen."

Sanne rose angrily. "How dare you! I was trying to help. I only wanted to make you see sense, Leander. I can see how this is already affecting you. Affecting us. Surely this is all best left to Minister de Meiren?"

"So, do nothing?" Leander turned away laughing in disbelief. As if he wasn't already under enough pressure with all that had happened, it seemed Sanne was intent on further worsening his mood, which was already unpredictable at best these days. On reflection, maybe he wasn't the only one who had changed. Sanne seemingly had her own agenda, though for what reason Leander wasn't sure. He only knew that this was neither the time nor place to air her grievances. A polite approach had failed, he realised; clearly it was time for something new.

"And this is an example of you helping me, is it?" he asked. "Presumably you think a nice walk or a spot of lunch might make things better? As long as you are the focus of my attention, that's right, isn't it, Sanne?"

He turned back and found the princess stood directly in front of him. "Focus of your attention?" She laughed dismissively. "Oh, King Leander, I doubt that will ever happen."

Leander's face creased with confusion. "What is this?" he asked, at the end of his patience. "If you've something to say then just come out and say it."

Sanne pursed her lips and narrowed her eyes. "The other day when we had lunch together you delayed our plans and told me you were busy. But what was so important that it kept you from me?"

Leander froze, but the guilt on his face must have betrayed him. He cleared his throat and said, "The investigation, I told you this already."

"The investigation?" asked Sanne, eyebrows arched with suspicion. "That's funny, because from what I hear, you spent the morning with the servant girl, Perrine Delport. You two were locked away in the solar for some time as I understand it. It's the talk of the palace, King Leander. Oh, how people must be laughing at me..."

Leander buried his head in his hands. "It's not like that," he uttered through gritted teeth. "I had some questions I needed to ask of her. She answered then left, no reason at all for you to concern yourself."

"Concern myself?" Sanne laughed, but the expression on her face was far from amused. In truth, she was hardly recognisable from the woman Leander thought he knew. She was no longer sweet and playful, but rather angry and spiteful.

"It's the lies that concern me, King Leander. I told you I would be here to support you, but I was also very clear what I expect in return. Don't ever think to take me for a fool. As for the girl..." A malicious smile appeared on Sanne's face. "I am princess of Eluria and future queen of Fermantia. What concern have I for a lowborn slut?"

The time for polite was definitely over.

Her grin disappeared as Leander's palm connected. She tumbled to the ground and reached to nurse her cheek, which had already turned red, gasping at the throbbing pain. From the way she had fallen, he could tell that Sanne hadn't expected the strike. She now lay shocked and furious, her arrogance already a distant memory.

"Don't you ever speak about her like that," he bellowed. "You made me do this, you know that? I told you it was all part of the investigation, but you wouldn't listen, would you?" He glowered at her heaped on the floor, tears of fear leaving lines upon her cheeks. To Leander, she now looked pitiful and grotesque, and he wondered how he had ever found her appealing. "I am king of Fermantia. I do not answer to the likes of you," he continued. "Where I go and who I see is none of your concern, do you understand?"

Sanne flinched and then nodded at the question fearfully.

"Good," said Leander. "Then perhaps we can end this foolish act. Neither of us ever really wanted this marriage, did we? The sooner we accept this and move forward, the better. Sadly, my concerns are too plentiful to accommodate your self-obsession. If you want to make your father proud and deliver his alliance, do what you do best; smile and look pretty. But while you're doing it, stay out of my way."

He turned and stomped away, leaving Sanne sobbing in the dirt. Striding chest out, chin high, Leander reasoned it was no less than she deserved. Why was it then, that he could hardly recognise the actions as his own? His heart pounded, his lips trembled, and tears filled his eyes as his walk slowed to a defeated pace.

Man. King. Leader of people.

But in his mother's arms, Leander was still just a boy.

His tears fell heavily, dousing the dowager queen's bedsheets. As always, she was there when he needed her. He wondered why it taken him so long.

"Now, now…" She held him close and ruffled his hair as she had when he was a child. "It can't be that bad, surely?"

The prospect of answering made Leander feel nauseous, but this had always been his safe space, something he needed, now more than ever. "It's Sanne," he sobbed. "I've done something awful."

"Well, now, I'm sure it's not the end of the world, Leander. When I was younger, my mother had a phrase she would use in her local tongue; roughly translated it means 'nothing you do cannot be undone.' I think that's rather relevant here, don't you?"

Leander sighed. "Except murder, of course." The confession was there on the tip of his tongue.

"Well, not murder, no, but I don't think you're here to tell me you've killed the princess. So, what did you want to say, Leander? Whatever it is, I'm sure you had your reasons…"

Leander cuffed a tear from his face, then locked eyes with his mother and said, "You don't know what I'm capable of. I struck her, Mother. I hit the princess. She only wanted to be there and support me, but I lied to her and lashed out when she questioned me. Just as Father did to you. Just like..." Tears interrupted his next words.

If his mother was sickened, she didn't show it. Her grip tightened as she pulled him close, rocking gently, casting Leander's thoughts back to younger, simpler times. "I hoped I'd have raised you better," she said softly. "I believe we can blame your father for the temper, but he never once displayed an ounce of your remorse. The important thing to remember is that no matter your actions, you are not your father. You're king now, and you can behave in whatever manner you decide. Just remember that power is not just about strength and stubbornness. True leaders accept their mistakes, make them right and never repeat them. I know that you're under quite some pressure at present, but heavy-handed behaviour, especially with women, is unlikely to endear you to your people, least of all your mother."

"You think that Sanne will accept my apology."

"Perhaps, though if I were her, I'd make you sweat a little first." She pursed her lips, and her eyes narrowed. "Come now, my boy, when did you start giving up so easily? The Leander I know is persistent and resilient. It doesn't hurt to make your old mother feel useful from time to time, but I'm afraid you're going to have to face this alone. You've already shown us the kind of king you hope to be; now it's time to let Sanne see the man you really are."

She released her grip and Leander sat upright, in awe of the woman he had the privilege to call his mother. How was it that she always knew the right thing to say? Finally, it felt good to give voice to his problems, and having started, he now found it more difficult to stop.

"It's not just Sanne—I can't get anything right at the moment. Perrine hates me for what happened with her father, and this business with The Ministry is a total mess."

Leander's hands became the subject of his mother's attention. "I see you've been biting your nails again. What have I told you?" she asked, glancing at the raw skin at the tip of his fingers. "A mess, yes, but not of your doing, Leander. The Delport girl, well, perhaps you were always too different to be together. You know I want nothing more than for you to be happy, but you are a king now, and with that comes a certain amount of responsibility. As to the regrettable situation with her poor father, I fear that you must shoulder some of the blame in your father's absence. Grief is a flame that burns bright but soon dwindles. I'm sure Perrine will, one day, find it in her heart to forgive you. Until then, try not to be too hard on yourself. Look forward, make good decisions and you'll soon realise that people will define you by your next action, more than your last."

With each word, fresh hope began to gather in Leander's chest. Maybe he could still win back Sanne's affection, and though things with Perrine could never be as they were, he dared to believe that she would, someday, forgive him.

As quickly as this newfound optimism appeared, darker thoughts resurfaced, hauling him back toward more immediate concerns. "Maybe you're right," he said, almost defiantly. "But during my time as king, we've still buried five ministers."

"A situation which you have now resolved from what I hear? Or is Emile's death not a clear indication of the man's guilt?"

Leander huffed. "Maybe, maybe not. The circumstances of Emile's death are suspicious to say the least. It just feels like everything I do seems to go wrong, make matters worse or winds up with someone else dead."

He sighed. From the corner of his eye, he noticed a portrait of his father hanging upon the wall. The king looked resplendent in gleaming plate armour trimmed with gold and a luxurious blue robe that complemented the sapphire gemstones decorating his elegant crown. But it wasn't the clothes that Leander was focusing on. Instead, the king's eyes seemed fixed on Leander with that same old disapproving stare he knew so well. He imagined what his father would make of him in that moment, the thought prompting a fresh sense of guilt.

"None of this would have happened if Father were here," he continued, voicing doubts that had tormented him for some time. "He wasn't perfect, but people respected or feared him anyway. Can you imagine the consequences of the murders during his reign? He'd have arrested the culprit soon after Bram was found, and that's assuming the murderer was foolish enough to even try it in the first place."

"Well, that," said his mother, "is something we will never know now is it, Leander? You're right to aspire to better, but mindless speculation does you no good in the end. Take each day as it comes and do your best. You never asked for any of this, and most importantly, it's not your fault that your father isn't still here with us."

Leander's breath suddenly caught in his throat. Could he really sit here and accept this sympathy? Could he bring himself to lie to his mother after all she'd done for him? Confiding in her had already given him a feeling of such relief, but Leander still had one secret he was yet to tell. Would there ever be a better time than this?

"You're wrong," he said, twisting away to avert his eyes. "Emile may have been the one to poison Father, but I was there in the room at Lennart's castle. I let him die before me and didn't lift a finger to save him. In my own way, I killed Father. I thought that Fermantia would be better off without him. I thought that I could do better…but look how that turned out. You know," he said, standing to pace and fixing on his own loathsome reflection in a mirror. "I convinced myself that I did it to protect you." He laughed. "But look at me, here, crying like a babe on his mother's shoulder. You've always been the one to do the protecting. Me—I'm nothing more than a foolish boy and a murderer."

Leander had no idea what reaction to expect from his mother. She sat, at first, in quiet contemplation, her face expressionless. Finally, she stood and walked over to stand at the mirror beside him. Her reflection portrayed a conflict of emotions.

"You didn't kill him."

"I did."

"You're wrong," she said, firmly. "I'm telling you, Leander, you did not murder your father."

Leander turned in frustration. "Did you not hear a word of what I just said? I let him die. What's the difference?"

"Trust me, that's not the same as murder," she answered, looking him in the eyes. "I know that better than anyone..." A sudden deep breath punctuated her sentence. "Why? Because it was me who killed your father."

"What?" Leander said vacantly, brows knitted with confusion. "You're lying," he added. "Just trying to make me feel better. You weren't even there, so how can you have possibly killed him?"

His mother turned away. "Your father always did enjoy his wine. It's something we started when the king was much younger. Whenever he travelled, I would gift him a bottle from his favourite vintner. He always said that the taste reminded him of home and that he would think of me when drinking it, a toast to our continued good health."

"You poisoned him?" Leander's mind raced to catch up. His own confession seemed like a different lifetime, but as he thought back to the night of his father's passing, his mother's story began to fall into place.

"I'd been doing it for months," she said. "Gradually of course, but the plan itself never changed. Your father, well, you'll remember how his behaviour had begun to worsen. The way he treated you and those mad plans to invade Tenevarre! In the end, he forced me to move my plans along a little more quickly."

Leander began to massage his temple, already he felt a fresh headache developing. "So, the cough," he said. "That was your doing?" He recalled the night of his father's murder, the king's chin and upper body stained with blood, the same carnage Leander had witnessed upon Bruno. He was prepared to accept Emile as a cold-blooded killer; it was harder to imagine his mother so cruel.

"I suppose the cough was a symptom of my intervention, but trust me when I say that your father's health was far from perfect."

"But you made him suffer for all those months before he died?"

"For you, Leander, and for the good of the people. Do you really consider your father the victim in all of this?"

As always, she had a point. Leander's shoulders slumped, crestfallen. He wasn't sure what hurt more, the act or the decision his mother had made, leaving him to carry the blame unnecessarily. Above all, he encountered that same helpless feeling. King Leander, ruler of all Fermantia, a clueless piece in a series of illicit games.

Sensing his discomfort, the dowager queen stepped forward to take him by the hand. "Surely you understand?" she asked, voice trembling with uncharacteristic worry. "I did what I thought was best for all of us. I believed you'd make a better king than your father ever could. I still do. Please Leander, you must see the sense in this..."

Leander tore his hand away from his mother's grip, a petulant response borne out of confusion. All told, his mother's actions were scarcely different to his own, yet their premeditated nature left him full of resentment and further questions. She'd killed his father—what else was she capable of?

"Is that all?" he asked, swallowing deeply. His hands shook at the potential consequences of his next question.

More than anything he wanted to believe it an impossibility, but with his mother's admission he was no longer so sure. "What I mean is, is there anything else you want to tell me?

His mother's brow furrowed. "Anything more...wait, are you accusing me of killing the ministers? Darling, I did what I had to, but surely you can't think me some rampaging killer?"

Despite feeling a little embarrassed, Leander persisted. "Is it really so ridiculous? Half a day ago, I might have agreed with you, but after what you've just told me..."

His mother's face softened, and she walked back to take his hand. "I'm sorry, Leander, truly I am, but you must believe me, I didn't kill those men. With your father I made a decision that will live with me for the rest of my life. The ministers' deaths I had nothing to do with, that I promise you. I've seen this before," she continued, staring at Leander as she had when he was but a child. "Your father was just as bad for worrying and overthinking. He was always convinced that someone was out to get him. Fear not, Leander, I've told you everything you need to know. As for the ministers…I think we can count Minister Roos as your murderer. Justice has been served, and there's no evidence linking either of us to your father's death."

She broke off and watched as Leander's eyes widened.

"What did you say?" he asked her urgently.

"Justice has been served."

"And the other thing."

"There's no evidence, Leander, nothing to worry about."

He laughed as the threads of mystery finally untangled themselves. "I have to go," he said turning and making to leave. "I know who has been killing the ministers."

The dead, he now realised, were never the target of hatred or jealousy, but victims of what they had seen and their failure to act. Seven men swore an oath to take the secret of King Yorick's death to the grave. Now, only two remained, and it dawned on Leander, he would be next.

CHAPTER 11

"Ah, my king, I'm glad you've summoned me," said Lennart. "The envoy from Vicentia has been asking about the treaty and when he might expect the paperwork. I told him that you've been busy, of course, but there are only so many times I can send the man away."

Leander smiled. "Yes, I fear Consul Rizzuti might well be very disappointed. Unfortunately, I find myself taken with one or two other priorities at present. Indeed, I am reconsidering whether this treaty is really the best choice for Fermantia."

"Your Majesty?" Lennart's eyes widened with concern. "The agreement was your idea. If you back out at this stage, you are likely to cause serious backlash."

Leander adjusted himself on his throne and reached for the comforting handle of the knife he wore in a scabbard upon his hip. The horrors of war had left him with a peaceable outlook, but he was king after all, and people close to him were dying. He felt it prudent to come prepared.

"You know," he said. "You seem to have no shortage of strong opinions these days, Lennart. The treaty is one thing, but then there's Emile and his death, which for whatever reason you are certain was self-inflicted. I wonder whether these opinions are truly for my benefit, or if, perhaps, you might have your own agenda?"

"Your Majesty?"

"It strikes me as unusual that someone of your undoubted experience and expertise has had such little success in identifying the murderer. You were close to Emile, were you not?"

"Well, I wouldn't say close, Your Majesty. He was my peer, but little more."

Leander's grip tightened around the handle of the knife. Even now, it seemed that Lennart was intent on bending the truth to cover his back. It did, however, seem that the minister was oblivious to his king's suspicions. Leander was happy to keep it this way, for now at least. He forced his anger down and asked, "Are we any closer to understanding how that knife appeared in Emile's cell? It was rather an extravagant looking blade, which should somewhat streamline our search."

Lennart's head shook. "No, my king, that's quite the mystery. I've spoken with the prison guards who conducted his search on arrival, two of our best men, and they assure me that the weapon was not in his possession. We have a record of all visitors to the cells, which may, perhaps, have flagged something suspicious. But having taken a look on your behalf, I've not found anything to report."

"Nothing at all?" asked Leander, voice laden with suspicion. "Then how do you explain the appearance of a prohibited weapon, or was this knife a magic knife, Lennart? Tell me, should I be concerned?"

Lennart laughed nervously, hands adjusting his collar. "Of course not, my king. Fear not, you are safe. As to the knife, I suspect the only explanation is not in witchcraft but human incompetence. The guards I mentioned are certainly two of our best, but not immune to an occasional error. Let us not forget that Emile was both minister and war hero— and resourceful at that."

"An error?" said Leander. "You're suggesting that Emile simply found a way to smuggle the knife?"

"It pains me to say so, but this is truly the only reasonable explanation. With Ciel, I am, of course, continuing my investigations and, if the guards are found to have been wanting, you can rest assured that suitable punishment will be administered."

To his credit, Lennart's pretence never faltered. Leander had to admire the man's quickness of thought. No wonder he'd struggled to identify the killer; Lennart was a master at apportioning blame. The consequence of a life surrounded by criminals, Leander concluded.

"So, incompetence is your answer then? I must say this does not reflect well upon you, Lennart. Perhaps this kind of ineptitude is the reason our inquisition has proven so unsuccessful. Five dead ministers, and us always one step behind."

"Of course, Your Majesty." Lennart's head lowered. "This is not my finest moment, but in the end, we have at least solved the mystery. Emile was apprehended and denied the opportunity of further victims. While regrettable, his death was surely the most likely outcome from the trial should it have happened. In many ways, this was the best conclusion for all concerned. You know how desperate the minister was to avoid the public shame that his father experienced. Meanwhile, you are a busy man with many responsibilities. In his actions, Emile has at least spared you a trial that might have stretched on for days."

Leander nodded. "Yes, I must admit it is all very convenient. Hardly the most reassuring outcome though is it, Lennart? On reflection, I wonder if I have been affording your opinions more credence than deserved. And if that's the case, what reason do I have to believe that you are right on this particular occasion?"

"Your Highness?"

"There is, of course, another possibility—Emile was never the killer, but always a target. Perhaps the minister had it all worked out, a risk that the murderer had to silence. There's no doubt a trial would have been detrimental to Emile's reputation, but I wonder if he was not alone in wanting to avoid our questions. And if it was not Emile…" he said, standing, one hand still clenching his knife. "Then it had to have been someone with resources, access to money and information. Can you think of anyone who might fit that profile, Lennart?"

The minister's face glistened with worry. "Surely, you can't think that I had anything to do with this?"

"Why not?" said, Leander, taking a few slow steps to close the distance between them. "You are perhaps the only person who has thus escaped my suspicion. One of seven men who swore an oath the night my father passed. Look around you, Lennart, only two remain. Would you have me believe this some kind of coincidence?"

"But Your Majesty, I've been doing all I can to help find the killer."

"Or so you'd have me believe." Leander edged closer. "Tell me, what have you actually contributed? From memory, I recall a lot of speculation and false assumptions, misdirection that may have ultimately prevented us from catching the killer sooner. With Emile's demise, the question remains as to whether the murderer is still at large."

He stopped with only a few feet between them and looked deep into Lennart's eyes, hoping to find the truth within them. By now, Leander was so sick of the lies. From Joran's liaisons to his own mother's murderous secret, his patience was exhausted. He was exhausted. His mind thought again to the portrait of his father, forever watchful, and he wondered if he'd judged the man too harshly after all.

Lennart raised his palms and pleaded, "See sense, King Leander, what possible reason could I have for wanting them dead?"

"Justice," said Leander, finally withdrawing his knife. "Or your own depraved view of it anyway. Perhaps I should celebrate your devotion to my father's memory, the willingness to murder five of your peers in his name. Except, I don't think this has ever truly been about my father, has it? I've no doubt that you respected the man, perhaps even loved him, but it was King Yorick's ideals that really appealed to you, wasn't it? Truth is, my father never cared for his people.

The two of you were kindred spirits with a shared disdain for all those born beneath you. Under my father's reign you were free to hunt and kill people like game. And it was a game to you, wasn't it? A pastime that you just weren't ready to give up."

"Nonsense—"

"No, Lennart, the time for nonsense is over. If you aren't the killer, then you're simply incompetent. Which is it?"

At knifepoint, Lennart made to speak, and then paused as if a new idea had suddenly taken him. "What about Ciel?" he said, trying once again to shift blame. "You're quick to pass verdict, but Ciel was every bit as much a part of the inquisition."

"Very good," said Leander. "I see what you're trying to do, but it's all just disappointingly predictable now. Need I remind you that the decision to introduce Ciel was yours and yours alone? The man's guilt would thus be yours by extension, though I do not believe he had anything to do with this. You see, Lennart, Ciel has something you do not: a soldier's oath, a sacred vow that unites every warrior of the Cadraelian Realm. The pledge to protect and fight for the wellbeing of a brother-in-arms. A promise that cannot and will not be broken, one that Ciel himself swore to our unit before the fateful siege of Ardalan."

"But, Your Majesty, please see—"

His sentence ended with a wheeze as Leander's knife plunged deep into Lennart's stomach. Leander removed the blade, watching as the minister crumbled to his knees, hopelessly trying to stem the wound.

"A very clever man, but in the end, perhaps a little too clever," said Leander. "Only now, with your death, has justice been served."

Lennart's body hit the floor, and his face glazed over with that same lifeless expression with which Leander had been recently all too regularly reacquainted, one he had hoped to leave on the battlefield. Crouching down, he wiped the blood-spattered knife on the motionless arm of Lennart's tunic. Once clean, his reflection stared back at him from the shining surface. He was no longer a fool, but a king inciting respect and perhaps even fear.

He hardly recognised the visage as his own.

A new day dawned on Cadrael—bright blue skies, and with them, fresh hope. A time to heal and to rebuild. Leander, for one, sat more comfortably and confidently upon his throne.

"Good day, Marcel," he said, addressing the Royal Chamberlain. "I gather you have been keen for an audience. Tell me, what news?"

Marcel bowed in deference, and then straightened his pristine tunic. "Thank you, my king; I know you've been extremely busy, what with the passing of the ministers and that awful incident with Minister de Meiren. Truly, it was a shock to all of us, but we are grateful for your continued health."

"Thank you, Marcel."

"You are welcome, Your Majesty. Now we must look forward to the better days that are surely only just around the corner. Recent events have left your staff somewhat depleted, but there were a few pieces of news on which I wanted to update you. I will endeavour to return with more detailed accounts when I have them."

Leander nodded with approval. "Your efforts have not gone unnoticed, Marcel. With men like you at my side, I'm sure that the future of Fermantia is in safe hands. The hard work starts today though, my good man. What news do you have on the incumbent ministers?"

"Thank you, my king." Marcel gave another bow. "On that point I can confirm work on a series of official offer letters. The letters are addressed to the respective next-in-line for each position and shall be ready for your signature before the end of the day."

"Excellent. Will each of them be summoned here to join us at the palace?"

"Correct, my king, for the investiture ceremony. I've no doubt that these men will be quick to accept and commence their duties, especially since you solved the case of the infamous Cadrael Killer, and the capital is considered a safe place once more."

Leander's smile widened at the unexpected prospect of a fresh start. Though the path to this point had been fraught with fear and terrible loss, it had given him the chance to move forward with a new ministry. Men sworn to Leander and the realisation of his ideals.

"Excellent," he said. "Fine work, Marcel. The new ministers can't come soon enough, I'm sure you'll agree. No doubt their presence will help to somewhat alleviate your burden. Only a matter of time and I'm sure you'll be back to what you do best."

"It's my honour, Your Majesty, certainly no hardship. As a boy, I always dreamed to be part of your ministry. Of course, a ministerial position was never my birthright, and my father took great pleasure tempering these ambitions. He told me that I would never get anywhere near the palace, but I made a promise that I would do *anything* to prove otherwise. The last few days have certainly been busy, but you won't hear any complaints from me, that I can assure you."

Leander nodded. "Very good. Any updates concerning our guest from Vicentia?"

"Requests for a royal audience have been persistent and determined. I don't suppose you've had time to complete and sign that paperwork? As you know, Queen Orsolina is not famed for her patience. I fear Consul Rizzuti is similarly restive."

Leander looked at the ceiling thoughtfully, rubbing his hands together. When he spoke, his words were slow and considered. "Tell the consul that his continued patience is greatly appreciated. Remind him the many unfortunate occurrences that have happened in recent times but assure him that the treaty is still utmost in our priorities."

"But Your Majesty, I understand that the provisional agreement is completed, pending your approval. Have you changed your mind, or is there something else to which I'm not privy?"

"Nothing in particular," said Leander. "However, it's fair to say that my attention has been somewhat compromised of late. At times like these, I believe my thoughts should begin a little closer to home, only then can we lay the solid foundations required for peace."

Marcel smiled like a proud parent. "Well said, Your Majesty. Rest assured I will assuage Consul Rizzuti with suitable discretion. I can't imagine Queen Orsolina will be expecting to change the world overnight."

"Quite, said Leander. "However, change the world we certainly shall. Were there any other updates you care to report? If not, I should like to invite Princess Sanne for lunch. The Princess is another unfortunate victim of our recent tumult."

For Leander, this would be his first time seeing Sanne since the sorry incident in the palace gardens. Though daunted by the prospect of making amends, he saw this as another challenge he needed to meet head on. If recent developments were anything to go by, he felt sure that luck was finally on his side.

"Oh," said Marcel. "Didn't anyone tell you?"

"Tell me what?"

"The princess departed the palace this morning for Eluria. I'm sorry, Your Majesty, I've been so busy and, well, I thought you must have already known. I must say, the princess left in something of a hurry. I'm sorry to pry, but is everything all right, my king? I had heard that the princess had been somewhat emotional of late."

It was all Leander could do to subdue the feeling of anger and embarrassment. Rolling his eyes he said, "Of course," in the most jovial tone that he could muster. "I'm sorry, I forgot. Completely slipped my mind what with everything that has been happening. Princess Sanne has been feeling painfully homesick these past days. The effect on her mood has been obvious to anyone, and we agreed that she would return home briefly before the wedding."

"So it's true!" Marcel's eyes suddenly glinted with excitement. "A royal wedding to plan for. Oh, Your Majesty, what fine news."

Leander wiped the sweat from his palms against the silk upholstered arm of the throne. "Yes, absolutely," he stumbled to answer. "Though all in good time, I'm sure you understand."

"Of course, Your Majesty. Something more to look forward to. I'm happy to provide one final update that should please you. The princess is not the only notable recent departure from the palace—Perrine Delport has relinquished her employment."

The news was like a knife to Leander's heart. The pain was so much that he wondered if he might have suffered less at Lennart's murderous hands. Insulted, lied to, and now abandoned by those closest to him, Leander felt his mood darkening once more; he only hoped it wasn't so obvious to his company.

Marcel continued, "I imagine this is good news, Your Majesty? Marriages are best when free from unnecessary complications. The girl undoubtedly has charm, but she has never been the same since the incident with her father."

"Yes of course, fantastic news." Leander forced a smile. "Another step in the direction of our bright new future, Marcel. Now if you don't mind, I need a little time to consider other issues, principally the withdrawal of our troops from the newly occupied regions of the Clanlands."

Marcel inclined his head. "Yes, Your Majesty. There was, however one more thing, which I would be happy to delay if you would prefer."

"Go on."

"Well, Master Huertroop—"

"Ciel?

"Yes, Ciel was here a little earlier. He said he'd found someone to translate your letter and that you'd know what I was talking about? Sadly, Mr Huertroop..." He cleared his throat, and then corrected himself. "Ciel rather, had to leave quite unexpectedly. The girl is outside if you can spare a moment, her name is Ana, one of our own staff no less."

Frankly Leander wanted time alone to scream and beat his fists against the wall until they were bloody, but if this was to be a brighter day for Fermantia, he wasn't about to let it darken with his mood.

"Of course," he said, with no small amount of curiosity. With Lennart gone, this letter was the only loose end that remained. Maybe it would provide the closure he needed to move forward. Perhaps it had been entirely unrelated all along. The name Ana was another mystery, prompting a distant echo of remembrance, but from where he couldn't tell.

Another bow, then Marcel said, "Perfect," before making toward the doorway. He exited then returned with company, a diminutive maidservant with jet-black hair whose head never lifted, choosing instead to follow her feet. Though her expression was hidden, the girl seemed nervous, a point which, at first, seemed unusual to Leander before he remembered that he was, of course, king.

"Welcome," he said brightly, as the girl drew to a halt in the centre of the throne room. He fixed on the Royal Chamberlain and added, "Thank you, Marcel. We'll be fine from here,.I'm sure there are other priorities requiring your attention." He turned to the armed guard stood at his right flank. "You too. Please wait in the corridor for further instructions."

With a look of surprise, which the young guard shared, Marcel said, "Only if you're sure, Your Majesty. There are men outside the door should you need them. I'll be back with further updates at the earliest opportunity."

The two men left, closing the doors behind them and leaving the girl alone in Leander's company. Not knowing what to expect from the content of the letter, Leander preferred that he, and he alone, should be the first to hear.

"I understand that you have something for me," he said, trying to encourage some confidence in the new arrival, who moved to unravel the letter in front of her. To his dismay, she proceeded to recite the indecipherable language that he had previously seen in writing. The intonation was flat, yet strangely musical. Crucially, Leander gained no insight as to the author's thoughts.

He laughed. "Is it me, or is it still not making any sense? I had hoped to gain some understanding in the common tongue. I gather that you're familiar with the language in question and that you've been able to translate it accordingly?"

"Yes, Your Majesty. As you wish." She straightened the letter and began to read slowly but steadily. "A father's blood left to dry on the sands. Seven lives as repayment, their blood on my hands."

For a moment, Leander was lost in puzzled silence. "Seven lives?" he uttered, then his jaw dropped. The maidservant raised her head and Leander's eyes widened with terror. For the first time, he could see the fullness of her face.

"You," he spat, sitting forward in his throne with disbelief. Finally, he recalled the name he'd been searching for, a name he'd heard in stories around a campfire. A name he'd last heard on the eve of the siege of Ardalan. The young girl left back in the capital, sister to two brothers who would never return. "Ana Veraza, isn't it? You know, you've caused me quite some trouble."

Ana presented a murderous grin. "Oh, King Leander, you don't know the half of it. I should start by thanking you for sparing me the day of my father's execution."

"A small mercy."

"Quite. And perhaps the only reason you're still alive today."

Leander's brain raced to keep up, but every new realisation made him feel bilious. "So, it was you all along?" he asked. "You killed the ministers?"

"Oh, now, Leander, let's not get ahead of ourselves. I can't tell you how long I've been waiting to speak to you."

Ana ran fingers through her long dark hair, and Leander sat back inviting explanation. Annoyance was second only to curiosity, and he began to consider each murder in turn. For one thing, he knew he was safe, at least briefly—if Ana's plans had been different, he would have already been dead.

Ana's expression turned serious. "I suppose you want to know why and how? Shall I start from the very beginning?"

Leander nodded.

"So, Minister Hoste, or Bram as he had me call him. I'd heard that he was something of a womaniser, but I never expected that to be an understatement. In the end it only needed a few subtle glances and the occasional touch of his arm to get his attention. The fat old pig was eager to continue our dalliance and took little convincing that Lower Cadrael was the most suitable location—"

Leander interrupted. "You? It was *you* with Bram the night of the coronation?"

"It was indeed. A risky move, but the room was full and not without distractions. I wondered if you'd even recognise me without my father's blood for decoration. In the end, I needn't have worried; your attention was taken by one or two others that particular evening, wasn't it, Your Majesty?"

Leander cringed. "But Marcel confirmed that you never left the palace."

"And he was right," said Ana. "I wonder how long it took Bram to realise I wasn't coming. Truth is, the minister was already drunk to the point of insensible. He travelled unaccompanied and told me I was his little secret. The dirty old fuck was hard with excitement, but the night didn't end the way he had planned."

"But if not you, then tell me, how did you kill him?"

Ana sneered. "Oh, I killed him the moment he agreed to leave the palace. The pie-eyed old fool was so drunk he'd already broken his glasses. In the end, he walked into my trap and didn't even see it coming. Lower Cadrael is a tough place for those who have lived there all their lives. For one of the six wealthiest men in all of Fermantia?" She scoffed. "I made sure all the wrong people knew to expect him; those most aggrieved by the decline of Lower Cadrael, and the late minister's part in this contemptuous neglect. In the end, old Bram got fucked alright."

Leander buried his head in his hands. Though the story had answered some of his questions, there was so much more he wanted to ask. He knew he should call for the guards, but Ana was clearly getting to something, and he knew this might be his only chance to hear it. Midday bells tolled ominously across the city.

"How long?" he asked. "How long have you worked here?

"Not long, I joined just before the coronation. I gather that your father's suspicious nature had caused him to maintain a small but trusted household staff. Perhaps the hateful fuck was not entirely witless, but his decisions had left the Royal Chamberlain somewhat hamstrung. With the imminent celebrations, reinforcements were needed, and I was, of course, only too happy to help."

Leander breathed a sigh of frustration. "And the others," he asked. "I doubt all were susceptible to your wiles."

"True, but remember there are many ways to crack an egg, King Leander. It was not long before the cracks themselves began to appear. The only higher power that Minister Dubeck ever served was himself. The man stood on an altar of gold pilfered from the church and the common people, while his opposition, The Sworn, fight for the dream of reformation. They were right to investigate the minister's finances, and I made sure they found appropriate evidence when they did. To call the institution corrupt would be a divine understatement. It's no wonder the church is so keen to cover up their guilty secrets."

"And Joran?" By now, Leander was flapping. "The man was scrupulous; don't tell me you also had a hand in his murder?"

Ana's eyes threatened to roll from her head. "Come now, Leander. You and I both know better than that, don't we?" She pouted. "Minister Rensen was a lovesick adulterer, though you can hardly blame Annelise Bekaert for indulging him—the only thing she ever shared with Bruno was a penchant for the male anatomy. Of course, Bruno was rather sensitive about his little secret. Annelise was the perfect facade as he fucked his way through Cadrael's rent boys. That was, at least, until he found out about Joran. An affront on his status and vanity, but not only that, one which threatened to expose him. I felt it only right to inform the minister of his wife's sordid liaisons. Men can be painfully prideful and predictable, and it was no surprise when he sought revenge against Minister Rensen."

"And Bruno?"

"Well, I must admit, that one was fortuitous. Evidently, Bruno chose the wrong victim, and it seems that Joran had been much more than a meaningless fling for Annelise. From what I hear, she gave quite the performance when you discovered her clutching her husband's body. I wonder which of the two men was responsible for her grief…"

Leander's jaw fell. "So it was Annelise Bekaert who killed him? The hemlock and the poison garden. It was right there all along. A woman's weapon…"

"Things start to become a little clearer when you know what you're looking for, King Leander. For days I'd managed to avoid you around the palace. On the rare occasion you were nearby, I'd turn my head or leave the room on pretence of busyness or modesty. Imagine my surprise when you arrived unexpectedly in the palace prisons. You were so close to finally solving your mystery; pity you didn't realise that Minister Roos had already solved it for you. You know, the man cried that first night you sent him to the cells. Cried for the damage it would do to his reputation. Cried at the feeling of helplessness, that harsh realisation that no matter how powerful you are, there's always someone more powerful. I wonder if he cried for the people and cities he destroyed in the Clanlands. Did he mourn the families left desolate by his careless displays of strength and wanton destruction?"

Leander chewed at his fingers, wincing as the skin broke painfully, leaving a metallic taste in his mouth. "You killed him then?" he asked solemnly. "You took revenge for all of his victims?"

Ana sighed. "It wouldn't have been any less than the man deserved, but no, in the end it was fear and pride that did for him. I smuggled the knife when delivering his last meal, instructing him that it was a gift from the hand of his king. I've been rather busy writing letters of late, but it took real craft to successfully forge your signature. Your written instructions stole any remaining hope from the minister, who was intent on avoiding the scandal of a protracted trial. Even more so when the outcome was predetermined. The man's incessant vanity never left him, not even at the end. So concerned was he with his own appearance that I almost expected him to raise from the dead and clear the mess of blood away. That or arrange it in some vainglorious mural to his alleged achievements on the battlefield. Nonetheless, I suppose he did the honourable thing in the end, leaving Minister de Meiren as the obvious culprit. Truth told, I didn't expect you to be such a cold-blooded killer, but we've already seen what fear can do to a man. Why should a king be any different?"

The threat in her words was not lost on Leander. In his mind he desperately tried to get ahead and fill in the blanks, hindered by the uncomfortable truth that, through Ana's machinations, he had needlessly murdered Lennart. He had to believe the girl's confession, but it was one thing to make plans and something very different to complete them. The murders required extraordinary access to people and information. One thing was for sure, Ana hadn't been working alone.

"Ciel…" he uttered without thinking, then shook the thought away. "No. He couldn't. He wouldn't." He paused again. Was it truly inconceivable? How much did he really know about the man anyway? With Ana expressionless, he added, "It can't be."

"No?"

"No. He…he was a soldier. He swore the oath. He was sworn to protect me."

Again, Ana brushed the hair from her eyes. "Ah, the oath. You do remember then. I'd be lying if I claimed to know the pledge in its entirety—something to do with fighting for the betterment of Fermantia, isn't it? And there's another part about protecting the life of your compatriot as though it were your own. Did you protect your compatriots at Ardalan, King Leander?" She folded her arms defiantly, challenging her king to answer the question. "Did you stand up for them when Minister Roos came calling for lambs to the slaughter?"

Leander stuttered. "I didn't...I couldn't."

"Couldn't or didn't, King Leander? To my mind, the two are very different. My brothers told me all about you in their letters. Told me you were different, that you cared and that you'd fight for them just as they fought for you. They were under no illusions as to what they were getting into, but in you, they thought they'd found someone worth following. Then you sold them out when Minister Roos came calling, didn't you? You knew the attack on the city was reckless, but you stepped aside and let it happen. You even gave him the men to do it. And why was that? Because it was easier, wasn't it? Easier than standing up to your father, easier than acknowledging that the men had families, hopes and dreams, and that no man's life is worth more than another. It was easier to do nothing, wasn't it, King Leander?"

"No, it wasn't like that." A sharp pain coursed through Leander's head, causing him to wince. That fateful day in the shadow of the walls of Ardalan flashed through his mind as a painful memory. Could he have done more to save those men? Would his father have listened? He supposed he would never know...

"Ciel, as you remember, was one of the first to scale the walls. He screamed *your* name as they descended upon the city. He made good progress too, until the main body of the opposition's troops intercepted him. A spear point through the leg left him helpless, sprawled in a bog of blood and butchery. That was, until my brothers, Rolan and Elias dragged him to safety. In the end, they carried Ciel out of the city and back to the surgeons before re-joining the offensive, but not before they made him promise that if the worst should happen, he, Ciel, would help look after their little sister. That was the last he ever saw of them. Ciel has been like a brother to me ever since."

The clues had been there all along, and Leander was furious with himself for not seeing what was right before his eyes. Worse still, he felt sympathy for Ana and her family despite her murderous intentions. He couldn't deny the blame was his. He reached for his knife, quickly realising it wasn't there.

Fittingly, Ana withdrew two knives of her own. "I wouldn't if I were you. Let's not do anything stupid—that includes calling the guards. You know..." she said, pacing with the confidence of someone in total control. "When I was younger, I wanted to be just like my brothers. I wanted to fight for you and your father, but of course the army has no use for women. I must have been a real terror for my mother." She laughed. "She wouldn't let me play with swords, but kitchen knives were easy enough to spirit away without her noticing. The problem with knives is that they're only effective against enemies in close proximity. That is, unless you learn to throw them accurately. Would you care to find out how well I can throw?"

Leander's heart sank and his arms went limp. He found himself entirely at Ana's mercy, but it seemed she had a reason for keeping him alive, and now, in conclusion, he needed to know what. "Why?" he asked, breathing heavily. "And why are you telling me all of this now?"

Ana paused for a moment. "Because my brothers were honourable men, who rushed back into Ardalan and ran toward death when it was easier to walk away. My father was the same, but you already know that. The man chose to stand up for what he believed in, even knowing it could cost him his life. That day at the arena, I never expected any clemency from your father or his shit-sniffers. You though, Leander, I hoped for better; I dared to dream that my brothers were right about you all along, and that you might spare my father in their memory." She shook her head in disgust. "What I saw that day was a frightened young man, a prince of Fermantia who was a slave to his own emotions. That day, you let fear compromise all the good my brothers once saw in you. However, I still saw it, King Leander. I still see it even now after everything that has happened between us. Why am I telling you all of this? Because I wanted you to know what it is like to live in fear, to experience the helplessness of feeling that everything in your life is impermanent, vulnerable, easily snatched away at any moment. Only now can you truly understand your people."

Enough was enough. "So that's what all of this has been for. An opportunity to test me. Some sick game for your entertainment," Leander snapped.

"Was my father not beheaded in the name of entertainment?" Ana snarled with the intensity of a wild animal. For the first time, Leander knew he'd been able to provoke a reaction. He wondered what to expect from the repercussions.

At length, Ana continued, "Come now, King Leander, surely you aren't about to defend the honour of your fallen ministers? Pride, greed, lust and anger, all sins to which The Goddess is so opposed. Those six men sent my father to his death. They took his life, and I've taken my vengeance."

"Except you haven't, have you?" Leander sat upright in his throne, his face now smug. "You never killed any of those men, not really. They were a loathsome bunch, that we can agree on, but their deaths were a simple case of life catching up with them."

Ana scratched her head in frustration. "King Leander, are you really this simple or just pig-headed? Killers aren't always those with the knife in their hands, you know that better than anyone does. Like the general who allows the slaughter of his men, or the prince who watches on in silence as an innocent man loses his head. Inaction is action's more dangerous sibling. This is life catching up with you, Leander. I wonder how you will react."

Leander's fists tightened with anger. Who was this girl to press him with ultimatums? Perhaps more importantly, what did she want?

"Enough of the games. You've made your point, so let me guess, I'm next? In your letter, you mentioned the blood of seven men, I presume this time you'll be the one holding the knife?"

Ana's eyes tightened with momentary confusion, loosening only with the emergence of a feline smile. "I think you might have lost count, King Leander. Eight men sentenced my father to his death that day at the arena, and to the best of my knowledge only one remains."

"My father?"

"Well, of course. I told you he had to die, didn't I?"

"But I didn't—" Leander silenced abruptly, unwilling to surrender his mother's secret. He still remembered the night as if it were yesterday, those dying moments, Ana's words of encouragement echoing in his mind. *The king must die,* she'd said outside the arena. With Leander's inaction, it came to pass. He sighed in the knowledge he'd been playing Ana's game from the very beginning. Outthought and outmanoeuvred—Ana Veraza was a mirror for all his weaknesses. He now began to wonder if he would be strong enough to survive.

"It may surprise you to hear that we want the same things, King Leander," said Ana. "Liberation for Tenevarre and peace throughout the Cadraelian Realm. Withdraw our troops and give people the chance to live free from fear and oppression. My homeland, Irazar, is long since devoured by the Cadraelian maw, but there is still hope for others if you'll give them the chance."

"Tenevarre," said Leander, chuckling with disbelief. "That's what this is all about? A treaty which I, myself, proposed?"

"Only to disregard it at the first sign of a threat to your person." Ana countered. "I hear the treaty is yet unsigned, Leander, why is that? Are your views on the wellbeing of others so changeable, or are common folk simply less valuable than you are?" She paused but found no answer forthcoming. When she began again, her voice was softer and pleading. "The treaty is a fine start, a milestone to surpass the achievements of your forebears. Stick to your principles and sign the agreement. Stand tall and fight for those who need you the most. Help them live safely. Let them be free."

"And what if I don't? I am, after all, a king. It's not in my nature to negotiate with scum like you, least of all those who have me at knifepoint."

Ana shook her head, and her teeth gritted with frustration. She might have expected to persuade him more easily, but despite their many differences, Leander retained his father's stubbornness.

"Then arrest me," she shouted. "Or die trying. Ciel is already long gone, so you'll never find him. He's a remarkable man, you know, not that you ever saw the best of him. He kept the oath he made to my brothers and deserves the chance to find peace of his own. Me...well, I have nothing left, your family made sure of that. I did all of this so that, in my heart, I would know that I had tried my best to make a difference. Question is, King Leander, when you look back on this moment, will you be able to say the same?"

Leander pondered her words in silence. The demands were clear, but the circumstances could scarcely have been murkier. Here was a common girl, a murderer no less, giving orders to a king. It hardly mattered that the course of action was, at its origin, Leander's own idea. The nature of the situation was deeply distressing; was this truly standing up and doing the right thing, or was he being forced into a decision as he had so many times before?

He scratched at his stubble and tried to see things through different eyes. Was he, Leander, the victim in all of this? Ana had risked it all to stand up for what she believed in, and here she was still fighting. Maybe Leander should thank her. After all, she'd ridden Fermantia of six sinful ministers. In her heartfelt words, she had reminded him of all he had sworn to tackle and change. At her essence, Ana was resourceful and headstrong, the sort of person who would only benefit Leander, if stood by his side.

He made to speak before a familiar voice interrupted him. The memory of his father's words, fraught with the usual tone of disappointment and disapproval. Benevolence aside, Ana was a murderer, and one that Leander had already shown lenience once before. Thinking back over all that had happened since King Yorick breathed his last, Leander realised how different things might have been following Emile's recommendation to have Ana arrested for treason. Weakness, procrastination or pure pig-headedness designed to infuriate his own father, Leander's actions had already ended lives and relationships.

Whatever his next decision, it would have far-reaching consequences. After much consideration, he knew what to do...

EPILOGUE

The wide doors of the arena parted, and Leander found himself assaulted by a wall of sound as he stepped out onto the hallowed sands for the very first time.

Adjusting to the blazing midday sun, he raised his hand to shelter his eyes, turning the action into a wave, which sent the crowd into deeper frenzy. From the seats surrounding him, adoring city folk called his name, showering him with flowers and compliments. Leander smiled as he basked in his moment of glory. This was his first significant public appearance since the coronation, and there was scarcely an empty inch in the arena.

A moment, and a spectacle, but Leander was pleased to face it in trusted company.

"Drink it in, brother," said Oskar, following along closely in his wake. Two accompanying guards brought Leander some security, but Leander's greatest assurance came with the sight of Ana Veraza in the centre of the arena.

Walking to meet her, he snatched a glance up at the royal balcony, where his mother dazzled with her usual poise and regal elegance. To her left sat Fermantia's fresh-faced new ministry, a selection of brothers, sons, and nephews: a new generation that Leander would mould to avoid the mistakes of the past.

To the other side, Leander's empty chair, and beyond it, the discomfiting sight of Princess Sanne with her father, King Jannick for company. The princess's face bore no reminder of Leander's temper, but she had returned to Cadrael cold and reluctant. In his optimism, Leander hoped that the princess would come to love him, but more important was the allegiance with King Jannick's Eluria, and, most pressingly of all, the conception of a royal heir. In this regard, love was not a necessity.

Pivoting to survey the full spectacle of the four-sided arena, Leander closed his eyes and let the sounds of adoration wash over him, cleansing any lingering thoughts of those torrid first days of his reign. This fresh start would bring closure on all that had gone before. Ana was watching his approach intently, but Leander found himself too lost in the moment to return her attention. Something about the girl still left him uneasy; however, the dynamic between them could hardly have been more different to that of their previous encounter. Above all, he was intent he wouldn't his nerves show.

He arrived at the centre of the arena, greeted by the Master of Ceremonies, who fell to one knee.

"Arise," said Leander, and the man obliged with admirable haste. He returned to full height then swept away to join Ana and her two armoured escorts. Leander cleared his throat, and silence descended upon the arena. The moment had arrived; his time had come.

"People of Cadrael," his booming voice echoed out. "You owe my presence to this woman, Ana Veraza," he said, gesturing. "A woman who, in adversity, fought for her own beliefs. A woman who opposed your king and his ministry, and a woman whose actions have taught me a valuable lesson. In his time, my father used this arena to make an example of those who conspired against him. Ana's own father was one such victim. Today we will watch as his daughter joins him."

The crowd erupted as Ana stumbled toward the guillotine, hands bound and with the attention of two armed men for encouragement. Long gone was the self-satisfaction she had shown in the throne room. Instead, her expression was now one of infuriating calm. The very sight caused Leander's fists to clench with frustration, but fear always came to the condemned eventually.

A trail of crimson carpeted the ground in welcome. The blood of Annelise Bekaert, murderous wife of the late minister, whose discarded head lay nearby already beginning to turn in the midday heat. A warning to all those who would seek to oppose Leander, not least Ana herself who knelt as instructed, allowing the executioner to secure her in place at the pillory.

Still, her face showed no emotion. Perhaps she had simply resigned herself to her fate, but to Leander's mind, it was one last act of defiance. An act which prompted unwitting thoughts of Perrine, and anger at the lack of respect she had demonstrated in leaving him. He pictured the servant girl similarly bound and condemned and resolved to have her found and returned to him for judgement. He saw now, how lenience and generosity could be mistaken for weakness, but on this, he would surely have the last word. In the immediacy, however, he had more pressing matters to contend with.

With the stage set, the crowd quietened once more. Leander cleared his throat, and thirty thousand spectators hung on his every word.

"Ana Veraza," he bellowed. "You are convicted of murder, treason and attempted regicide under Fermantian law. Your guilt is incontrovertible, owing to the detailed confession, to which I, your king, was a first-hand witness. This leaves but one further formality..." He broke off and looked to the royal balcony, where all six ministers were out of their seats in waiting—a sight that provoked an eerie ghost of a memory. "I ask, will any of you stand for this girl?"

One after another, they returned to their seats, just as Leander himself had instructed. A fitting ending to a sorry saga. A grim smile of satisfaction unfolded on Leander's face, and he made no effort to contain the excitement in his voice.

"Ana Veraza, you are sentenced to death. May The Goddess find mercy that I could not."

With his final word, the guillotine dropped, the crowd gasping as Ana's severed head hit the sandy ground with a thud. A surge of noise and celebration followed, masking Leander's own considerable sigh of relief.

The nightmare was finally over, atonement for his own mistakes and foolish compassion. Too late, Leander had learned the lesson his father had sought to teach him. His weakness had allowed Ana Veraza to taste blood, but her antics left him only one course of action. For Leander the time for mercy and wishful optimism had passed. He had no choice but to put the bitch down.

Oskar's hand suddenly gripped Leander's shoulder. Over the din, he called, "Congratulations, Your Majesty. Cadrael is safe and the people adore you. Not bad for a king only yet in his infancy. Tell me, what else do you have up your sleeve?"

"We are to meet with Queen Orsolina," said Leander. "Today is a good day, but change is afoot, and I fear I have been a little too accommodating. Above all, our enemies must not perceive us to be weak."

Oskar's eyes narrowed. "What do you mean?"

"I've had fresh thoughts concerning the future of Tenevarre," said Leander coldly. "As you know, it was once the property of Fermantia. I'm of a mind to take it back."

One way or another, Leander knew that history would remember his name. The adoration of the crowd assured him that he was no normal man but one who stood above all others, and that, in the face of adversity, he would shape the future.

"You're just like him, you know," said Oskar. "I'm sorry I didn't see it sooner."

Oskar wasn't smiling.

Neither of them were.

ACKNOWLEDGEMENTS

This book was written in the late summer of 2023 in the months leading up to the birth of my daughter, Steele. Not knowing what to expect from fatherhood, I rushed to get the book completed before her arrival, so I should begin by thanking her for the productive deadline. In the end, it was she who was late!

Next up, I must thank my wife, Breana, who has always encouraged me to develop my craft and explore new challenges. She was the very first person to read the book and helped guide it toward the finished article. Ultimately, she is my inspiration.

From an editing standpoint, I am extremely grateful for Charlie Edwards-Freshwater; a wonderful friend and a brilliant writer. As a true murder-mystery aficionado, Charlie was a fantastic choice to edit this book, and he exceeded all expectations. Any good ideas in this book were probably his.

Completing the group is Natalie Milne, aka @TheBookishDesigner, who created all of the visual aspects of the book. It isn't easy to bring an author's vision to life, but Natalie's patience and enthusiasm helped make this process as stress-free and effective as possible, and I'm so happy with the results. Highly recommended.

Image Credits: Blacklight_trace & Maxger @ iStock

Thanks to all of you who have continued to follow my work beyond Pillars of Peace, and to those for whom this book is a first. I hope that in either case, you enjoyed the story and found the mystery extremely frustrating.

Truly, this book (like many others) could not have existed without Agatha Christie's work, and for that I must finish by thanking the queen of the genre herself.

ALSO AVAILABLE

<u>Pillars of Peace</u>

The Look of a King: Pillars of Peace Book I
No Place for Peace: Pillars of Peace Book II
Where Heroes Were Born: Pillars of Peace Book III
A Dagger in the Dark: A Pillars of Peace Novella

Cyrus is a storyteller frustrated by the mundane trappings of village life, while Prince Augustus struggles to meet high expectations after an upbringing of royal privilege in the bustling capital.

As both young men attempt to forge their own paths, a royal assassination unexpectedly closes the gap between them. The nation of Easthaven is thrown into war with their oppressive neighbours, and so begins a conflict from which neither Cyrus nor Augustus can walk away—a conflict with far-reaching consequences beyond either of their imaginings.

A story of family, friendship, hope, and love, the *Pillars of Peace* trilogy is an unpredictable and fast-paced coming-of-age tale that asks what it means to be a hero and what it takes to be a king.

ABOUT THE AUTHOR

Tom was born in 1987 in Chelmsford, Essex. As a boy, he fell in love with the fantasy worlds of video games, J.R.R Tolkien, and Philip Pullman.

Despite an early passion for storytelling, Tom obtained a BA in Tourism Management before a varied career in the travel industry, bringing to life another of his passions. When he is not working, Tom is an avid fan of his beloved Ipswich Town. He also writes and performs music and enjoys long walks with his wife, daughter and their three dogs.

Tom currently lives near Colchester, Essex, and *A Killer and a King* is his first standalone novel. He previously published the *Pillars of Peace* series, comprised of a trilogy and accompanying novella, which was largely written during the coronavirus pandemic with huge influence and editing support from his wife, Breana.

Contact Tom: tomdumbrell@aol.com
Instagram: @tom_dumbrell
Twitter: @tom_dumbrell

Suggested Reading
Joe Abercrombie – *Shattered Sea* & *First Law* Trilogies
Agatha Christie – *And Then There Were None*
Tom Hindle – *A Fatal Crossing*
Chris Wooding – *Tales of the Ketty Jay*
Scott Lynch – *The Gentleman Bastard Sequence*
V.E. Schwab – *The Invisible Life of Addie LaRue*

Printed in Great Britain
by Amazon